BY REBECCA DENGATE

HUGG Universe Series
Envy
Exit

Standalone Novels
Traces of June

TRACES OF JUNE

REBECCA DENGATE

✦ Lyons & Brown

Cover design: Damonza
Editing: Kim Smith, Kim's Editing Solutions
ISBN: 978-0-6451951-1-8 (paperback)

 A catalogue record for this work is available from the National Library of Australia

PROLOGUE

TUESDAY 13 OCTOBER 1987 AT 1:35PM, 349 PPM CO_2

A shadow passed over Alejandro as the woman entered the café. He looked up from his notebook, because what he caught out of the corner of his eye—wavy copper hair that fell to the bottom of her shoulder blades, shapely mouth set in porcelain skin—intrigued him.

The woman stopped, surveying the room. She had moved out of the way before stopping, so as not to inconvenience anyone coming in. With little evidence, Alejandro decided she was shy; there was a self-consciousness to her, as if she'd be more comfortable alone in the café. Her eyes darted around, giving the impression of barely repressed nervous energy. *First date, or maybe blind date?*

Alejandro watched her surreptitiously. *I'm a writer*, he thought, ignoring the fact that he'd only written two thousand words in the last month. *It's my job to study people.* Also, he was eighteen. He noticed women. Including this one, even though she was too old for him by at least a decade.

He began composing a description of her in his head. A fine pattern of puckered skin ran up the inside of her right arm, like the fjords of a coastline; a burn scar, Alejandro realised belatedly. She wore jeans—strangely fashioned so that they sat low on her hips and tight around her ankles—and a jade T-shirt a size too small for her. Her breasts were shaped like—like what? Like ripe melons, he decided. But softer.

The woman ordered from the counter, and took a sandwich to a table near the window, where she sat facing Alejandro.

Alejandro shook his head and returned to his notebook, where his two thousand words were waiting. He was beginning to admit that he'd do anything to avoid writing, because writing was hard.

Another woman entered the café. Alejandro looked up and did a double-take—although he tried to hide it, so it ended up as more of a jerk—because it was her again. Different clothes, but same hair, same face. Her posture was more confident, yet there was a tightness around her eyes, a weariness.

Twins, you idiot, he thought. Yet, to a close observer like Alejandro, they were *exactly* identical. Even the tiny mole above their collarbone was the same. The café was nearly full, but no one else was paying any attention whatsoever. This woman was dressed in a knee-length skirt and a blouse. Her hair was loose in the same casual style as her twin.

The woman turned and stared at Alejandro, sending him reeling with confusion. *Do I know her?* Because she looked like she had recognised him, but he was sure he'd never seen her before. Her or her double. But then she broke eye contact and looked straight at the table where her double was sitting.

The first woman was gazing at her double, the woman who had just entered the café, in shock. Her double walked over and sat on the opposite side of the table. Alejandro would bet any money that the two women had never met before. So—*reunion with a long-lost sister? But . . . one who is identical in every way?*

The two women talked, and the first seemed upset. Alejandro was wondering how he could move to a table closer to them without seeming creepy when the first woman stood up abruptly and left.

Alejandro closed his notebook and tucked it under one arm, his bag in one hand and hot chocolate in the other. He was normally shy around women, but he sensed that if he didn't act now, he would wonder about this forever. As he slid into the seat that the first woman had just vacated, he caught a faint whiff of campfire smoke.

"Hi," he said.

The woman smiled tiredly, without a trace of surprise that some strange man had joined her. Her hands, folded together on the table, never stopped their infinitesimal movements: squeezing, fiddling, twisting.

He coughed. "I couldn't help noticing your twin is, in fact, exactly identical to you. So, are you clones, or what?"

"Clones?" she repeated, surprised. She laughed, a hollow sound with no joy, and shook her head. "Good one."

Three years ago, in 1984, scientists had found a way to clone a sheep. It didn't seem crazy to Alejandro that they could have cloned a human by now. But then, he wasn't a scientist.

Alejandro took a sip of his lukewarm hot chocolate. The woman's expression was strangely inscrutable; even when she was laughing or smiling, there was a blankness behind it.

"I'm a writer," he said. "I'm burning up with curiosity right now. If you'd rather I left you alone, I'll go, but you seem unhappy, and maybe you would like to talk about it."

"You want some advice?"

"Uh . . . sure," Alejandro said.

"Forget your writing, unless it's going to inspire people to act on the climate crisis. Rebel. Fight. Anything that will make some noise. Not that it will make a difference, but it will make you feel better. The world is going to hell even now, and I can't help you."

"Oh-kay," Alejandro said slowly, drawing out the syllables, "nice to meet you, thanks for the advice."

The woman pursed her lips and nodded, eyes slightly wide, humouring him.

She was crazy, and he knew he should leave, but still he hesitated. "Is that based on inside information? From the future?"

It was a joke meant to keep her talking, but her face went blank at his words, and it was that, more than anything else, that convinced him that *she*, at least, thought she was from the future.

"You *are* from the future!" he said, half-believing it.

"Yes, I'm from the future, my mission is to convince you to *save the world*, Alejandro Gomez."

Alejandro leapt up, eyes wide.

The woman laughed and pointed to his crotch. No, she was pointing to his notebook, where he was clutching it, to the words he'd scrawled ironically across the front: *Alejandro Gomez, writer extraordinaire.*

Alejandro deflated and sat down again. He should probably leave this clearly crazy woman alone, but he still didn't understand what was going on, and he wanted to find out.

"I'm June," the woman said. "Let me tell you a story. It isn't a very interesting narrative, but the stakes are about as high as you can get, so listen carefully. Normal atmospheric CO_2 levels—that is, levels that persisted for ten thousand years before the industrial revolution—were about 280 parts per million, or ppm. Currently, the CO_2 levels are 349 ppm. Next year, the Intergovernmental Panel on Climate Change, IPCC, will be established. In 1989, fossil-fuel industries create the Global Climate Coalition, which issues propaganda aimed at convincing the public that climate science is too uncertain to act on."

Alejandro scratched his head as he listened. *Plausible*, he thought. But also, maybe she's not from the future. Maybe she's a robot. She didn't talk like a normal woman, and her eye contact was off kilter, her gaze bouncing off his at the wrong time, and darting around the room far too fast.

"In 1990, the IPCC issues a report saying that temperatures

have risen zero point three to zero point six degrees Celsius, partly due to human emissions, but it's not until 1995 that they definitely say that humans are responsible for climate change. By then, reports are popping up about actual warming in polar regions, Antarctic ice shelves breaking up, that kind of thing. And CO_2 levels are 359 ppm. By 1997, research into renewable energy is making real progress. At an international conference, the Kyoto Protocol is established, which sets targets for nations to reduce greenhouse gas emissions. Unfortunately, the US rejects it. That's where you're from, isn't it? The US?"

Alejandro nodded mechanically. Even though she couldn't possibly be from the future, he began to feel like she was telling the truth.

"Yeah. So anyway, Australia signs up to the Kyoto Protocol with a promise to *increase* its emissions based on 1990 levels, which apparently made some kind of sense at the time. By 2001, IPCC words its reports more strongly, saying global warming is 'very likely' with highly damaging results."

The two men at the table next to them had stopped talking and were openly staring at them. As was the waitress, the tray balanced on her hand, forgotten.

Alejandro found his mouth was open slightly and closed it. June smiled to the room at large.

"We're writers," she announced. This broke the spell. The waitress whisked her tray away to a far-off table while the murmur of conversation resumed.

"Do you want me to go on?" June asked in a quieter tone of voice. She had stopped twisting her hands together and was now playing with the ends of her hair.

"Yes," Alejandro said. "Please."

"Okay. In 2003, a heatwave in Europe causes thirty thousand deaths. CO_2 levels reach 375 ppm. Finally, climate change captures people's attention and appears in books and movies. In 2005, Hurricane Katrina rips through New Orleans and surrounds, and causes eighteen hundred deaths. That's just one of many. Natural disasters are—have always been—a steady drumbeat of devastation, but now the drumbeat is speeding up and getting louder, but that's hard to spot for the average Joe."

"You can't possibly know this," Alejandro said.

"Oh yeah? Take a look at this," June said. She pulled out a shiny black rectangular thing, shielding it from the view of anyone else with her body so that only Alejandro could see it. Then she unfolded it, somehow, and held down a button on the side. A tiny ghost-like Earth formed above the object and spun rapidly, stars circling it, until it dissolved into text: *Fantinia*, it read. The wood grain of the table was faintly visible through the text. Then the text vanished, and the top face of the object lit up with intricate, colourful pictures.

June folded the object and tucked it away.

Alejandro ran his hands over his face. "Your credibility is rising. What *was* that?"

"Phone," she said. She flicked her eyes upward. "Loading graphics that appear after a reboot. Very annoying."

Alejandro nodded uncertainly. Rebooting was something you did to computers, he was vaguely aware, but that device was too small to be a computer. "Are you a spy or something?"

She laughed. "A spy?" she said derisively. "No. Everyone in my time has one of these. *Everyone.* I'm no spy, I'm a software engineer."

"*You*? You're a software engineer?"

She stared at him blankly, as if she were unable to grasp why he might find that strange, which shook him. She wanted him to believe that she worked with computers? He supposed there might be a few women working as software engineers, and perhaps there would be more in future . . .

"Go on," he said grudgingly. It was stupid, but he was getting gripped by her story.

"Fine," she said. "Droughts, storms, floods, and extreme temperatures are the biggest killers. In 2007, IPCC notes that the cost of reducing emissions will be far less than the cost of the damage they will cause. Also, sea ice all over the world is found to be shrinking faster than expected. This becomes a theme over the next two decades; scientists always seem surprised. It's happening faster than we expected, and the effects are more severe. In 2009, a bunch of emails—um . . . correspondence—between climate scientists is released, supposedly showing climate change is a conspiracy, but it's all overblown and misinterpreted, and the truth comes out, eventually. Skip a few years, 2015, and researchers point out that the risk of crossing certain tipping points, certain thresholds, is growing. For example, the Amazon rainforest turning into grassland, or large-scale emissions of CO_2 and methane from melting Arctic permafrost."

"God," Alejandro said hoarsely, all his attention on June. *It's fine*, he tried to tell himself as his stomach clenched, *it's not real.* But it felt real, and her phone was either real or magic.

"Also that year, the Paris Agreement starts, superseding the Kyoto Protocol, but with similarly lacklustre outcomes. In 2016, though, renewable energy becomes cheaper than fossil fuels for the first time. In 2018, IPCC publishes their most hysterical report to date—which is still understating the truth, because they can't be seen as alarmist—saying that we have to hold warming to below one-point-five degrees Celsius or face terrible consequences. A fifteen-year-old Swedish schoolgirl leads strikes across the world for climate action. But the politicians deliver empty promises, if they make any promises at all. Between 2019 and 2022, the world is busy with a different kind of disaster, and in 2023 to 2026, yet another one. Still, in 2021, the president of the twenty-sixth global climate change meeting, COP26, cries because they've failed yet again. CO_2 levels are at 409 ppm, after a year of releasing thirty-six point four billion tons of CO_2."

Alejandro wanted her to stop, but he needed to know what happened next, so he nodded mutely. He was holding back tears.

"We're still emitting greenhouse gases, although we're emitting less each year. In 2023, there's an ultra-heatwave combined with power grid failure in California and Nevada that kills sixteen thousand people. In 2028, flooding in India causes three hundred thousand deaths. Here in Australia the bushfires are out of control, with larger areas destroyed than ever before, and a whole generation of us panic when we smell smoke."

Alejandro's eyes were drawn to the scarring on her arm. June didn't seem to notice, because her eyes were focused somewhere far away.

"The world *is* changing," June continued. "But it's hard. Obviously. So in 2029, with a CO_2 level of 435 ppm, we released twenty-nine point eight billion tons of CO_2, despite all the promises, despite all the targets set by governments from all over the world. And the Thwaites Glacier collapsed, locking us in for sixty-five centimetres of sea level rise within the next decade: up to your knees, in other words. Likely several metres by the end of the century."

Goosebumps rose on Alejandro's skin, on the nape of his neck, and on his bare arms. He felt sick. *Twenty-five inches of sea level rise guaranteed, and maybe six or seven feet?*

June shrugged. "And that's all I know. I'm guessing the politicians at the table over there are worried about the Soviet Union. Or perhaps Australia was never that concerned about the Soviet Union. But whatever they're discussing, it's probably inconsequential. Trust me," she said absently, looking at the table. "This is the big one."

She drained her tea and put the cup down with a clink. Not being Australian, Alejandro hadn't recognised the men at the far table as politicians. Although he probably wouldn't have recognised them even if they were American politicians, because he didn't follow politics.

"Oh yeah, and maybe get your money out of stocks, there will be a big crash in October," June said. She made eye contact, and he was struck by the cool detachment in her eyes. He sat frozen and nauseated.

After a moment, she stood up and walked out of the café and out of his life.

He thought of her often after that, though, especially after Black Monday, when on October 19 that year a global and unprecedented stock market crash took place.

But this is not his story. It's hers.

CHAPTER 1

FRIDAY 30 AUGUST 2030 AT 1:18PM, 435 PPM CO$_2$

June waited in the corridor of Old Parliament House, Canberra, clutching her phone. It would be poor form to arrive for her interview at the wrong time. After a great deal of thought, she had decided the correct time was somewhere between five and ten minutes early. But she couldn't resist turning up on a nice round number, twenty past one.

She slid open the door to MediSlice. Her chest ached somewhere deep, and her senses were tuned too sharp. She wanted to flinch from the world. *Where was he?*

MediSlice had been subdivided into smaller rooms, joined by a hall. The white moulded ceilings and dark wood frames were old-fashioned, similar in style to the rest of Old Parliament House. The narrow book-stuffed office in front of her was empty, as was the glass-walled meeting room next to it. Down the end was a kitchenette, lights off.

No Elijah. And no sign of Phoenix Simpson, the founder of the start-up, and the guy who was supposed to interview her.

"Hello?" June called.

At the other end of the hall, a pot plant sat on a table beside a green leather sofa. Around the corner was a computer lab, round empty desks visible through the glass walls. A closed door opposite was labelled, oddly, Travel Room. Underneath, a stop sign read "DANGER HIGH MAGNETIC FIELD **STOP** IF YOU HAVE ANYTHING METAL ON YOUR PERSON." She twisted her engagement ring off her finger. Three diamonds, a large one and two smaller ones, like children on either side of their mother. *Don't think of that.*

"Is anyone there?" June said, putting her engagement ring on the window ledge nearby.

She knocked on the closed door, and, getting no response, opened it. Inside the small windowless space, a flatbed fed into a softly rounded, white-panelled cylinder. A magnetic resonance imaging scanner, or MRI, oriented with the foot of the bed towards the door. She averted her eyes from the flatbed.

This was like no MRI June had ever seen before, and she'd seen a lot of them. The company she used to work for, Deep Scan, booked MRIs through the hospitals when they needed to test their code. They couldn't afford an MRI onsite, and their hardware was standard.

The guts of this MRI were spilling out, connected to equipment June couldn't identify. A tangle of cables erupted from the machine and snaked along the back wall before disappearing through a hole into the next room.

On the left, a small partition with a glass window faced the MRI, which June assumed housed a desk and controls for the MRI technologist. Next to June was a white Ikea cube storage unit filled with what appeared to be clothes. Every surface, including the back of the door, was covered in glossy brown hexagons. Some kind of acoustic shielding, perhaps.

June closed the door and retrieved her engagement ring. She sat on the green leather sofa in the hall and waited. After all, she was early.

Phoenix didn't show up at 1:30pm. Ten minutes passed, then twenty. June had attempted to dress up but was now regretting it.

She hadn't noticed that the cuff of her fanciest grey jumper was unravelling. The waistband of her black pants was loose.

I should call Phoenix, June decided. But she didn't, because she thought it might be rude.

Another ten minutes passed before the MediSlice door slid open. June had been winding the loose thread from her jumper cuff around her finger and fretting about how scruffy she looked, and she hastily unwound the thread and stood up.

She recognised Phoenix from his photo on the MediSlice website, although he was better-looking than his picture. His tawny skin and long neck were from his mother, who was a dancer. His narrow jawline gave him a boyish look, even though he was in his early thirties, just a few years older than June.

He stared at June.

"Hello," June said. Phoenix seemed to be waiting for her to say something else, but she wasn't sure what. "I'm here for the interview," she said.

"Right." He shook her hand, barely making eye contact. No apology for being late.

June had a sinking feeling that she wasn't going to get the job; his body language was signalling a hostile *no*.

Maybe Phoenix was just in a bad mood, with something on his mind unrelated to her. She didn't know him well enough to tell. He took her to the glass-walled meeting room, which was dominated by a single wooden table. The table looked like it dated from when Old Parliament House was built, as did the chairs around it, and probably also the sofa in the hall.

June and Phoenix sat opposite each other. The drawn blinds obscured the view, but let in thin bars of sunlight from outside.

A whiteboard on one wall showed scribbled ovals with arrows between them, labelled with names like "collider" and "accelerator." The module names were unfamiliar, but she was reassured by the ovals and arrows, because that was what ended up on the whiteboard at every meeting when her team discussed software.

June bet herself that the whiteboard marker sitting on the shelf below the board had dried out.

"So," Phoenix said, with a sigh that was just small enough not to be rude, "Jane. Why do you want to work for MediSlice?"

"June."

"Sorry?"

"My name is June," she said. "Not Jane."

"That's what I said."

But it wasn't, she was sure of it. Phoenix asked her a technical question on an obscure sorting algorithm, attempting to write part of it on the whiteboard. The whiteboard marker was dried out, as June had suspected, so Phoenix had to fetch one from a different room. He left, his thick expressive eyebrows drawing together.

Phoenix's phone, which he had left on the glass-topped wooden table, showed an incoming call. The phone vibrated furiously in waves, then projected a tiny holo above the screen; a bright-eyed woman, strikingly similar to Phoenix, perhaps his sister. It was an old-school phone, not foldable, but new enough to have holo technology.

June quietly freaked out, biting her fingernail and trying to breathe.

It's a test.

What was she supposed to do? She didn't have any idea how to handle this situation. She sensed it would be inappropriate to answer it, but should she get up and find Phoenix? Or take his phone to him?

The phone stopped, to June's relief. After a moment, it buzzed as a message came in, which showed over the lock screen. On it was an image of a boulder with a date carved into it: "August 2029." Grey-green shrubbery surrounded the granite boulder. The date carved into the rock was just over a year ago. The message was obscured by other graffiti, the most obvious of which was dated 2016.

June didn't recognise the location, but it looked similar to the bushland around Canberra. *Weird.*

Phoenix returned just as the phone screen turned off. He picked up the phone, checked it, and then continued with the interview as if nothing had happened.

June, unnerved, fumbled the sorting algorithm question, even though she was sure Phoenix wasn't a software engineer—although she could tell that he did write code—and he had probably just looked the algorithm up before the interview so he had a technical question to ask.

Her anxiety turned to anger. Firstly, the presence of that specific knowledge didn't predict her general skill as a software engineer. Secondly, Phoenix seemed annoyed that she was able to answer it. Why? Was it a gatekeeping question that was meant to keep her out?

June wondered whether he didn't want to hire her because she was a woman. Being a female software engineer cut both ways; some managers were keener to hire her, but some didn't believe she could do her job until she proved herself to them. Not that it mattered. She wasn't really here because she wanted the job.

"Where do you see yourself in five years' time?" Phoenix said.

"I see myself as Chief Technical Officer at MediSlice."

Phoenix didn't even smile at her joke. To work at MediSlice, she had to get along with Phoenix. It wasn't going to work out. She stopped caring about the interview, especially when he then asked her a stupid "creative thinking" hypothetical.

"If you had a chance to go back in time, to any time period, and change one thing, what would it be?" Phoenix asked.

That was even more annoying, because of course she thought of Elijah. Her emotions hit her like a tsunami, and she feared for a second that she would cry, turning this interview from bad to comical.

But worst of all was that she didn't know what she could have done differently. They had had a great relationship, as far as she could tell, but Elijah wanted something different, which meant someone who wasn't June.

"I would go back and tell the Raiders not to bother hiring Curt Maxwell," June said.

Phoenix checked his phone again.

"Really? The decisions of a local footy team are more important than, say, Hitler?"

"Join the hordes of time-travellers who were trying to knock him off? Not to mention the numerous attempts by citizens from his own time. No. It's pointless."

"Saving the lives of six million people is pointless?" Phoenix said coldly, looking up.

Maybe if she hadn't been smarting over Elijah and feeling utterly insignificant, she would have answered differently, but she was in a restless, brutal mood.

"Yes. History is nothing but a litany of suffering, of all different forms. War, natural disasters, genocide. And if you're going to save all of them, what kind of world is left?"

The anger faded from Phoenix's face, replaced by a kind of respect. He looked at her properly for the first time during the interview. June stared back at him steadily, wondering what he saw. She'd dyed her hair red with henna after the breakup, which she now regretted. She preferred to be as unremarkable as possible, and red hair was more distinctive than her natural brown. Her clothes hung off her; she had been slightly overweight before, but could now be described as slim as her appetite had disappeared. Her white skin would be called pasty on a male software engineer, but would probably be described as milky on her. She had breasts. Maybe they were like some kind of fruit. She didn't know.

"Okay," Phoenix said. "Do you have any questions about MediSlice?"

June shook her head. Phoenix gave a faint smile.

"Everything we've discussed today is covered by the NDA you signed, don't forget," he warned her. A Non-Disclosure Agreement with unusually savage penalties. MediSlice definitely had something to hide.

"Yeah," June said.

"Okay, well," Phoenix said. "I'll let you know the results of your interview within forty-eight hours."

His phone buzzed aggressively, the screen lighting up. June looked at the picture on the phone screen—the carving on the boulder—and a revelation hit her.

The picture on Phoenix's phone.

The seemingly random hypothetical.

A sick, cold excitement filled her, squeezing her heart so it beat with a single heavy *thud*, even as the rational part of her mind was incredulous. Confused, she turned the facts over in her mind, looking for inconsistencies. The carving was weathered, all right, and the nine at the end filled with lichen. It had to be older than a year, especially since graffiti from 2016 was sprayed over the top.

It looked like someone from August 2029 had gone back to 2016 and carved the date on a boulder.

Of course, a crazy person in 2016 could carve "August 2029" on a boulder.

"Can you see yourself out?" Phoenix said to June, answering his phone and sliding open the glass door.

"But—" June said, still reeling with the idea that MediSlice might do *time travel*. Surely not? But then she remembered the sign on the MRI lab reading "Travel Room."

Phoenix swept out the door, talking on his phone, leaving June staring crestfallen after him. After a minute, June collected herself and wandered out.

Of all the interviews to bomb.

———

June carried a bowl of noodles into the living room, avoiding the Lego and other objects—was that a potato masher?—strewn across the floor. She checked for toys before she sat on the armchair; the robot she'd sat on last week had left a tender bruise on her backside.

"Greenhouse gas emissions have decreased by twenty-eight percent on 2005 levels," said Australia's Prime Minister, Peter Larden, from the TV. "We've beaten our Paris Agreement targets. All Australians should be proud of that."

Hannah came in, holding a bowl of ice cream. On the TV, a German politician whose name June couldn't remember leaned forward.

"Meeting your arbitrary and frankly stupid target is irrelevant," she said. "Australia is responsible for thirteen percent of global emissions, because you've refused to stop—"

"TV, channel seven," Hannah said, and the soothing sound of cricket commentary filled the room. She sat on the sofa and tucked her legs up under a blanket. A blissful expression spread across her face as she ate her ice cream. The house was quiet now that Hannah's kids were asleep.

The dark circles under Hannah's eyes had appeared soon after she had her first child, Rahul, and had only intensified in the four years since then. It was rare to see her sit down, unless she was feeding Amy. Rahul was keeping her busy; he was going through a phase where he said "mum" every few seconds, often followed by interesting facts. *Mum! Did you know that octopuses squirt ink but people don't?*

"How did the interview go?" Hannah asked, glancing at June.

"Not great. No chance I got the job." June stirred her dinner, which was still too hot to eat.

"Probably for the best," Hannah said, mostly to herself. Her spoon clinked against her bowl.

"Excuse me?"

Hannah looked at her. "Oh come on. Jess happens to mention on social media that Elijah's working at MediSlice now and suddenly you have an interview there."

June flinched. "I—"

"It's okay. I understand. But I'm glad you didn't get it."

June sat in the near darkness of Hannah's living room, remembering the weeks post-breakup, where she'd seen Elijah every day at work. She ate her dinner mechanically. It tasted like cardboard.

Three years of living together, and within a few hours of him breaking up with her, all trace of Elijah was gone from her rental apartment. *Keep the ring*, he said, and she had. But she saw him every day in the open-plan office at work, which was practically like living with him. June averted her gaze whenever she saw him. Elijah did the same.

He skipped meetings, and he seemed to forget what he was saying when June came around the corner. June startled whenever she heard his voice, and could no longer focus long enough to trace the source of the bugs she was meant to be fixing. Their teammates were rattled. Their manager, furious.

They only managed to keep it up for a week before Elijah took leave. June quit her job, broke the lease on the apartment, and moved from Melbourne to Canberra to live with her sister. Only to find out a few days ago that Elijah had also quit and was working in Canberra, at MediSlice.

She wondered whether she could use the time machine to fix their relationship. But their relationship was great, until it no longer existed. The moments she'd spent with him were her best, and she didn't want them to vanish.

"If you could go back in time, what would you change?" June asked Hannah.

Hannah looked baffled.

"It was one of my interview questions," June said. After her interview, she'd searched for Phoenix online and found a series of teleportation papers which listed him as the primary author. The ability to transport objects through space was a hot field of research, albeit one that hadn't made it out of the lab yet. With Phoenix's background, it was entirely plausible that he had invented time travel.

What would Hannah say if June told her that MediSlice did time travel? But she knew how Hannah would react: she would refuse to believe it. June, on the other hand, was a seasoned sci-fi nerd. She wasn't at all surprised time travel was real, only surprised to find it had been invented here and now, and that she was apparently among the first to know. She knew from books and movies that she should be hysterical, probably wondering out loud whether she was crazy, but instead, she just felt satisfied.

The thought amused her.

"I wouldn't change anything if I went back in time," Hannah said, but June noticed her furtive glance at June's right arm, where the scarred skin went from the inside of her wrist all the way to her elbow. "If I did, it would change my kids, right? Any change would mean a different sperm fertilised the egg. That's too high a price for me. I don't regret having kids, you know."

Which was an interesting thing to say, because it hadn't occurred to June that Hannah *would* regret having kids. Which meant that either Hannah assumed June didn't like kids, or that Hannah did regret having kids.

"You haven't spent much time with them," Hannah continued. "I know it seems like they're difficult and messy. And loud. Also, an insane amount of work. And yes, they've derailed my life."

Hannah thought for a bit more. "Also, I don't get to sleep for longer than four hours at a stretch anymore."

June pursed her lips and waited, amused.

"And I pee when I laugh sometimes now. But—*but*—I love them so much. It's hard to explain," Hannah said. "I guess—I mean, they're just so cute."

"I know," June said, and meant it. She loved children, but if she had children of her own, they would trust her unquestioningly to protect them, when she couldn't. Given the climate crisis, they wouldn't be safe, and June couldn't fix that.

But clearly Hannah didn't realise that was her reason. June fiddled with the ends of her hair.

"It's not about—" June started, but her phone buzzed, and when she flipped it open and read the text, she forgot what she was saying.

MEDISLICE: The job's yours if you want it. Call
me back to discuss salary. -Phoenix.

"Ah," June said.

"What's up?"

"I got the job."

Hannah stared at her, alarmed, then her forehead creased in
sympathy. "That's going to be . . . interesting," she said.

"Yep," June replied. On the TV, someone hit the ball over the
fence, and the crowd roared.

"June, sometimes you—what I mean is, you're not always—
June, Elijah's gone for good, right?"

"Oh, yes, absolutely," June said. She kept her eyes fixed on the
TV. "No question about it."

"He hasn't hinted that there's a chance you could get back
together?"

"No. Not at all."

"Okay then," Hannah said. She glanced at June's left hand, at
June's engagement ring. "I'm sorry. You made such a lovely
couple. But it's good that you're clear on that."

June nodded. She grabbed her half-eaten bowl of noodles and
mumbled something about calling Phoenix. As she left the room,
she heard Hannah say "oh, Jesus" softly to herself.

In her bedroom, she sat on the edge of the bed, considering her
future. She hadn't thought about getting the job when she
applied. She'd had a clear picture of walking through the start-up
space on her way to the interview and running into Elijah in the
corridor, maybe, or passing by his desk. The start-up office in her
imagination glowed white, with modern cubicles housing a few
dozen employees; nothing like the small, antiquated space she
had seen. She had pictured herself talking to Elijah with absolute
poise, although she had known, even then, that she would be
awkward and hurt, and that the conversation would change
nothing.

The whole point of the interview was to see Elijah—she ached to see him—and then, after the interview went so badly, she hadn't even considered that she might get the job.

She wondered what it was that MediSlice actually did with the time machine. If she had known before the interview that they had time travel technology, she would have said confidently that they were developing it into a commercial application. There were any number of ways it could be worth a fortune. But something in Phoenix's eyes convinced her otherwise; he was a man with a mission. And she guessed that mission was to solve the climate crisis, because that was *the* intractable problem facing humankind.

She sighed softly and called Phoenix.

"Yeah," he answered shortly.

"I don't think I can take the job. I'm sorry," she said, and, to her at least, the regret was plain in her voice. Hannah was right: working with Elijah again would be a disaster. Which was a shame, because the job sounded perfect.

"Right. Fine," Phoenix said.

And that was that. She pulled her suitcase from under her bed and began packing; she had a plane to catch the next day, to spend a week in Queensland visiting Aunt Katie. When she came back to the living room, exhausted, Hannah had gone to bed, but the house was still a mess. June quietly tidied up and cleaned for an hour before she went to bed, thinking about the possibilities of a time machine.

CHAPTER 2

Some bright spark on the internet had decided that everyone needed to say "I care about the climate crisis" when introducing themselves, because it was hard to convey that information otherwise; a way of putting climate up front. Of course, this had been seized on by companies as a very cheap way of showing they cared too, and since then, you couldn't buy a cup of coffee without hearing "I care about the climate crisis."

June slammed the door of the taxi. She'd heard it from the flight attendants, the captain of the aeroplane, and even the information desk at the airport, but not from the taxi driver. There were still climate deniers. Merton, Queensland, population ten thousand or so, was probably a hotspot of them.

The opposition to climate change had fallen into camps.

There were those who believed it was too late and too hard to fix climate change, so we had to keep burning fossil fuels and adapt, which was a popular notion with the fossil-fuel industry, never mind that adaptation was impossible.

There were the happy preppers, who waited for civilisation to end, believing they could survive it by growing vegetables. That would work for other forms of apocalypse, just not this one.

There were the people who believed the climate was changing for the better.

And then there were the people who believed the UN was run by aliens resembling yellow bobble-headed dolls and that the US President was part of a vast conspiracy to mind-control the population to stop burning fossil fuels, which—if she succeeded—would cause an ice age.

The roar of the taxi's engine receded, leaving sudden silence, absent from the usual city-noises June was used to. Katie's ground-level Queenslander house sat before her, white weatherboard planks grey in the twilight. The covered veranda was shadowy from the heavy storm clouds overhead. Fragrance from the frangipani tree in the front yard lay thick in the warm air. Rushing water gurgled from somewhere nearby; the house backed onto a billabong, but June didn't remember it being so noisy.

June stood and eyed the house dubiously. *What was she doing here?* When she booked the holiday, it sounded appealing. Hannah encouraged her; June couldn't tell if it was because she thought Katie needed the company, or whether she thought June needed the break. Or perhaps Hannah just wanted her house to herself.

June had pictured Aunt Katie being there to welcome her. Instead, the house was shuttered and dark. She'd received a text from Katie when she landed: *I'm so sorry, June. Bandit got a tick yesterday and was in overnight at the vet in Townsville. I'm picking him up now, but I won't be back until 8. Key's under the mat.*

June slapped a mosquito on her forearm with a yelp, leaving a smeary black and bloody mess, and hefted her bag across the path, skirting around the puddles. The lawn was a green submerged carpet in places; they'd been having a lot of rain.

June found her room and unpacked, suddenly bone-tired. Rain pelted the roof; at first a few discordant drops, then a loud beating on the corrugated iron roof. While she was eating dinner—

reheated leftovers she found in the fridge—she received another text.

> KATIE: Canargen Creek crossing is underwater, I'm going to have to stay in Townsville. See you tomorrow, ok?

June replied, texting with one hand and eating with the other, sitting in the pool of light the hanging light fixture provided.

> JUNE: Will Merton flood?

Katie didn't answer until June was in bed and nearly asleep. June had changed into her berry-pink cotton short-sleeve pyjama top and shorts and had claimed the single bed in the guest room, sinking into the mattress supported by a metal frame that creaked, the lamp on the table beside her casting a warm glow on the blue-painted panelled walls.

> KATIE: No, don't worry. The billabong might come up to the back step, but it never gets higher.

June checked for flood warnings and was reassured to find there weren't any. She answered Katie and put her phone down. The night was warm, the air soft on her bare legs and arms. The rain beat down outside, the sound of sloshing drainpipes and heavy drumming soporific. Later she heard a siren, and someone shouting, but she lay immobile in her bed, comfortable on the edge of sleep.

In June's dream, Elijah entered her room wearing an old T-shirt and boxers, his hair mussed. He spooned her, cosy with sleep-warmth, and she was suspended in that moment. Her body was alive at every point his smooth skin grazed hers. Every time he embraced her, the cacophony of thoughts inside her head harmonised to a single tone that lasted the length of the embrace.

June sat up in bed abruptly, thinking she'd heard a bang, but unsure whether it was part of her dream. The dim holo that rotated above her phone read 6:02am. The room smelled strange; it was gummy and dank in a way that she hadn't noticed before. And her door was open—she hadn't left it open—

Her heart beat wildly as she struggled to reach the lamp. She patted the base of the lamp and the wall near the bedside table before eventually finding the switch. But the lamp stayed dark. Grabbing her phone instead, she turned on the flashlight and struggled out of the sheets, swinging her legs over the side of the bed.

June whimpered involuntarily as her feet landed with a splash on what should have been carpet. Water flowed across the carpet under her metal-framed bed, glinting white in her flashlight, and turning the light-blue wall darker where it lapped above the skirting boards.

The water was up to her ankles, and shockingly cold, given that even the water coming out of the cold taps in this house was usually warm. Her first thought was that a pipe had burst some-where in the house. The house was on stumps, probably knee-high, so surely the water couldn't be coming from outside?

But there was too much water. This was bad, but now June understood what was happening, her breathing evened. She waded across the room into the hall, swearing as she stubbed her toe on something she couldn't see. The hall light wasn't working either; she guessed the power was out. Gum leaves, twigs, and debris floated on the muddy brown surface; pages from a note-book June recognised from Katie's kitchen, a biro, a wood sculp-ture of a swan from the living room, and a garbage bin. As she passed the bathroom, she caught a glimpse of water gushing out of the toilet, dark leaves flowing over the rim like fishes escaping the bowl. The smell of sewage made her gag.

Her feet hurt; the water was painfully cold.

Water rushed noisily under the front door. June wondered whether she should try to block it out with something, but it seemed pointless. *Should she call emergency services?* She called Katie instead, wading to the front door so that she could have a look outside.

She unlocked the front door and screamed as the door shoved itself against her, a much higher level of water outside—up above her knees—rushing in. She dropped her phone, turned around and threw her bodyweight against the door, forcing it closed, but certain it wouldn't stay shut with the water outside pressing against it.

Yet it did. Now her heart was pounding again; it was one thing to be flooded and another to see the higher water rushing in from outside.

June bent down and patted the wood floor around her feet, feeling for her phone in the freezing muddy water, trying not to think of the sewage that contaminated the water. At least her phone was waterproof.

She trod on her phone, but when she picked it up, it was speaking.

"—hello? Hello?" the phone said. June could barely hear the speaker over the rushing water.

"Katie, is that you?" June yelled.

"June! Are you all right?"

"Your house is flooded, what should I do?" June shouted. She waded to the kitchen, not really sure where she was going, and was astonished to see out the kitchen window that the garden and street had turned into a river. It was getting light outside; the sun hadn't risen yet, but it was about to. As she watched, a wave of water came from another direction, much higher. From out of sight, someone screamed.

Katie said something garbled.

"I can't hear you," June shouted. She felt a cold sense of unreality.

Photo albums, she thought. *Passport?* But she didn't know where any of that was, and probably the photos were all digital these days anyway.

"Katie?" But the phone had disconnected.

Her legs were numb from the cold water and painful anywhere the numb hadn't reached. She considered what to do next. It didn't feel dangerous inside, yet, but she thought she should find somewhere that was safer. So she left, opening the front door and letting the water gush into the house. Walking out was like walking up a waterfall, against a strong current, but it wasn't too bad on the veranda. The billabong behind Katie's house had broken its banks, engulfing the neighbouring houses and covering the street. But from the front door she could see farther up the street, which was uphill, and there the ground was clear.

It wasn't that far away. Across the flooded street and up the footpath and she'd be on dry land. Or wet land, rather, but importantly, not underwater. If it was knee-deep on the veranda, the water at ground level would perhaps reach mid-thigh. The alternative was to climb onto the roof, which she could do quite easily by mounting the railing on the enclosed veranda and pulling herself up. But then she'd be trapped on the roof, which might eventually be inundated.

She bit her lip and waded across the veranda, wishing she had shoes. Her sneakers had been by the front door, so they were presumably floating around the house somewhere. The icy water swirled around her thighs as she climbed down the underwater steps, the water level eventually rising to her crotch.

Wincing, she walked as quickly as she could across the yard, hoping she didn't tread on anything sharp. Her feet were so numb she might not notice if she did. Then the water got shallower, and she reached dry land. The edge of the road had been eaten away by the flood, but looking up the hill, it was as if the town wasn't flooded. Except for the roar of water behind her. June shivered.

A silver Toyota Prado came around the corner and drew to a stop beside her.

The driver was about her age, June guessed, lithe and muscular. From his features and skin tone, he was perhaps of Aboriginal or Torres Strait Islander descent, but she wasn't sure. The front passenger seat was occupied by a wide-eyed elderly woman, who watched the floodwater and paid no attention to June.

"Want a lift?" the driver said to June. "There's no towels, sorry, but they'll have some at the evacuation centre. And dry clothes."

"Thanks," June said. She climbed in the back and buckled in.

The driver introduced himself as Yarran, and his passenger as Elle.

June's body shook with the occasional shivering fit as Yarran drove the car through town.

June didn't know where she was and didn't care. She was safe now. In the front of the car, Yarran and Elle were conversing. June couldn't hear properly and stayed out of it, until she realised they were talking about climate change.

"—worse in my day," Elle said. Yarran caught June's eye in the rear-view mirror and rolled his eyes.

June didn't catch what Yarran said to Elle then.

Elle scoffed. "We'll adapt. We're tough." But there were limits beyond which humans couldn't adapt.

A distorted voice sounded from what June had thought was a particularly overbuilt cell phone. Yarran picked up a handheld UHF CB radio, chunky antenna protruding from grey plastic, and held down a button on the side.

"Please say again. Over."

The distorted voice said something June couldn't make out.

"Are you kidding me?" Yarran said and let loose a string of expletives. He finished with: "Useless bloody nitwits. Over and out."

"What? What is it?" June said.

The car braked and June was thrown against her seatbelt, which locked instantly. Ahead, the street was flooded. A wave approached from a different direction.

"They released seventy-five thousand megalitres of water from the dam," Yarran said. Elle pursed her lips and grumbled under her breath.

"That's . . . bad," June said.

"You think so?" Yarran said.

"Isn't it?"

He turned around in his seat to stare at her curiously, and she felt her face warm. *Of course it was bad.*

A wave of water came into sight at the far end of the flooded street, several feet higher than the surrounding water and travelling fast against the flow of the floodwater. Yarran reversed, cruising away from the floodwater just as it reached where they had been parked.

The wave chased them as Yarran sped up the street, the churning brown water carrying along a fridge, tree branches, and broken chunks of plasterboard. June slumped against the backseat, feeling the vice-like tension release from her chest as they accelerated away from the wave until it receded from view.

Yarran braked again. June craned her neck to see water flowing over the road ahead of them. She couldn't tell how deep it was. On the other side, the road rose gently, clear of the floods.

"Can't we go a different way?" June asked.

"This is the only road out," Yarran said grimly, and he swore.

"Language!" Elle warned him, holding her phone up to her ear. "Yes, it's Elle Langford, we're trapped in a vehicle—what? No, we need help urgently. There's three of us . . . no, you don't understand, we need help now. What do you mean? Don't hang up!"

The water was steadily rising in front of them, lapping at white-picket fences on either side of the road.

"They can't help us," Yarran said. His hands tightened on the steering wheel. To call emergency services and have them say *sorry, you're on your own* was unfathomable to June, although she thought Katie would have something to say about that. Something pointed about how June, a latte-sipping city dweller—

never mind that she didn't drink lattes—was spoilt. That out here in the bush, they had to rely on each other.

"We can't cross that!" June shouted to Yarran, who was staring at the water as if it were a dangerous snake.

"We've got to, this whole area is going to be underwater soon," he said implacably, and the vehicle rolled forward, splashing through the water. Elle shrieked and clung to the seat, chanting something that June couldn't make out. Prayers, perhaps.

June sank back against the seat, defeated. *She was going to die. They all were.*

Her fingers were tingling, numb; her heart racing so fast she thought it would give out. All sound was replaced by a single whine in her ears.

The car bumped along through the increasingly deep water, and she caught a glimpse of her waxy face in the rear-view mirror. Then the car stalled.

Elle swore—shocking, but funny from someone who had objected to Yarran's milder curses—and Yarran chuckled in response. June sensed that he was somehow enjoying being in danger, which was crazy.

They weren't very far from the edge of the floodwaters, perhaps three metres, but the fast-flowing water was impossibly treacherous. They wouldn't make it.

"Okay, out we go," Yarran shouted. He touched the buttons on his door, winding down all windows in the car, but as he did, the car rocked, then came free from the ground. It bobbed in a way that a car never should, as if they were suddenly on a boat.

June couldn't seem to move. Not panicking, just lethargic, trapped beneath the weight of knowing she was doomed. The car slowed down, floundered, swept into an area where the water didn't flow as strongly. Elle and Yarran were climbing out the windows, but June just sat there, dazed, as the car tilted. It boosted her into the air, sinking on the left side. Brown water cascaded into the window opposite June and into the passenger-side front window.

Someone yanked June out, scraping her shin painfully on the window: Yarran, fierce expression, blood dripping down his face from his hairline. He was standing in water up to his thighs, braced against the current. He held June's arm painfully tightly as the water tried to pull her downstream.

She found her feet. She half-walked and was half-dragged towards the nearby shore, clinging to Yarran. Elle was on the soggy, grassy verge already, coughing. Their car bumped away downstream, now submerged, only a triangle of roof showing above the water.

"What the hell was that?" Yarran bellowed at June as he sloshed forward. The floodwaters flowed smoothly past. "Why did you give up?"

"I thought we were dead," June said weakly.

"You can't know that. It's not over until it's *over*, okay?"

Their next step plunged them in up to their necks, and June shrieked as the floodwaters swept her off her feet.

CHAPTER 3

She caught a glimpse of Yarran upstream, struggling ashore, before her head was struck hard enough to make her dizzy. Something struck her thigh, and in response she tried to pull her legs up close to her chest. She tumbled through the water. It was like being in a waterslide but with greater turbulence; it dunked her and she choked and coughed, spluttering as she tried to get her head above water. The flooded houses and trees slid by as fast as if she were driving. *Elijah!* Some part of her mind called out, because he'd always been there when she needed him, but no, he was thousands of kilometres away—

She had only an instant to realise the water was going to slam her into a tree before—

Grabbing at the branches, she skinned her hands, but she managed to hold on to one, and pull herself back, hand over hand, until she reached the trunk. She hugged it, able to grab her own wrist with her other hand, locking herself to the tree. The water tugged her downstream, a relentless out-of-control *pull* that she had to use all her strength to resist. But she found a spot that she could balance in, by wiggling sideways, so that the force pushed her against the tree, rather than trying to drag her away.

A wheelie bin swept by, bright-yellow lid open. *Recycling night*, she thought incoherently.

She shivered and tried not to notice that her arms hurt. This all felt familiar, even though June had never been caught in a flood before. Her mind made up these scenarios and forced her to live through them, usually while she was trying to sleep. Perhaps it was because she had been caught in a fire as a child that she went through life waiting for the other shoe to drop.

A helicopter flew over. June yelled and tried to wave, but nearly lost her grip on the tree, and she had no idea whether it had seen her.

Her eyelids kept trying to close. She tried to fight the drowsiness with rising panic, but her strength was fading. Hypothermia, maybe? She didn't know, and it didn't really matter; to sleep was to die.

With a sense of betrayal, June realised that she was going to die. Betrayal and bewilderment, because the government was supposed to prevent her death. Why hadn't they been warned to evacuate? She had a sense that it was unfair to die, but of course it wasn't; her actions had led her here. Maybe if she had climbed out of the car window when she was supposed to, rather than wait to be rescued, she would be ashore now. Or she could be safe, back in Canberra, if she hadn't decided to visit Aunt Katie. She could be on Katie's roof if she had decided to stay with the house. Merton rarely flooded, and never like this. The piles the houses were built on were normally enough to prevent the houses from being flooded.

She could be dry right now if floods hadn't become more frequent and more dangerous. She'd heard Aunt Katie talking about it, after Merton's last—and worst—flood, just two years earlier. Fires were also more intense. Fires drove Merton's residents out of the hills onto the less fire-prone floodplain, which was also a tempting place to settle because the occasional and light floods had made the soil fertile. Fires made floods worse, because they stripped and hardened the land, preventing water from soaking in. And warming air held more water, so rain was literally wetter.

June had always believed climate change was going to kill her someday, even if rationally she knew it might not, but she had expected many decades of happiness with Elijah first. It wasn't supposed to happen today. She decided to take the job at MediSlice if she made it out of this. And if it meant she had to work with Elijah, well, maybe that was a good thing.

Over the noise of the river, she heard a roar of a different pitch. An aluminium dinghy was heading upstream, steered by a man in a baseball cap.

"Help! I'm over here," June tried to yell, but her voice was weak, like it was in dreams sometimes.

The boat turned around, and the man bent over the side. For a moment she feared the boat was leaving, but then she realised it had caught on something under the water, and that the man was trying to free it. She held on, arms burning, shivering with cold, willing herself to wait.

She always thought it would be a fire that got her, not a flood.

The boat shot forward in June's direction, and June sobbed with relief. She grabbed the edge and clambered aboard as soon as it got near her. The man driving barely looked at her; he seemed intensely focused on their surroundings and on trying to control the boat. He had the kind of grizzled, weather-beaten look that June associated with a certain type of Aussie man; stoic, competent men—of any age—who had few words and little patience. June sat in the boat and clung to the side as they raced through the turbulent brown water.

A few minutes later, they arrived at a section where the water was slower, and the man beached the boat, jumping out and helping June out. She tried to thank the man, but instead vomited on a bush.

She was taken away, helped by someone in a navy uniform with warm hands, but it was a blur; a nauseating, bumpy ambulance ride, and then June was sick again and again and had diarrhoea in a toilet in the evacuation centre. Sometime later, she was helicoptered out to Townsville University Hospital and put in a hospital bed, Aunt Katie fussing over her.

Yarran and Elle were okay, a nurse told her, when she asked repeatedly. The drip in her arm tugged as June shifted. She was relieved, but also had time to be ashamed that she had frozen in the car and had needed Yarran to rescue her. *She was alive, strangely*. It seemed like only a temporary reprieve. Climate change wasn't any more dangerous than it was yesterday, but her perception of its urgency had changed, because it had happened to her rather than faraway people. It was personal. She resolved to call Phoenix and accept the job, as she'd promised herself when she was clinging to the tree in the floodwater.

Whenever she was close to sleep, suddenly she'd be back in the roaring water, struggling to keep her head up, and she'd jerk awake and start shivering again. At one point, the television mounted in the corner showed coverage of the flood, and she was sure that she saw the car they'd been in. She saw a bird's-eye view of it stranded on an island—a suburb, just a bit higher than the surrounding area—and saw the car plunge through the floodwaters. But perhaps it was a dream.

———

Almost a week later, June cycled around Lake Burley Griffin. The interesting thing about Canberra was how much visitors seemed to hate it, calling it a lifeless concrete jungle. Canberra definitely had an abundance of paving and wide roads, but the suburbs were leafy, and surrounded by large bush reserves. The city went to bed sensibly early. Good for raising children, residents said. Planned by architect Walter Burley Griffin for seventy-five thousand people, the population was now approaching six hundred thousand. Griffin's stroke of genius was the artificial lake in the centre of Canberra.

She stopped her bike and stood looking at the lake, feeling as if she were on a holodeck. She'd nearly died, but that was in a different town, and nearly a week ago. Even Hannah had stopped asking if she was okay by now. Katie had taken the government buyout of her property and was preparing to move to Bali. The government was efficient at compensating flood victims these days; they'd had some practice.

Canberra was in drought. The Queensland floods had eased, and there was only the occasional news article showing that they had ever happened. But June remembered. She kept getting flash-backs, and the feeling she was getting now—that none of this was real.

June resumed pedalling.

She met Phoenix at the lakeside, breathing heavily as she dismounted from her bike. They had arranged to meet at a café on the lake's edge, just a kiosk with a handful of tables nearby. On the pavement near the bike rack, someone had spray-painted "Fossil fuel = death," which she *knew* was fine, but as a programmer made her feel itchy, because they just assigned death to fossil fuels, rather than suggesting the two things were equal.

A kayak slid past, slicing the freezing air silently. Ducks quacked as they crossed the wooden deck, brown feathers bright in the sunshine. Flooded Queensland was so remote it seemed like a different planet.

"Nice weather we have today," June said, as Phoenix put his coffee and banana bread on the table. Small talk was annoying to her, but she understood its importance. She had read that it was a negotiation for an increase in intimacy. Once she understood that, she could do it easily. If Phoenix accepted her comment, they could move onto the next level where she could say something a bit more personal. But Phoenix just smiled dourly. *Negotiation over.*

He gave her another NDA to sign, but withheld her contract.

"Before you sign this, I have something to tell you," he said.

"Yeah, I know. I figured it out," June said, speaking loudly to be heard over the noise of the coffee machine in the café. Her sweat was beginning to cool, but the sun was warm on her back.

She punctured her orange juice bag with a metal straw. The translucent skin of the juice bag was made of algae that would decompose when she put it in the composting bin nearby.

"No, Jane, listen. This is something you can't have figured out."

"Really?" June said sceptically. He still hadn't figured out her name was June. "Okay. Tell me then."

Phoenix looked around furtively. A group of cyclists in lycra sat at a nearby table, talking and laughing.

He lowered his voice and leaned towards her. "What we do at MediSlice," Phoenix said, and he paused dramatically, "is time travel."

"Yeah," June said. She drank her orange juice while she waited for the important part. The pat of butter on Phoenix's banana bread was melting.

Phoenix blinked at her.

"Your MRI is in a room marked 'Travel Room'. I saw the picture on your lock screen of the graffiti," June said. "Between that and your research interests and the time travel hypothetical question in the interview, it was the most logical explanation."

Phoenix looked bemused.

"Are you going to eat that?" June asked, gesturing to the banana bread. The scent of cinnamon and butter was making her mouth water.

The outrage on Phoenix's face answered her question.

"Okay, okay, never mind," June said.

He seemed to reconsider. "Do you want half?"

"Yes, please."

He sliced it and put half on a serviette, giving her the plate. *Polite*, she thought in surprise.

"Do you want to know how the time machine works?" Phoenix asked.

"Sure," June said.

She shifted her chair forward to let one of the cyclists wheel her bike out. The banana bread had a firm glazed crust but was soft and warm on the inside.

"You know how virtual wormholes exist in spacetime foam and pop in and out of our reality constantly?"

June stared at him blankly.

"You don't," Phoenix said, apparently struggling with the idea that she wouldn't know that. "Well, they do. They only last a Planck time, but that's sufficient to make the teleporter I was trying to build into a time machine. The teleporter was sending apples across the room roughly one time out of ten. I couldn't understand why until I had a conversation with the guy next door to MediSlice, who mentioned the previous owner of the MediSlice office space kept finding apples all over the place. Because, you see, many of the wormholes had one end in the past. So, if you send the matter stream through the wormhole, the matter materialises in the past."

June waved her hand impatiently as he took a bite of banana bread, seeing that he was about to launch into more detail. "That's not interesting to me. At MediSlice, you have invented time travel. Since you haven't publicised it, I assume you want to use it yourself for something. The important part is what that mission is."

"You must have guessed it already," Phoenix said.

"I think I have, but I'd like to hear it from you."

"We're going to save the world, Jane," he said. "We're going to find some tiny nudge, some butterfly wing-flap, that means that we're not facing down the climate disaster today with so little chance of success."

June stood up at that and paced around the table for a moment, because she was overwhelmed with hope, which stung, and made her heart beat too quickly. She never could contain her too-large emotions. Couldn't hide them as well as she was supposed to.

The surface of the lake was perturbed by wind into a miniature landscape of grey-brown mountains, blue where they reflected the sun, rising and falling as if in a time lapse.

Erase the floods. Erase the fires. Erase the heatwaves that had bats boiling alive in the trees, the heatwaves that left stands of trees apparently untouched but dead. Turn the world into a place that wasn't continually trying to kill people—to kill her.

She was approaching her thirties, and her schoolmates were turning up in all kinds of vital roles. The world now belonged to her generation. It didn't, however, belong to her; she was still apart from it, just trying to make it through without anyone noticing that she didn't belong. Which was a pity, because she was starting to realise that some influence would be useful. The world needed changing, but she was powerless to change it, or so she had thought.

Phoenix watched her with a slight frown. A wattlebird landed on the table next to them, cocking its head to inspect the crumbs on June's plate.

June sat down. "Yes. Oh, yes, please."

"You get why it's climate change and not any of the myriad other problems facing us, right? One of my other employees, when she signed up, didn't understand why we weren't tackling war or poverty instead . . ."

"Yeah, I get it. Climate change will end civilisation. War will pass," June said.

"It *threatens* to end civilisation. But it also exacerbates and multiplies poverty. Fix it, and we'll be fixing a bunch of other problems. Although there's many problems it won't fix, obviously."

"Where do I sign?" June asked.

He pointed to a section at the bottom of the contract.

"My name is actually June. Did you want me to put that down, or should I put Jane?"

Phoenix raised his eyebrows at her in an unamused fashion. June chuckled to herself as she signed.

———

The odour of burnt toast wafted in, and June sat up, resting her back against the frame of the bed. The light outside was flat and pale where it hit the planks of the fence. Weeds flourished between the stones in the narrow space between the house and the fence.

In the morning light, her new job seemed crazy. A time machine? It raised a lot more questions than it answered. Where were all the time-travellers from the future attempting to change the past? But she put her doubts aside.

The first thing she checked was whether Elijah had messaged her; he hadn't.

She had made a fool of herself, because she had been upset when he hadn't replied to her message. After a few days, she'd accepted that he wasn't going to reply.

Did he know that she had a job at MediSlice?

> JUNE (5 days ago): How are you? I hope you are well. You left your climbing gear behind, where should I post it?

> JUNE (2 days ago): Please answer me.

> JUNE (2 days ago): How could you?

The words could be read aloud with a minimum of passion, but when she sent them she'd been sobbing, and each minute that went by without a reply had hurt. She never expected to play the jilted lover and certainly hadn't expected to do it with so little grace, but that was where she ended up. *How could you?* was her shriek into the void, but now she was embarrassed.

The news was all bad on her phone. Hundreds dead in the floods in Thailand; she read that with a new horror, understanding now what it had been like for them. Pakistan threatening to use nuclear weapons against India. North American wildfires continued to rage. In Jakarta, a man mowed down fifteen pedestrians in an SUV, killing eight. Work on the Australia–Timor power link had gone over time and over budget, and the Oceania power grid probably wouldn't be online until next year.

June sighed and got out of bed.

Rahul—five in March, as he proudly told everyone, even strangers—passed her in the carpeted hall as she went for breakfast, wearing his Batman costume and mask. He was a quiet, focused child; fascinated with machines and not that interested in people.

"Are you Batman?" June asked.

"No," Rahul said, pained. "I'm Rahul." He walked away, but looking back at her in a distressed fashion, as if worried she'd lost her mind.

In the bathroom, Hannah had overheard the exchange and was snort-laughing. "He's like you," she said, her voice tinny in the tiled room. "Overly literal."

June smiled wryly, because what was normal in a five-year-old was frequently not appropriate for an adult, so Hannah was really commenting on June's personality. A psychologist years ago had suggested that June might be autistic, but June had never followed up on it. She was strange, she knew it, but what good would a diagnosis do now? She was comfortable with who she was.

Pranav, ready for work in his navy scrubs, was trying to make toast with one hand while cradling Amy in the other. His plate clattered on the quartz benchtop.

"Here, could you—" he said, handing Amy to June.

Amy was warm and light in her arms, a whiff of laundry powder emanating from her pink stripy onesie. She looked up, her ever-so-wide brown eyes staring straight at June, and smiled.

It was the smile of someone who didn't have to worry about what was for dinner or what the other person thought of them or what kind of mood the other person was in or any of the million other things humans worried about, frequently simultaneously. It was a toothless grin of pure pleasure, a grin that said *looking at you has made me feel happy.*

June smiled back, with a mixture of delight and sorrow. Pranav finished buttering his toast and took Amy back with grateful thanks. June took one last look at Amy before leaving.

Parliament House was a half-hour ride. Her breath made visible clouds when she exhaled. For some stretches, the bike path was nothing but a painting of a bike on a narrow car lane. Cars drove unnervingly close to her, and she thought, again, of taking public transport, but Canberra's buses took forever to get anywhere, and the light rail didn't go anywhere useful; they were still building lines, even though it had been running since 2019. She was safe, at least, from self-driving cars, since the Beacon app on her phone transmitted her position to them.

She arrived at Old Parliament House. Smoke scented the chill air, rising from a campfire at the Aboriginal Tent Embassy across the road. The demountable building next to the tents had been painted with the First Nations flag: yellow sun on a black and red background. A crackle of raucous cockatoos burst from the gum trees in front of Old Parliament House and flew towards the lake.

Her phone had buzzed while she rode. She checked it as she chained her bike in front of Old Parliament House.

Message from Elijah.

Oh God. Her hands trembled as she read the message.

> ELIJAH (12 minutes ago): Hey, I'm sorry, I haven't been checking my phone. Are you okay?

She stood next to her bike until her breathing returned to normal.

The message was so lacking in context. Was it a breezy formality, or a heartfelt request for information? *I'm not okay.* Would he care if he knew she'd been seconds away from losing her grip on the tree and drowning?

June had never been great at reading between the lines in the first place, but this message was impossible to interpret.

> JUNE: I'm okay, thanks. I just started a new job.

The rose bushes next to the bike racks were covered in new spring growth and heavily mulched with fragrant woodchips. She took a deep breath and went up the stairs into Old Parliament House. The three-storey, white-painted building was semi-classical, with attention to symmetry and proportion, but little ornamentation. The donations box in the entrance hall reading "Donations Make a Difference" was for the Museum of Australian Democracy, which made up the larger part of Old Parliament House.

June whispered *new job* over and over as she walked down the green-patterned carpeted corridor that led to the start-up space. The words were stuck in her head and saying them out loud was comforting. Every muscle in her body was taut.

CHAPTER 4

June entered MediSlice cautiously, fight-flight-freeze reaction happening in preparation for seeing Elijah. But just then her phone pinged with a message from him in the MediSlice group chat Phoenix had invited her to: Elijah was off sick.

"June," Phoenix said, entering the hall. He was followed by a gaunt, white-haired man.

She looked up from her phone, trying to contain her reaction to Elijah's news; a mixture of relief and disappointment that he wouldn't be in. Elijah had Covid-19, he had said in the message.

Phoenix's eyes flicked to June's scarred arm, then to her face, before he appeared to internally dismiss it as unimportant. It was the first time he had seen her in short sleeves, June realised.

"This is Ted McNamara, he's going to give us an obscene amount of money," Phoenix said, glancing at the white-haired man.

Ted gave June a shrewd look and nodded as if that were a reasonable thing to say.

"I care about the climate crisis," Ted said ironically. June thought the phrase was grating and performative. With his tone, though, Ted seemed to be mocking anyone who used it, which was rude.

June gave a close-lipped smile.

"Just a sec, June, I'll show you to your desk," Phoenix said, and he took Ted to the break room, then returned and led June to the computer lab.

"We have a problem," Phoenix said to June as they rounded the bend in the hall. "There's meant to be an intersect check performed prior to dematerialisation, but it's not working, and actually has never been working."

"So the trips you did . . ."

"I could have ended up in the same physical space as a chair, every cell fused to it," Phoenix said grimly. "Or worse. Can you fix it as soon as possible? Ted needs to make a trip, and he doesn't have much time."

They arrived at the glass room opposite the travel room, and Phoenix pointed out June's computer. Unlike the desk in the meeting room, her desk was unmistakably modern, curved plastic and particleboard.

"I haven't even seen the codebase yet," June said. "Am I the only developer?"

"Elijah works on the code too, but he's on the embedded side."

Hearing Elijah's name struck June like a physical blow, which must have shown, because Phoenix looked at her curiously.

"You know Elijah, right? He used to work at Deep Scan too."

"Oh, yeah. Him," June said, trying for a dismissive tone and failing utterly.

Phoenix gave her a quizzical look and left her to it. June sat in the dim computer lab and booted up her computer. Each desk was partitioned into quarters, high enough to block the view of anyone else at the table. Faint light filtered through the window blind.

A poster on the wall was a scene from the bottom of a shallow seabed; colourful leaf-like plants anchored to the sandy bottom rose up towards the light. In between, round striated discs hugged the ocean floor. *The Garden of the Ediacaran*, the text said.

In the silence, June scrolled through the code Phoenix had written, trying to intuit its structure, although the sense she was strongly getting was *spaghetti*. Her disbelief increased with every line she read.

In her last job, she'd been given code written by some of the smartest people she'd ever met: radiologists, computer vision and machine learning researchers, and computer science PhDs. She had learnt quickly that expertise in one field didn't necessarily translate to another.

Some of them passed as software developers. But most of them didn't.

They made rookie errors, such as cutting and pasting huge blocks of code from one part of a file to another. She'd spent days tracking down why some output had NaNs—Not-a-Numbers— and had fixed the bug, only to find the nearly identical code block a hundred lines away already had a fix in it.

They panicked, they were clearly uncomfortable with coding, they did things the wrong way. That's fine, it wasn't their job.

And then this code.

It was a nightmare, and not only because it was badly written, but also because it was not written to be understandable, and because there was so much of it. One file ran to twenty thousand lines of C++, mostly of math operations—linear algebra, vector calculus, and stuff she didn't even recognise. This was a brain dump in code form.

But the code worked. That was the difficult bit. It had been refined; any attempt to change it would break something. No tests, of course. A bug tracker started by someone called Mitch had hundreds of bugs logged, although oddly there was no Mitch in the group chat.

Of course, it was going to be more complicated than she initially thought. When was life ever otherwise?

———

Phoenix had been working for almost five hours straight. Every time she went past his office to get to the break room, he hadn't moved, but it didn't seem like he was working on anything. He just bounced a tennis ball: wall, floor, catch. She could hear the faint rhythmic thumping from the computer lab.

In Phoenix's windowless office, a large standing lamp in the corner created a soft pool of light. Strung-up glowing fairy lights threw strange-shaped shadows across the far wall. Books were piled high on his desk and on the floor, like rock stacks in a national park. His desk was covered in scientific papers with highlighted passages.

June refilled her water bottle in the break room and went back past his office. The thump of the tennis ball had stopped; Phoenix had his head in his hands as he stared down at his desk, unblinking. They were the only ones in the office. The MediSlice group chat had four participants besides her. The two she hadn't met were Blythe and Harry. Blythe had messaged that she wouldn't be in because her daughter was sick. Harry was apparently a historian that Phoenix had just hired.

June worked on the intersect check, which from the history of the file had been commented out since almost the beginning. The commented-out code didn't compile, but reading through it, June knew it wouldn't work anyway. She rewrote it and tested it as much as she could without materialising actual objects.

At 1:09pm, she suddenly realised she was starving. Phoenix hadn't moved. She went downstairs to the café and bought two vegemite-and-cheese sandwiches and bags of apple juice. Old Parliament House was beginning to feel like home; she passed the House of Representatives on the way, the lofty dark-wood chamber empty and silent but for one lone tourist with a camera.

When she cleared her throat by Phoenix's office door, he looked up and scowled.

"What is it?"

Pushing a stack of papers on his desk aside, she put a sandwich and drink down. The condensation from the juice bag made a wet circle on the wooden desk. The sandwich was in a white paper bag, freshly made, and smelled delicious.

"What's that?" Phoenix said shortly as she made to leave.

"I thought you might be hungry," June said from the doorway of his office. One of the books on the shelf above him was precariously close to the edge, pushed by the other books as if it were a penguin forced into testing the waters.

"You bought me food?" he said, sounding startled.

"Yeah," June said, with a small smile. She didn't like him much, but everyone needed to eat. At least her indifference to him meant she didn't care if she was acting in a socially inappropriate manner.

"Oh," Phoenix said. His eyes looked bright in the dark room; his face lit from below by the paper glowing white in the light of the lamp. It was clear he was exhausted.

"Also, I've fixed the intersect check. I'm not sure how to deploy."

The surprise on his face was satisfying. June herself was proud she had fixed the bug so quickly.

"Thanks," Phoenix said. "For the lunch as well. I'll show you how to get the binaries to the machine soon."

"No worries." She leaned against his door. The relaxing scent of books permeated the space.

"I have questions. We can't travel in space, can we?" June asked.

"No," Phoenix admitted. "I should have packed up and gone to Rome as soon as I realised I was building a time machine. But it would be very hard now, with everything built in place. I didn't document as I went, but even if I had, I'm afraid that if I tried to rebuild the machine it would just, mysteriously, not work. So, I've decided it's not worth the risk. It does limit what we can do, though."

"That makes sense. So, who's Ted?" June asked.

"Angel investor," Phoenix said. "He wants to go back to 2002 and be an extra in *Lord of the Rings*. Spend 120 days—including ninety nights—filming the Battle of Helm's Deep at a dry creek quarry in Belmont Regional Park."

June looked at him with dismay.

"I don't like it either," Phoenix said. "But Ted's got cancer, and this is his dying wish. More importantly, we've exhausted our supply of tritium, a radioactive isotope of hydrogen. It costs fifty thousand dollars per gram. We can't use the time machine until we obtain more. Ted has agreed to supply us with enough for thirty trips."

Phoenix picked up the tennis ball from his desk, turning it in his hands.

"The part that scares me is that this is not a trivial trip," Phoenix said. "Ted appearing in *Lord of the Rings* will create changes that could easily cascade and propagate. The life of the extra he's replacing will take a different path, for example. But this is Ted's price for the tritium."

"It could destroy our chance to fix the climate crisis," June said. "What if the world is so different that there's no time machine to send anyone to the past?"

"Then how could we have changed the past in the first place?" Phoenix asked. "I don't know. This is the first big change we're trying. Which I would obviously not have agreed to if there were any other way."

He twirled the tennis ball on one finger, deft and sure. "I wouldn't have worked ninety-hour weeks for the last five years on the time machine if there wasn't an immediate crisis to solve. A crisis that I believe can only be solved with time-travel technology. But that doesn't seem to be how time travel works . . . you see a change you want to make, you go back and make it, and when you return, the change is in effect. Only you remember how it used to be. The same effect should happen if you travel back to the future the normal way—by which I mean one day at a time."

June leaned forward in her chair.

"Don't you have a theoretical model that predicts what will happen?" she asked.

"Actually no. The models have diverged from reality. I've been trying like hell to understand why. Best guess is that if I went back —to, say, 1980—and changed the past to prevent the climate crisis, to the extent that there was no time machine to pick me up, I'd remain in the past, and the changes would propagate forward naturally. By 2030, my younger self would be doing something entirely different in a cooler world, and I, a sprightly eighty-three-year-old, would be keeping my head down."

June contemplated this. "How would you survive?"

"Betting, maybe, but the outcomes aren't certain anymore in a changed world. The theory says just the oxygen molecules I displace should be enough to change the weather, which cascades to changing lottery numbers, and eventually everything. But that isn't consistent with what we've seen so far. I'd make a living somehow. Or maybe I'd end up on the streets. Doesn't matter. First, we have to figure out a change that's guaranteed to work, which is not as easy as it sounds. And before that, we have to give Ted what he wants without destroying our timeline. He doesn't care if he gets stuck in the past, because he's dying anyway, but I do. I've been trying to figure out how to get him in and out with minimal impact. I believe his appearance in *Lord of the Rings* is unlikely to change the climate crisis, so it won't change the course of my life, and therefore the time machine should still exist."

June nodded slowly. They were both silent for a moment.

When they did change the past to fix the climate crisis, everything would change. If a price for carbon had been established in the 1980s, there would have been more research and development for renewable technologies. Earlier electric cars? No wars over oil?

Everyone was reacting to the climate crisis these days, one way or another. The sudden absence of that in people's minds would leave a gaping hole. Perhaps there would be something worse, something she had no way of imagining. Or something infinitely better.

Would I have had a child with Elijah?

Phoenix put the tennis ball down and looked at her. "You're not what I expected when you showed up for your interview an hour late."

"What? I wasn't late."

Phoenix hesitated, perhaps surprised by the certainty in her voice.

He pulled out his phone and opened a calendar app, which showed that her interview had been at half-past one—the time she had shown up. Phoenix stared at the calendar event silently for a moment, then looked at her in dismay.

June smiled at him. "It's fine, don't worry about it," she said, suppressing laughter.

She left the book-filled, cramped office, emerging into the light of the hallway, liking him a bit more after the horrified look he gave her. As she walked away, she heard the tennis ball thump the wall again, then smack on the carpet.

CHAPTER 5

The next morning when June arrived at work, she finally met another MediSlice employee. A woman sat on the leather sofa in the corner of the hall, her back against the wall and one leg tucked under her, engrossed in something on her phone. Blythe, June guessed. She was in her early forties and smartly dressed.

Blythe—if that's who she was—looked up with a haunted expression as June approached her.

"What is it?" June asked.

"I was reading about the ultra-heatwave. Bangalore. They're still counting the dead, but at least tens of thousands."

The term "ultra-heatwave" indicated a wet-bulb temperature of more than thirty-five degrees Celsius, which meant humans couldn't survive without artificial cooling. Sweating didn't work. Even in the shade with water, people would cook and die in a matter of hours. That's why they were called ultra-heatwaves; hotter heatwaves happened all the time, but if the wet-bulb temperature was below thirty-five, they weren't ultra-heatwaves. There had been four ultra-heatwaves since 2023, with death tolls that depended largely on whether the power stayed on or not.

June had read about the Bangalore heatwave. The power grid

had failed at one point. It was now over, a cooler change having come through in the last few hours; it was about 3:00am in Bangalore and the temperature was hot, but survivable. It wasn't even summer there; it was the monsoon.

She sat on the couch next to Blythe. The leather felt firm and cool. The lace curtains on the window down the end of the hall billowed.

"Well, we're going to change all this. They won't have died," Blythe said.

June nodded. "We have zero chance of surviving as a species unless our mission succeeds."

"You're a doomer?" Blythe raised an eyebrow. "Not zero chance, I think, just low. Low enough that our mission is vital."

June stared at her in consternation. Survey after survey showed almost half the population believed humans were doomed, and June was among them. It was a quiet belief; it was easy to assume that anyone who was scared of an apocalypse was probably hysterical. The situation couldn't really be that bad.

But it was that bad. June knew that the world was ending, which had annoyed Elijah—because a feeling the world was ending was unreliable, he said—but the evidence was on her side.

Blythe untucked her leg and leaned forward, resting her elbows on her knees, looking at the green 1920s style carpet. Blythe's blond ponytail cascaded over her shoulder. Dark roots, June noticed. Her earrings were silver, which surprised June, but perhaps sterling silver wasn't magnetic. June figured she should probably introduce herself.

"I'm June."

"I wouldn't have guessed," Blythe said.

"Oh, I thought Phoenix would have told you," June said.

Blythe suppressed a smile at that, and June realised belatedly that Blythe was being sarcastic.

"Well, I'm Blythe, in case that wasn't clear."

There was something self-contained about Blythe; a polite but firm boundary that June sensed she wouldn't give up easily.

"Do you hear that?" June said.

Sounds filtered in from outside through the open window; a car engine revving, faint conversation, a snatch of birdsong, but over that, a persistent beeping.

"Hear wh—" Blythe started, but then she turned her head. Her expression was one of growing alarm. "That's strange, sounds like the battery is low."

June tried to follow her as Blythe rushed into the travel room, but Blythe stopped her at the door and told her to wait.

She reappeared after a moment. "It's okay," she said, exhaling quietly. The beeping had stopped. "Are you wearing any metal? Cardiac pacemaker or defibrillator? Cochlear implants, metal clips on arteries? Other implants? Have you ever had any metal injuries to your eyes?"

"No, none of that. Oh, except my ring," June said, removing it and placing it on the windowsill nearby. Her jeans were elastic-waisted, and her puffer jacket had a plastic zip. Her T-shirt bra wasn't underwire. She couldn't stand the feeling of hair ties in her hair, so it was always loose. She didn't wear jewellery normally, although she had decided she liked her engagement ring; it provided her fingers something new to fiddle with.

"Oh, and my phone," June said.

Blythe glanced at it. "That's a Fantinia 2028, isn't it? That one's non-ferrous, so not a problem."

June left it on the windowsill with her ring anyway. Blythe stood aside so June could enter the travel room. A large battery to the right of the MRI had a power bar showing it was almost empty, but it was no longer beeping.

"The battery power cord had come loose. Good catch," Blythe said, her tone suggesting it would have been a serious problem.

"Thanks," June said, but she didn't really understand why it was so important.

The small downlights that dotted the ceiling were like stars in the dark room; one close to the MRI played over the curve of the scanner, picking out the lines where the panels came together tightly on the glossy white plastic. June imagined herself on the flatbed, being fed into the MRI, and felt the hair on the back of her neck rise.

"The machine runs off mains, but we have a backup battery in case the power goes off mid-trip," Blythe said.

June tore her eyes away from the flatbed. "But it's a time machine. If we do lose power and exhaust the battery when someone is out on a trip, we can always retrieve them later, right?"

"Actually, no," Blythe said. "The machine stores your MRI scan, called a trace, and uses that to bring you back. If it loses power, the trace is lost, and you can't be returned."

"Oh." June's voice was steady, even if her mouth was dry. "Shouldn't you have a backup battery then?"

"The battery is the backup. You know how reliable the power supply is here. If power goes out, it gives us twelve hours to find another battery—easy—assuming the power isn't back on before then, which it most likely would be."

With the door closed and the MRI off, the travel room was quiet and somehow peaceful, like an art gallery. The brown hexagonal tiles that covered the ceiling, floor, walls, and doors contained hydrogenated boron nitride nanotubes, a shield against cosmic rays, Blythe said. Red cables ran from the MRI machine to the far wall. Blythe took June back out to the hall and into the room adjacent to the travel room. A cylinder lay on its side, taller than June, taking up the whole room: a collider. It must have been built in place. Thick red cables ran down the length of the blue-painted metal.

The collider, Blythe told her with enthusiasm, was the smallest that had ever been built. It created ten-trillion-degree heat resulting in a quark-gluon plasma. Physics wasn't June's strong suit, but she nodded. A large fire extinguisher was mounted on the wall near them.

They returned to the travel room and sat behind the control desk, which provided a view of the MRI through a pane of glass.

An oscilloscope on the desk showed a waveform of some kind, the screen horizontally refreshing every few seconds.

"It's scanning," Blythe said.

"But no one is in the past, are they?"

"Actually, our angel investor, Ted McNamara, is on a trip."

"Oh! But . . . why isn't he back already, then?"

"We scan in real time. One second of scanning is one second in the past, which is fine, provided we know the time the person is going to turn up. We start scanning from an hour before the agreed rendezvous time and continue scanning from then."

Ted would spend months in the past, only to return hours after he left. Or, if he were delayed getting back to Old Parliament House, he could be gone for days—it depended how late he was. June was used to things that shouldn't be possible, after all, she'd grown up in an age of moon landings, smartphones, and bacon paste that could be sprayed from a tube. And time travel books and movies were rife. But seeing the machine, she simply felt she was in an elaborate social experiment, in which her reaction would be filmed and scrutinised. The machine was just for show and wouldn't transport anyone anywhere; after all, this was Canberra, not a far-off important city such as New York or London.

The interface on the monitor was locked with a passcode.

"Phoenix added the passcode," Blythe said. "So that people weren't tempted to make unauthorised trips. To change their personal past, for example."

Behind every sign is a story. "Did someone try to?"

"Yeah," Blythe said. "I did."

June waited for Blythe to elaborate, but she said nothing. Behind her confident facade was something tuned too tight. June, who went through life trying to pass as normal, picked it instantly; it takes one to know one, as they say. A hint of unhappiness which showed in the strain in Blythe's voice. A certain wide-eyed quality, like a frightened animal, carefully masked.

June followed Blythe out of the travel room and went to work in the computer lab.

––––––

When she looked up, it was 2pm. Ted had returned; everything was apparently the same, but would June know if it were different? Her memories would have been rewritten when Ted changed things and would be consistent with the new timeline, so June wouldn't see any changes. Ted would be the only one who remembered the world the way it was.

Phoenix had been in his office with Ted for hours, asking him questions about history and trying to figure out what Ted thought was different. Not much, from what June overheard, but then Ted hadn't been back for long. Phoenix seemed to be going through a list of questions that focused on a time period immediately following 2002 and comparing them to Ted's previous answers. Who won the FIFA World Cup? What's the official currency in Europe? Tell me what happened to the space shuttle *Columbia*. What were the 2002 Bali Bombings? Who is our prime minister? Why is India at war with Pakistan? The questions were eclectic and seemed mostly inconsequential, but June knew she couldn't have done better.

June's computer desktop was littered with open files, browser tabs, and notes to herself. She twisted a frond of hair around her index finger.

Someone came up the hall towards the computer lab and June glanced up, expecting it to be Phoenix, but it was Elijah, who stopped as he saw her through the glass.

Elijah slid the door open and entered.

June stopped breathing. She had decided he wasn't coming in today, because he hadn't shown up to work that morning.

"Hi," she said, standing up, which made the chair rotate away a bit. The partitions on the desks came to waist height; she reached out and steadied herself on the edge of one. Elijah stood near the door, feet apart, arms crossed. Strangely solid and existing outside of her imagination, wearing the polo shirt with the tiny Tux penguin embroidered where the pocket usually was, the one he got at a conference. His hiking pants were belted tight around his slender waist.

"Hey," he said in a low tone, frowning as he no doubt noticed her hair—now henna-red—and the engagement ring she wore. He closed the distance between them, until he was close enough to reach out and touch.

She'd forgotten how stern he looked when he wasn't smiling; his mouth all but disappeared in a disapproving line. His dark eyebrows grew together in a faint monobrow, right now lifted on the left in a concerned expression.

"I'm sorry about the text messages," June said.

"Don't worry about it," he said. At five foot six, he was barely taller than her, and she'd always liked that. They were on the same level, partners; it felt more intimate than a conversation with someone looming over her. Then his expression softened, and he dropped his arms to his sides. "Are you okay, June? Really?"

"I'm okay," June said, hating that her voice cracked as she said it. "Your climbing gear is there." She indicated a reusable shopping bag beside her desk, sitting on the green-patterned carpet.

"Thanks," Elijah said, but he just stood there.

"It's great that you're working on the firmware," June said. Elijah was the embedded developer at MediSlice, in charge of the firmware for the MRI and collider modules. He'd been angling to join the embedded team at Deep Scan for years without success. Privately, he was scared he wasn't a good enough developer; he barely scraped through some courses at university. But that was information left over from their former relationship and perhaps an example of why she shouldn't be working with him.

"Yeah. Listen, June, did you know I was working here?" Elijah said, shifting his weight.

"No," June lied, but heat rose in her cheeks. She hoped he

would think it was from the accusation. She stared at her desk, at the bright monitor.

"Only I saw Jess referred to my job on social media, and you two are friends."

"I didn't see it. But as I'm sure you're aware, there aren't that many companies in Canberra for C++ developers with biomedical expertise."

"All right," Elijah said in a measured tone, but she could read every eye saccade, vocal inflection, and muscle twitch of his just as well as he could read hers, so she knew he thought she was lying.

He watched her with a mixture of grief and pity, and it was that look that brought her composure tumbling down, because she missed him so damn much.

The room blurred, making the lights in the hall smears of white as her eyes filled with tears. She was furious at her lack of self-control. Furious, and ashamed, because she was emotionally mature, dammit, not the kind of person to stalk someone who had rejected them, and furthermore not the kind to *lie about it*.

"June—"

"Shut up, just shut up," she said, wiping her eyes and turning away from him. "Yeah, I knew. In my defence, I found out *after* I moved to Canberra."

"It's okay," he said. "Breaking up is hard, I know that. Probably harder for you than most—"

"What's that supposed to mean?" June said. Yeah, she was different, but—

"Meaning, I was your first real boyfriend," Elijah said, more gently than he needed to.

"Oh. That," June said, deflating. She sat in her office chair again, looking up at him.

"So . . .?" Elijah said.

"So what?"

"This is the part where you offer to resign."

"What? *No.*"

"June—"

"This is bigger than us, Elijah. Look at what we could accomplish here."

Also—if she were forced to admit her most private, shameful desire—*I'm not giving up on you.*

Elijah was silent for a moment. "Right. Because you believe we won't survive without changing the past."

"Yeah," June said, but that was a tired argument. Elijah believed in climate change, he just also strongly believed that technological solutions would save them. He was always showing her the National Energy Market updates. How much solar power was on the grid, how fast wind power was increasing, the decline of coal. And there was a lot of good news out there, but June didn't think it outweighed the bad.

"We tried working together. Would it be fair to say that it was a failure?" Elijah said.

June rolled her eyes and nodded reluctantly.

"And yet here we are trying it again, apparently?"

"At least we could give it a shot," June said. "You don't own this place just because you happened to get a job here first."

Elijah drew in a deep breath. "I can't force you to resign, obviously, and I'll try to work with you as a colleague. But June, we're not getting back together," he said. "Okay?"

"I'm not an idiot," June said. Except that she felt like one. She typed a line of code, even though it wasn't syntactically correct and was never going to compile.

Elijah nodded to himself, then took the bag with his climbing gear from beside her desk.

"Your hair looks fantastic, by the way," he said, with a faint smile, and left.

June rubbed her face. The first meeting was bound to be difficult.

———

June wheeled her bike through Hannah's gate into the backyard, parking it in the undercover carport. Washing hung limply on the Hills hoist in the middle of the yard. She sighed deeply and let herself in through the back door, her throat tight.

Pranav was in the living room, sitting on the couch, but as June entered, he rose and paced through to the kitchen in an aimless way. His red-rimmed eyes didn't seem to register June; he just straightened a picture on the wall, turned and shuffled out again.

June froze, wondering what had happened, but it wasn't until Hannah came in that she realised. The news was reporting that as many as eighteen thousand might have died in the ultra-heatwave. June swallowed. Lost in her own drama, she hadn't remembered Pranav was from Bangalore.

Hannah's face was drawn and lined. "His father," she said, in almost a whisper, her voice cracking. "And his niece, Zikshita. She had just turned three."

June nodded numbly, her eyes watery as Hannah hugged her. June had never met Zikshita, but she'd seen pictures and videos of the gorgeous, dark-eyed girl. Zikshita had loved dressing up, equally happy as Spiderman as she was a princess.

We're going to change all this, June swore to herself as Hannah let her go.

CHAPTER 6

t was a relief to be out of Hannah's house, even though Pranav had left a few days earlier, flying to India for the funerals, so the house was quieter than usual.

There was a strange man in the break room, standing at the small table in the dark. Phoenix was in his office just down the hall, door closed. June turned on the light, and the man spun around to look at her. A tray of sandwiches sat on the table in front of him, algae wrap pulled back, as well as some juice and soft drink bags.

"Who are you?" June asked.

The man grimaced apologetically, gesturing to his mouth and chewing faster. His button-down shirt looked new, as did his jeans and sneakers. There was something a bit plastic about him; the unnatural symmetry of his features, perhaps, or his hair, black and glossy as a currawong's feathers. He could have been a model for a clothing catalogue. June suppressed laughter as she waited for him to swallow.

"Harry Wang," he said in an American accent, flustered. "Sorry to startle you."

June came closer. Harry, yes, the historian from the group chat.

The sandwiches were on a catering platter, tiny white crustless triangles of chicken and lettuce, or ham and cheese.

"You're an American?" June asked.

"Yes. Yeah," Harry said. "From Illinois. Visiting academic, just completed post-doc—history—at the University of Canberra. I met Phoenix in the library, and he offered me a job."

June took a mug from the cupboard and filled it with boiling water, making tea. She took a biscuit from the glass jar.

"Why were you in the dark?" she asked.

"Oh! I, uh, couldn't find the light button."

"Right," June said slowly. Did Americans call a light switch a light button? She swivelled to look quizzically at the light switch, which was mounted on the wall in a prominent position and was not at all easy to miss.

"Do you want one of these? Blythe brought them in. They're delicious." Harry took another bite of his. The silver band of his wedding ring glinted in the light.

"I'm a vegetarian," June said. Also, it was 8:53am, which she thought was too early to eat sandwiches.

Harry looked pale. He grabbed a serviette and spat his mouthful into it. "I didn't know."

"I don't mind if *you* eat them," June said, fascinated. She'd never been great at social interactions, especially first meetings, but it was dawning on her that she was doing okay here, and this was weird because of Harry.

"No, I meant—" Harry threw the serviette in the bin near the table. "I meant, I didn't know they were meat."

"Ah," June said. "You didn't realise they were chicken?"

"I thought they were fake meat."

Fake chicken was definitely around, and June had eaten it on occasion, but she couldn't see how anyone could possibly mistake it for real chicken. She threw her teabag in the compost caddy and carried her cup carefully to the door, biscuit balanced on the side. "Coming to the meeting?" she said.

"Right—meeting," Harry said. He was probably thirty or so, but he seemed much younger.

Harry followed her into the meeting room and sat beside her. The wooden chair creaked as she sat down; the green leather upholstery was firm behind her back. The chairs and table were stained with age, probably dating back to when Old Parliament House was built.

Blythe came in with a cup of coffee, in conversation with Elijah. June couldn't meet his eyes, because she didn't know if he was going to acknowledge her presence and didn't want to find out.

"—don't even need an inflator," Blythe was saying. "We find a wormhole, Planck-sized and lasting only a Planck time. When we want to come back, we find another one. The quantum foam is teeming with them, after all."

Harry caught June's eye and dramatically mimed shooting himself in the head. June looked at him with amusement. She wasn't terribly interested in physics, but she didn't find it as intimidating as Harry appeared to.

"But what about the differentiator?" Elijah said. "You need a time difference between the two ends, right? Like, you'd have to take one end on a super-fast trip to get time dilation to kick in, or anchor one end near a neutron star where gravity slows time."

Blythe was shaking her head. "No. That's the thing. There are trillions of wormholes with one end in the past. We can tell the distance in time the wormholes represent by looking at their length, so it's just a matter of searching through the foam until we find one that takes us to where we want."

Blythe, with her long-sleeved black top and silver nose stud, struck June as the kind of scientist whom reporters love to interview; photogenic and articulate, someone to get the public interested in science.

Eventually the conversation between Elijah and Blythe subsided, and everyone sat around the table waiting for Phoenix. The others looked at their phones, perhaps finding the silence awkward, but June enjoyed it. She watched Elijah's reflection in the sheet of glass that covered the wooden table. Outside, a lizard ran up the bark of the plane tree.

There should have been a bigger team here, June thought. Social scientists, economists, psychologists, more engineers, and specialists for carrying out missions. Engineers weren't suited for this kind of thing. She wondered why Phoenix hadn't hired more people, wondered whether it was arrogance; whether, like many engineers, Phoenix thought that technical skills were the only skills. It probably hadn't occurred to him that he needed to hire other specialists.

Then again, to involve more people was dangerous, she perceived dimly; Phoenix could easily lose control of his invention if it became public, or if it were misused, destroying the integrity of the timeline. This was a start-up, run by pioneers, too busy trying to make stuff happen to consider whether they *should*. No oversight, no rules, and the only ethical framework they had was the one they brought with them. Often, to be an engineer was to have enormous power, and it was easy to lose sight of the responsibility that came with it.

An analogue clock set in a wooden box was mounted high on the outer wall of the office, visible through the glass wall of the meeting room. Phoenix came in at 9:04am, carrying a tablet.

The door screeched as he slid it open. Blythe had been reading something, and she dropped her phone onto the table with a clatter, her face contorted with fear. June looked at her with concern, and Blythe smiled at her, but the smile was more like a grimace.

Phoenix took a seat at the head of the table, tablet in front of him, having missed Blythe's startled reaction.

"Okay. Well, mission accomplished," Phoenix said. "Except that the majority of the Helm's Deep footage was cut, after the director, Peter Jackson, decided people wanted to see main characters fighting, not extras. But there are a few shots where Ted is visible."

Phoenix held the tablet up and swiped through a few pictures, captured frames from Helm's Deep, all of which were clearly Ted fighting Orcs, teeth bared and with a look of joy on his face.

"Ted is happy," Phoenix said. "And we have tritium, so we can make trips."

"What changed, other than the movie?" Elijah asked.

"At first he said barely anything, but over the past few days I have been getting messages with changes he's noticing," Phoenix said. "Very minor stuff. A brand of ice cream that doesn't seem to exist anymore. A shop that moved. He says the water tastes different. Honestly, some of this could be his imagination."

He interlaced his fingers in front of him. Elijah looked satisfied.

"It's . . . improbable that nothing major changed," Blythe said.

Phoenix nodded slowly.

The silence gave June a chance to jump into the conversation, something she always struggled to do in a group of more than three participants. She always misjudged, either speaking at the same time as someone else, or leaving it too long and missing the gap. But here was a gap—

"It's possible the changes aren't apparent to Ted. For example, perhaps he replaced someone who was an extra originally, and that person instead went to music college and is now a highly acclaimed classical composer. If Ted doesn't listen to classical music, he wouldn't notice the difference," June said.

Phoenix turned his tablet off with a click. "Right. And Ted participating in Helm's Deep wasn't a change that was designed to cascade into major changes. I think we call ourselves lucky that it didn't disrupt the timeline and move on."

"But you know what I think," Harry said.

Phoenix rolled his eyes while Blythe looked amused. Elijah glanced at June, and she saw he was equally puzzled. At his glance, something loosened inside her; *he didn't hate her*, she thought.

"What do you think?" Elijah said.

Harry's eyes gleamed as he leaned back, opening his hands as if showing them something physical. "The past resists change."

It didn't sound very scientific to June, and obviously Phoenix thought it was rubbish.

"We don't have enough data to suggest that," Phoenix said wearily. "So, obviously the earlier humanity had acted, the easier it would have been to fix the climate crisis. What's the earliest we could have acted?"

"Stop the industrial revolution?" Elijah said. June was about to tell him she thought it was a bad idea when she noticed that others were laughing.

"Personally, I'm not averse to the idea, but there are obvious issues with it," Phoenix said. "The later the change is, the more accurately we could predict the consequences, but an earlier change would have been easier. Let's ask our resident historian. Harry, take it away."

"Take what away?" Harry asked, sounding puzzled. Which was strange, because in June's experience, "take it away" was easily understood by Americans.

"Tell us your opinion. Please. We found out about climate change in about 1980, right?"

"Actually, the earliest report of climate change was 1896, when a Swedish chemist, Svante Arrhenius, worked out that burning coal and petrol for energy could raise global temperatures. Our modelling has become more sophisticated over time, but nothing major has changed in the field of climate science since 1979. But it's always been a problem of how much of a threat it would take to push us into action, and what degree of certainty is needed for the kind of sacrifices required. Would you make these sweeping, painful changes to society—yes, I realise that seems funny now," Harry said, when Elijah laughed. June smiled wryly. If the world had plotted a course in 1979, they could have reduced emissions at a leisurely rate.

Phoenix kept pushing Harry to tell him what intervention would have the most chance of fixing climate change without having too big an impact on the course of history, but even June could tell that Harry was uncomfortable, or perhaps unready, to make that decision.

After some back-and-forth, Harry committed, but unhappily. "The Pink Palace meeting might be key," he said. "A meeting that took place in October 1980, at The Don CeSar—a hotel known as the Pink Palace—in the Gulf of Mexico. It was attended by scientists, engineers, economists, fossil-fuel execs, US government officials from the EPA, the Energy Department, and so on. It was supposed to be the meeting to propose policy, but it was a wash. The attendees barely agreed on anything. If there had been a strong advocate for producing a carbon tax or similar, it might have made all the difference."

"Why that meeting?" Phoenix asked.

"Well. It's early enough that you shouldn't encounter resistance from the fossil-fuel lobby, yet late enough that there's some solid science to base policy on. To wit, the Charney report, *Carbon Dioxide and Climate: A Scientific Assessment*. The 1979 oil crisis is still fresh in people's memories, spurring research and development into renewables. If you get a strong policy *then*, one that can guide America through the next few decades, the impact of reducing emissions might not be too great."

Phoenix nodded. They divided up tasks to prepare for the mission: costume, travel documents, attendees' personal details, how Phoenix could gatecrash it, and more. June felt a rising sense of unreality. Once Phoenix travelled back in time, parts of her entire past could be rewritten, and she had mixed feelings about that. *But it's worth it.* It had to be.

The break room had a protein bar printer, about the size of a textbook, which incubated genetically engineered yeast and produced a maximum of five protein bars a day. The only inputs were electricity and flavour sachets. June had heard of the printers but hadn't used one until today. She watched the printer head dash back and forth over the dispenser bed, building up a solid bar, layer by layer.

Sunlight streamed through the window and the glass jar of biscuits, bouncing around the pastel yellow walls and making the varnished wooden cupboards shine. The aroma of coffee filled the room.

Phoenix came in. June took one look at him and burst out laughing. He wore a bushy eighties moustache, presumably a fake, and his hair was slicked back against his head. His wide-shouldered oversize blazer and matching pants were out of the eighties too.

"You look like my grandad," June said. She laughed again, looking him up and down.

"Yeah," he said seriously. June couldn't keep her eyes off his moustache; it suited him but was utterly incongruous in 2030, where the fashion was to be clean-shaven. Phoenix filled a water glass from the cupboard above the sink.

The protein bar printer beeped, the head withdrew, and the front window slid open. June removed the protein bar. It was warm in her hand as she took it to the tiny table against the wall. She sat down and took a cautious bite. It was spongy and overly sweet. Although chocolate-flavoured, it had an unpleasant aftertaste.

After a moment of debate, she decided not to spit it out.

"I don't like them either. But they are filling. Did the authorisation code I generated for you work?" Phoenix said. He rinsed his empty glass and placed it in the drainer.

June stood up. "Uh, yes," she said, before bursting out laughing again. "The tests went fine. I'm sorry," she said, gasping for breath, "I just can't take you seriously."

She held onto the cupboard, tears of laughter in her eyes.

Phoenix looked baffled, with a slight trace of amusement, like someone who sees there's a joke but doesn't get it. He cast a shy glance at her before walking away. June fell about again when she saw the gap between his pant cuffs and white sneakers. She finished her protein bar and was still chuckling as she went up the hall towards the computer lab.

———

Around 5:00pm, June heard a humming sound.

"He's back," Blythe said, coming into the lab.

June left her engagement ring on her desk, and she slipped her shoes off because her boots had metal zips. *He failed*, she thought, but she felt nothing but curiosity as to why.

In the travel room, the MRI clanked. It emitted a series of loud tones, irregularly spaced, as if it were transmitting morse. The volume increased as the bed travelled through the scanner until it was near deafening. June put her hands over her ears, muffling the noise.

Blythe wore a fake moustache. When Blythe noticed June staring, Blythe grinned and handed her one. It was soft and hairy, with sticky plastic on one side. June rubbed it between her fingers, enjoying the sensation, and put it on. Elijah arrived, and June laughed helplessly at his expression when he saw their fake moustaches. Blythe offered Elijah one too, and Elijah winked conspiratorially at June as he pasted it on his upper lip.

His wink made her heart race.

Harry was at the library, but anyway, he had a pacemaker, so he had to stay out of the travel room with its MRI magnets. The magnets were always on; the only way to shut off the magnetic field was to allow the coils to heat up until they were no longer superconductors.

They stood in the stuffy room under the glow of the downlights, waiting.

Phoenix appeared. As soon as June saw him, it felt like he'd been there for hours and she'd only just noticed. Her brain couldn't cope with him materialising instantaneously.

Blythe was shaking as if suppressing laughter. June, too, was keeping her face neutral only with great effort, but behind her amusement was the tang of fear. But no one would force her to use the MRI.

Phoenix pushed himself up from the MRI flatbed, his moustache drooping over the corners of his mouth.

"That was not really—" he said, then his eyes widened as he saw them wearing fake moustaches. June raised her eyebrows at him, trying to look innocent, and Phoenix choked with laughter, only for the rest of them to fall about too. Their laughter was oddly muted in the room; the shielding was not just for cosmic rays, but also acoustic dampening for the extremely loud MRI. June, trembling, was nearly crying with laughter. Part of it was relieved tension, because she was still here; the future clearly hadn't changed. Part of it was sensory overload. She wondered how much of Phoenix's hysterical laughter was due to him still being here too.

Phoenix was the first to calm down, and he shooed them out, stern-but-amused. The hall felt bright and airy after being in the travel room for so long. June wiped her clammy hands on her pants. They reassembled in the meeting room.

"Okay, so obviously the Pink Palace meeting didn't work," Phoenix said. "I made it to the summit, with some difficulties, which I won't go into here. Except to say that people are really freaking racist back in 1980. I mean I knew that, but to experience it . . . and I thought today's society was bad. Anyway, I was prepared to argue strongly that climate change was real, and that it was imperative that we act. But here's the thing: they already knew that. But they also knew that it was going to cause a lot of grief to legislate. Maybe we should request that American energy policy take into account the risks of global warming, someone said. No kidding. But, hell, every time I tried to speak up, this tall guy, what was his name . . ." He tapped the table for a moment, then snapped his fingers. "Pomerance, that was it. He was practically shouting at people. Usually saying exactly what I was about to say. Everyone else was treating it as an interesting hypothetical problem. The meeting was a shambles. We didn't propose any policy. The moderator ended up submitting a statement that was more wishy-washy than the description of why we were all meeting in the first place."

Blythe was biting her thumbnail, but she stopped when she realised June had noticed.

"Maybe Pomerance was from the future too," Blythe suggested, folding her hands in front of her on the table, and everyone laughed except Phoenix, who looked thoughtful.

"Anyway. I will try to find out if I've made any changes to the timeline. But my feeling is that I haven't. It's clear we have more work to do."

———

After the meeting, Blythe left work, and Phoenix went back to his office, so June ended up naturally strolling down the hall side by side with Elijah.

"Listen, please don't resign," Elijah said. "I'm sorry about what I said on Friday."

"Sure," June said. "Don't worry about it."

But her good mood was leaching away fast. She hesitated, then stopped mid-stride near the door that led them out of MediSlice. "Elijah, why are you here?" she said.

He turned back to her. "What?"

"You know I've always believed that humanity is doomed because of climate change," she said, uncomfortably remembering long evenings where she was full of gloom about the future. Elijah had held her and stroked her hair, trying to reassure her, which in retrospect probably had been bad for their relationship.

"But you don't believe that," June continued. "You think we're going to be fine."

Elijah nodded seriously. "Not exactly fine. We're still dramatically under-reacting to the real risks, however, I don't see the future as very malleable. If it is, great. But if it isn't, we're likely to survive anyway, because our worst-case scenario still results in a liveable planet. But I think we can agree that we've caused serious damage to the ecosystem already and are going to cause more. It would be worth changing the past to avoid that, in my opinion."

"Even if it changes your personal past?" June said, trying not to look as pathetic as she felt. Because she didn't regret the time she'd spent with him. His endlessly playful conversation. Getting competitive with video games. Travelling around Europe, Japan, Thailand, and Nepal.

"Even if we can make a big change to the past, I don't believe that would necessarily change *my* past," Elijah said.

"But what about the butterfly effect?" June said.

He laughed. "Butterfly flaps its wings in New York, the weather is different in San Francisco? I believe there will be heaps of minor changes. But those minor changes are mostly *minor*. There aren't many moments when a person's life changes utterly. It's easy to imagine that rain instead of sunshine on a particular day would have made a difference—one person never met their lover because they stayed in rather than going out, or they were hit by a car because the road was wet and visibility was bad. But in reality, how probable is it? Yeah, the car skidded, but they probably dodged it. Or the lover they were going to meet would have only been a passing fling anyway." He stuttered at the last, realising perhaps that it was a sensitive topic, but to June it was hypothetical, and she was focused on his meaning.

"You're saying your life wouldn't have been very different if climate change had been dealt with in the eighties."

This was a foreign concept to June, because her life definitely would have been different; the notion of being optimistic about the future was a heady and unfamiliar sensation.

"Basically, yes," Elijah said. He then blushed deeply for no reason that she could see.

"Anyway, I'd better—" and he gestured down the hall towards the break room.

"Sure," June said, wondering what his flushed face signified, but he was already gone. June shook her head and went back to work. It was five past six when she realised she was making stupid coding mistakes and needed to stop. Also, she was ravenous.

On her way out, she passed Phoenix's office. He was bouncing a tennis ball off the wall, staring blankly, pages of notes and equations all over his desk. He caught her eye and waved to her, and she nodded in return. She had wondered whether he was taking the responsibility of the time machine seriously enough when he allowed Ted to go back for such a trivial reason. But the dark circles under his eyes reassured her that he felt the weight of it; the weight of their future in the balance.

Outside Old Parliament House, the sun had just set, leaving a rosy twilight. The fragrant air swirled around her as she set off on her bicycle. She felt giddy.

When Elijah broke up with her, he made it seem like it was a terribly difficult decision, and that he'd rather not leave her. But he wanted children, and June didn't, because bringing children onto a doomed planet made no sense. At first Elijah had said he didn't mind, but when he held June's niece, Amy, in his arms, she saw the look on his face and knew that she was in trouble.

June had never considered a future that didn't end in an apocalypse, because for her whole life, humanity had been wrecking the planet. But now it was different. A few nudges, as Phoenix said, was all it would take. And if humanity had a future, that changed everything, including how she felt about having children. She blinked back the tears that had welled up; the idea of having children with Elijah, knowing that they would have the chance to grow up on a thriving planet, was the most painful kind of hope.

CHAPTER 7

The next morning was another meeting. June was stiff afterward. She hated the chaos of meetings; the reminder that people thought so differently to her that they might as well be aliens. Or maybe she just hated sitting for so long. Either way, they bounced ideas around without reaching any conclusions.

Although it was cold, June thought she would take her lunch outside. The Senate Rose Garden, to the left of Old Parliament House, was bordered by a tall, thick hedge. Bees buzzed above the expanse of green lawn, lazy in the sun.

June followed the path all the way to the fountain. Water gushed into the mosaic-lined pool with a gentle burble. At the end of the fountain, the mosaic continued down the paved path, which was covered with a wooden pergola and lined with benches on either side. Fragrant wisteria twined up the pergola posts and tangled over the top, shading the pathway with a mass of greenery. The wisteria had bloomed early this year.

Gentle *thocks* and sounds of exertion came from the tennis courts nearby, although the courts were screened from view by espaliered roses. June put her bag down, sat on the edge of the fountain, and trailed her fingers through the icy water. The tiles at the bottom danced and played, distorted by the moving water.

Elijah cleared his throat, and June started. He sat in the shade of the pergola, on the bench nearest the fountain, half-hidden behind the beam and the cascading wisteria blossoms. His biceps made fine curves where his arms emerged from his shirt.

"I'm sorry—" she said, getting up.

"It's fine," he said, smile a touch too polite. "We're colleagues, right? Join me."

June sat next to him, more nervous than on a first date. Not that she had had a first date with Elijah, because he had asked her out and she had turned him down.

But then one day, one particularly bad day, she'd been crying in the women's toilets. Safely alone, as there were only two women in their department of thirty, and the other was on leave. Elijah had noticed her missing—he always noticed everything— and had waited for her outside the toilet, real anguish in his face, holding a cup of tea that was cold by the time she emerged with puffy eyes. She drank it anyway, sitting with him in a meeting room. She didn't want to talk about it, and he didn't push, but they talked about other things. His presence was comforting.

By the time they finished talking, it was dark, it was raining, and he said he'd drive her home. In the back of his car were all his belongings. He confessed, shame-faced, that his share house had been sold, and he hadn't found somewhere to live in time. Also, he had very little money, having lost most of his savings in the cryptocurrency crash.

She insisted he move in with her, and he accepted reluctantly. Just for a week, he promised, and she knew him well enough to know he meant it. He spent the week doing rental applications, but when he finally got a place a week later, neither of them wanted him to leave.

Elijah sat just an arm's reach away now, but light-years from the man she remembered.

"I overreacted when you arrived," Elijah said, "and I'm sorry.

But also, I'd really appreciate it if you'd stop wearing that," and he nodded at her engagement ring.

"Of course," June said. She slipped it off now and put it carefully in a zipped pocket of her bag.

June removed her curry from her bag—it was hot in her hands —but she was not hungry anymore. Elijah had a plate of sandwiches from the catering pack Blythe had brought in.

"Who was Mitch?" June asked, having seen his name in the bug tracker and deduced that she had taken over his job.

"He was a software developer here. I never met him. Blythe said he only lasted a few weeks."

"What happened to him?" June asked.

"He decided the world needed to know about the time machine," Elijah said dryly. "He sent letters to various people, which he copied to his blog. He only got eleven YouTube views— and three of those were us—and he was the focus of a Twitter pile-on, so yeah."

"You're saying that I might not be sued if I break the NDA and go public," June said. "I might just be laughed at."

"Exactly right," Elijah said, and they both laughed.

June fell comfortably silent. She wanted badly to close the gap between them, to snuggle in like she used to. Elijah's laundry powder was heavy in the air, mingling with the scent of sweet wisteria blossoms.

Even though it was spring, the chill of winter was still in the air, although the bitter cold that had gripped Canberra for months had ended. Spring should be a time of hope, but June had always preferred autumn. Spring turned too quickly into summer, and summer meant fire. June touched her wrist with cool fingertips, tracing a line where the burn scars came to an end. This summer in particular was meant to be a bad one, since the drought had been going on for so long. The states and territories hadn't been able to do many prescribed burns this year because it had been too dangerous.

"What if we change the past?" June said. "Can you even imagine a future that doesn't have an axe hanging over it?"

"I don't see it that way," Elijah said, a bit stiffly. "But having climate change under control would be good."

She didn't want to get into another argument, so she tried to think of a new topic of conversation. Elijah was going to finish eating and leave soon—she had no right to his time—and somehow that broke her heart all over again. He was just a warm body next to her, his thoughts invisible, but she recognised in him a thousand memories of their shared past. Remember when Rahul was a toddler, and he hit you in the head with a truck because you were pretending to be a tiger and threatening to eat him up? Remember when we camped at the coast and it rained all weekend and we spent the whole time in the tent, eating bread and peanut butter because it was too wet to cook with the gas stove? Remember the sketches we made of the ideal yet unrealistic house we wanted to build one day, with the library and gaming room and underground pool?

June was so sure that she wanted him back. She wanted to approach this subject delicately, to speak in the language of subtext and implication, but she didn't know how. Her way was to say what she felt. She knew it made her awkward.

"I'm starting to think about a future where climate change isn't an issue. And in that future, I think I would want children," she said.

She hoped for a look of joy on his face, but he looked panicked instead. Elijah was an only child, raised by his father. June, with her two sisters, and many aunts, uncles, and cousins, couldn't imagine how quiet that must have been. Hence Elijah's insistence, at the end, that he needed to have children.

"I guess it wasn't just whether or not we were going to have a baby," June said ruefully.

Elijah stared intensely at his plate. "It was, but . . ."

"But what?"

"You know when we play chess, and you're losing, and you resign?"

"So what?"

"So, you could still win. But you never try."

"You broke up with me because of the way I play chess?" June said. This conversation wasn't going the way she wanted, but she hadn't imagined her chess skills were going to be criticised.

"No, I mean, that's your approach to the climate crisis too. Assume the worst. Assume you have no agency, no ability to change anything."

"That's rich coming from a meat eater," June said, annoyed. "I'm the one who wanted to reduce our carbon footprint."

A tennis ball hit the rose-espaliered wire mesh fence, making it rattle. Someone on the court laughed.

"I'm not talking about our carbon footprint. The whole notion of personal carbon footprint is rubbish, you know that."

"Yeah. But then what? I don't own a coal plant I can shut down. And it's not like you're doing anything about the climate crisis."

"I'm not doing anything because I don't believe action is required. IPCC's worst-case predictions for warming that it made in 2014 are no longer possible—we're definitely not going to have five degrees of warming by the end of the century. I know we're not on track for the most optimistic scenario, but every year that goes by brings us farther away from the most disastrous ones. But if I believed what you did, I would be fighting somehow."

"I am doing something," June said. She stood up. "I'm trying to change the past."

"Right," Elijah replied. "But you never tried to change the future."

He was still staring at his plate, not looking her in the eye. The wisteria swayed in the breeze as she walked away, not looking back.

———

That night, at 8:16pm, someone knocked on her bedroom door. For an instant, June was afraid that her tears hours earlier had left a mark, even though she was certain that they couldn't.

"It's me," Hannah said, voice muffled. June had come home from work early for once but had cooked dinner for everyone, then shut herself in her room. Light had leached from the world, leaving the fence outside her window grey, and then it had disappeared entirely. Pranav had returned from India earlier that day. June heard the drama that was getting kids to eat dinner, and the drama that was getting kids to bed, including Rahul's tantrum because he wanted to take teddy in the shower, but she had played computer games on her laptop right through the whole thing, under blankets in her bed because she was cold. Hannah's house was like many other houses in Canberra, poorly built in the sixties and renovated to modern taste with white walls and sleek bathrooms, but without any underlying improvements that addressed the lack of insulation.

"Come in," June said, pulling her headphones off. She felt much better after crying; it had blown the fogginess away, leaving her clear and sharp. Perhaps she should cry more often.

Hannah opened the door. She surveyed June, who was sitting up in bed with her laptop on her lap, a half-eaten packet of Tim Tams on the bedside table beside her.

"Oh no," she said, and grimaced in sympathy. "That bad, hey?"

"I'm fine, this has made me happy, actually," June said, as she reached over from her bed and closed the curtains over the night sky visible through the window. "I mean, fight with Elijah, minus ten points, but computer game, eight points, and Tim Tams, six points, so actually, I'm ahead by four points."

June shifted her feet, and Hannah flopped back on the bed and stared at the ceiling. June's room had no decorations. It was a guest room, after all, and only meant to be temporary.

"How's Pranav?" June asked.

"He's okay. We're okay. He's trying to get visas for his sister's family and his mother to come over here. India's power grid . . . and with the heatwaves . . ."

Instead of finishing the sentence, Hannah sighed. Pranav's father and niece were frequently on June's mind; she didn't think she had the right to grieve for them, because she barely knew them, but their deaths rattled her. She couldn't seem to forget them. She had read some analysis after the ultra-heatwave, talking about how Australia had to speed up its work on the Australia–Timor power link. Had the Oceania grid been online, the death toll would have been far lower.

"Are you okay to share a room with Rahul for a bit, so his sister's family can take this one, assuming we do get them visas?" Hannah asked. "We'll put his mum in with us. It'll be crowded, but . . ."

"Of course," June said. She thought of Pranav's sister and her husband and son squeezing into this room, no Zikshita with them, and blinked back tears.

"Thanks, sweetie. Thanks for making dinner, too. You didn't have to do that."

"It was nothing," June said.

After a pause, Hannah opened her eyes. "Want to talk about your day?"

"Nope," June said. Her problems seemed tiny, suddenly. Hannah rarely asked about her work, because June was adept at giving technical explanations which were boring for Hannah.

"Fair enough. Want some big-sisterly advice?"

"Always."

"You're working too hard. Remember that the company doesn't care about you. You don't owe it all your time," Hannah said.

"But the work is important," June said. "Like change-the-world important."

"Since when do you care about changing the world?"

This was uncomfortably close to what Elijah had said, but June could see what she was getting at. She thought about it. Before she could say anything, Hannah sat up.

"Maybe it's because you're living with me. It's different when there are kids around," Hannah said. June waited for Hannah to finish, even though she knew what Hannah would say next, because she'd said it before. It was inefficient for both of them.

"I mean, everyone says that you always want to change the world when you have kids, but I didn't understand until Rahul started to ask questions. I think before you have kids, it's impolite to question why things are the way they are, because you're like a guest in the world, but once you have kids, you're more like a host," Hannah said.

People didn't like it when you interrupted them, June had discovered. She used to think she was doing them a favour by saving them from having to complete their sentence—she didn't mind being interrupted herself—but it turned out people disliked it.

"You've told me that before," June said politely.

Hannah laughed. "What are you doing this weekend?"

"I haven't made plans," June said, knowing that she was about to be lectured on the importance of socialising. But June didn't know many people in Canberra and didn't feel like getting to know anyone right now. She was content to ride her bike around on weekends, visit museums, and read books. Some friends from Melbourne, including Deep Scan colleagues, were still in contact. June missed them, but she found long-distance communication terribly awkward. Also, many of them had been Elijah's friends first, which had made things doubly hard after the breakup. Some friends vanished, but to her surprise, the breakup made her closer to others. Until she left Melbourne, anyway.

"You should get out and date. Follow Elijah's example," Hannah said.

"*What?*" June said.

"Oh shoot," Hannah said, clapping her hands over her mouth

in a frantic gesture. She dropped her hands and looked at June in anguish. "I assumed that was why you were upset. I'm so sorry."

"Better that I know," June said evenly. Hannah scrutinised her, but June returned her gaze calmly, and the advantage of being naturally inscrutable—and of being known as somewhat unemotional—was that she could usually keep her feelings private if she wanted to.

The rest of the conversation was on autopilot, but Hannah left eventually, after giving her a hug. June closed her laptop screen slowly, shaken.

She took her engagement ring out of the jewellery box on her bedside table. She loved the symmetry and the feel of it; the weight of such a tiny thing, the smoothness of the band, and the machined edges of the diamonds. Turning it over and over in her fingers, she unfocused her eyes until all she saw was the occasional flash of a diamond facet catching the light.

One day long ago, before she knew Elijah well, she and Elijah had been at a restaurant with most of the Deep Scan team, and the waiter had balanced a stack of empty plates with forks on top in such a way that they were about to slide off. Before June could react, and before anyone else at the table had even noticed, Elijah had grabbed them and repositioned them on the plate. He noticed things more than others, as if he were more present somehow. On that particular day, when June had watched him save the cutlery, he gave her a kind smile, which, even though she barely knew him, had made her warm inside. He noticed things about June, too, brought to her attention the myriad ways he valued her.

Until he didn't.

But dating meant nothing; if anything, it showed her he wasn't in a relationship. It wasn't over.

———

June had forgotten to charge her phone for three days in a row, and the batteries were dead. She could charge it at work, but in the meantime, her Beacon app wasn't running. As she rode down Northbourne Avenue, she hoped like hell that self-driving cars would recognise her without the app transmitting her location to them. A bus indicated and pulled into the bike lane to pick up passengers. June sighed, stopping. There weren't that many self-driving cars in Canberra, anyway, and who was to say they were more dangerous than distracted drivers?

June arrived and was chaining her bike up outside Old Parliament House when a man interrupted her. Handsome, well-groomed in a smart-casual suit, very white teeth, hair shot through with silver. He smelled like cologne.

"Excuse me," the man said. "Do you work at one of the start-ups here?"

"Yeah," June said, wary. "Why?"

"Ethan Williams; I care about the climate crisis," Ethan continued. "I'm looking for someone."

Ethan held a photo out. It was a picture of Blythe, unquestionably, but younger, slimmer, and more confident looking. She wore a pair of horn-rimmed glasses, and black hair so short it was practically shaven. "Look familiar?"

"No, sorry," June said. Ethan nodded as if that's what he expected.

"Okay," he said.

June tried to walk away, but Ethan followed her. "Can I give you my number in case you see her?"

"I don't think so," June said. "Leave me alone, please."

"This woman, Alisha, is missing. Her family is very worried about her."

June walked up the stairs, ignoring him. "All right, you have a good day now," Ethan called after her.

June turned left into the start-up space, but she was afraid she was being followed, so on her way she ducked into the House of Representatives and loitered for a few minutes. She left when a group of schoolchildren entered.

She slid the MediSlice doors open and went straight to the

collider room, where Blythe sat cross-legged in front of the giant cylinder. It was open, like a giant tree that had been chopped in two. It even had concentric rings, but made of metal, with clusters of fine blue wires connecting the inner rings to the outer rings. A smaller core cylinder protruded from the inside. Blythe had parts arrayed in front of her, and tools out, but she was staring at her phone. She had a tattoo on her shoulder; most of the tattoo was under a strap of her dress, but a curling leaf stood out in sharp black against her pale skin.

June watched over Blythe's shoulder. June assumed it was going to be about the bushfires at Noosa, but apparently not, because some Americans were talking.

"—bad state," Senator Gomez was saying. "As many of you know, the acidity of the ocean is greater now than at any point in the past two million years because of the carbon it has absorbed. Carbon dioxide reacts with seawater to increase the acidity. This reduces carbonate, which is causing problems in creatures that use it. At the base of our food chain live planktonic snails called pteropods. These are now disfigured, pitted with holes, because of the lack of carbonate. If the base of the food chain collapses, the entire food chain goes, and we end up with slime. That is not a world any of us want to live in."

The news moved on to the bushfires at Noosa. Orange skies and walls of flame higher than skyscrapers filled the tiny screen. A child clung to his grim-faced mother as they boarded a boat and pushed away from shore.

Blythe sniffed, and June realised two things at the same time. Firstly, that Blythe was crying, and secondly, that Blythe probably didn't know June was there. She wasn't sure how to solve those problems. She felt a stir of anxiety. Blythe cupped her phone in her hands.

June coughed, solving problem two, and Blythe jumped.

"Um, I'm not often required to provide emotional support, so I don't know how to do this. But. It'll be okay? Can I get you anything?" June said, feeling stupid already.

As a software engineer, most of June's classmates—and later, colleagues—had been men. She never saw any of them cry, although she assumed they must occasionally, as she did. Not in front of anyone, though.

"I'm fine," Blythe said, turning off her phone and folding it away. She wiped her face. She'd removed her silver nose stud and ear-piercings—probably so that she could work with the active MRI—making her look strangely bare; younger, almost, although that might have been because June had caught her in a vulnerable state.

I should have left her alone, June thought, her face radiating heat from the shame. She wrung her hands. Blythe seemed embarrassed, but June was sure that she wasn't as embarrassed as June was.

"Anyway. What can I do for you?" Blythe said.

"A man was looking for you outside Old Parliament House. Ethan Williams. He said you were a missing person. He showed me your picture, but he called you Alisha."

Blythe paled.

"I didn't tell him I knew you," June said quickly.

"Thanks," Blythe said. She looked at June's face, but didn't quite meet her eye. "That was my ex-husband. I was in an abusive relationship."

"Okay."

"Will you tell me if you see him around again?"

"Sure . . . so, the unauthorised mission you went on, was that about your marriage?"

"No," Blythe said quickly. She looked at June as if she were about to say something else, but just sighed. "I've got to call my husband," she said, picking up her phone and flipping it open. June stood up. She glanced over her shoulder as she left, to see Blythe's face filled with fear.

Elijah was in the computer lab at his desk. June hadn't seen him since their lunch yesterday. The room was dark except for the glow from around the edges of the window blinds; June knew Elijah preferred it that way.

He looked at her when she slid the door open, and she wondered if he was going to apologise, or if he expected her to.

They were silent for a moment, June forlorn, and in the stillness Elijah swallowed. She smiled tentatively, and he nodded back.

June sat in her chair with her back to the window and played with the ends of her hair. Elijah's upper body was hidden by the partition, but she could see his legs, and could see that one of his shoelaces was undone. June started working, but she didn't stop hurting.

Ideally, he would do some work in mending their relationship, but she didn't have any right to expect it. What she wanted was for him to go to great lengths to win her back; to grovel, to be torn up inside when she wouldn't accept his advances immediately. But he wasn't going to do that, so she would just have to approach him like he was the injured party.

She sighed inaudibly.

CHAPTER 8

Each evening before bed, June read *The Wheel of Time*, working her way through the fourteen volumes. Rand and his friends against the Dark One and the Forsaken. She sat in bed in her quiet anonymous guest room with its bare white walls and view of the weedy space between the house and the fence. The nights were still cold, and she left the electric blanket on until she was ready to sleep, but she still woke up freezing in the middle of the night.

During the day, she sat in meetings until her backside ached. Rapid climate change was a worse foe than the Dark One. It was slippery, insidious, and slow acting. People died in climate-related events every day, all over the world, but since there wasn't an obvious enemy, how could they attack it?

One wall of the meeting room was transformed into a collage. It was plastered with a history of climate change, mostly curated by Harry and annotated with his neat handwriting. Despite his fear of mathematics, he was studious, always working away with a stack of library books. He created a timeline of conferences, meetings, hearings, publications, and publicity, all linked together with their outcomes. Photos and bios of hundreds of people who influenced events were added to the wall. Presidents Carter, Reagan, and Bush Snr, and vice president Al Gore. A sea of acronyms, which came to be as familiar as her own name to June, for all the organisations that might have played any part in trying to stop climate change: the United Nations Environment Programme (UNEP), the World Meteorological Organization (WMO), the United States Environmental Protection Agency (EPA), the American Petroleum Institute (API), the US Energy Department and its Office of Carbon Dioxide Effects, the National Security Council, and many others.

After the third day of meetings, Phoenix said with a sigh that he hadn't realised inventing a time machine would be the easy part. They had, by consensus, decided that they had been too hasty in sending Phoenix to the Pink Palace meeting and made up for it now with exhaustive research.

June came to think of the meetings as Save-the-World meetings. First, they had to understand the history properly, the points at which things might have been different, the triumphs, and the disasters. Day after day, they discussed what had happened, and what could have happened differently. As the weeks went on, the weather warmed. By late September, spring was finally in the air and with it a languid feeling.

"We should focus our attention on the decade between 1979 and 1989," Harry said one day. "And on America, the largest emitter at that time, because they were in a position to lead the world then. That was the golden decade, when the largest oil and gas companies were willing to make changes, if someone had stepped up and led."

"Why, what happened after that?" Blythe asked.

"Between 2006 and 2016, fossil-fuel companies spent more than two billion dollars trying to oppose action on climate change —ten times as much as was spent by environmental groups. The Global Climate Coalition went from a body that shared news of proposed regulations, to running a press campaign emphasising the uncertainty in the magnitude and timing of climate change, to outright claiming that the fundamentals of climate change were uncertain."

The rest of them listened silently. Outside the window, a magpie warbled.

"I don't understand why the fossil-fuel companies resorted to such behaviour after being willing to cooperate," Blythe said.

June—who had started speaking at the same time as Blythe and stopped herself—had missed the gap in the conversation to say that fossil-fuel companies were even now behaving questionably, pretending that they could claim negative emissions from cancelled projects that would have produced emissions.

"My theory—my personal theory—is that it's because of the rise of inequality that was taking place at that time," Harry said. "We know that, beyond a certain point, inequality can lead to a loss of trust in society and a rise in antisocial behaviour. A feeling that you're being treated unfairly prompting you to act however you want to get what you can, because if you don't, someone else will."

"Mos maiorum," Elijah murmured, just as Phoenix said, "the collapse of the mos maiorum, as it were."

"The collapse of what now?" Blythe said.

Both Elijah and Phoenix started to explain at the same time, and Elijah looked aggrieved as he let Phoenix finish explaining what mos maiorum was. Blythe glanced at June and flicked her eyes upward in exasperation, but she was also smiling in amusement, so June wasn't sure how to interpret that and gazed at her curiously for a moment. Mos maiorum was the set of societal norms in ancient Roman times, apparently, and their rejection led to the beginning of the Roman Empire's decline.

Phoenix started off by shooting down every mission idea, but after Blythe pointed out what he was doing and said that they were going to have to take risks, he went quiet for a while, then agreed to one of the mission ideas.

June relaxed after she realised that no one was going to force her to go on a mission. She was curious about the past, but she didn't want to subject herself to the MRI with its claustrophobia-inducing space and overwhelming noise. The rest of them were keen to go on missions, except Harry, who was banned from the MRI room because of his pacemaker. And Phoenix: they had decided to ban Phoenix from future missions, in case something went wrong with the time machine, since he had the best chance of diagnosing and fixing any problems.

Elijah went to a meeting in Woods Hole, on the southwestern spur of Cape Cod, to try to influence the Charney report, *Carbon Dioxide and Climate: A Scientific Assessment*, to add in urgent warnings. The Charney report was the science that the Pink Palace meeting—the one Phoenix had been to—had used to try to work out policy. Elijah reported, with bemusement, that they had filled mesh produce bags with lobster, clams, and corn. They boiled the bags in a cauldron and ate the contents. Apparently, it was called a clambake. Then they sat down and discussed the fundamentals of climate change for a few days. Then they almost ran out of time to try to figure out why the temperature predictions from a group of scientists called the Jasons didn't match the predictions of the Mirror World computer simulations.

Elijah took the place of a scientist they knew was invited who didn't show up, doing his best British accent. He waited patiently as they had a shouted long-distance phone call with the researcher who created the Mirror World simulations, then he offered to help the scientist tasked with working out why the figures didn't match—which Elijah was an expert on, given all the papers that had been published subsequently on the topic—but he was politely rebuffed, and he hadn't been able to persuade the scientist to change his mind.

When Elijah returned, the mood at the debrief meeting was sombre. At least he had made it back, and hadn't damaged the timeline, but on the other hand, he had not managed to influence the outcome of the meeting at all; the Charney report was as they remembered it. Harry's words echoed in June's mind: *the past resists change.*

By unspoken agreement, and even though Phoenix told them to knock it off, they all arrived before 8:00am, and usually didn't leave until 7:00pm, except Blythe if she had to pick up her daughter, or Elijah, if he had a date. Phoenix always worked those hours, but he made it clear he didn't expect them to. Yet, they crowded into the break room every night to eat together; pizzas, dals and naan, vegetable fried rice, or sesame noodles. June was there because she wanted Elijah. Elijah was single, so he didn't have a family to go home to. Phoenix lived alone, June knew. Harry apparently just enjoyed everyone's company; perhaps, as an American, he didn't know many people in Canberra. His wife and children were in America and he talked about them often, clearly missing them. The big mystery was Blythe; June expected her to go home early to her family, but she rarely seemed to want to.

As night fell outside the window, the glow faded from the pastel yellow break room, leaving it bleak, but the steady conversation and laughter continued. June was careful never to sit next to Elijah, and she thought he was doing the same, but they worked well together, pretending to be colleagues. That evening, after the team broke up, June had an attack of self-doubt. *Elijah didn't want her back.* She had been stupid to follow him.

Hannah and her husband and kids were out, but had left the kitchen a mess. June was doing the washing up late at night, listening to "World Spins Madly On", and her whole body convulsed as she cried.

She sobbed while scrubbing saucepans and loading cutlery into the dishwasher. She didn't hear Hannah come in, but suddenly Hannah appeared and hugged her, mostly with concern but also some amusement. Probably because being broken-hearted was something everyone went through, a rite of passage June had delayed, but not avoided.

Yet Elijah seemed to only go on first dates; she'd heard him discussing some of the more disastrous ones with Harry. His complaints were a litany of ways that the women he'd dated weren't like June, or at least that's what it sounded like to her. And he looked at June in a tender way, sometimes, which made her think that it wasn't over for him. Outside the meeting room window, past the terrace, the plane tree flowered, and work went on.

June's phone pinged at all hours of the day as they shared questions, jokes, links, and messages via group chat. When her phone was unfolded, there was a constant stream of animated holos dancing above it. She and Blythe messaged each other privately as well; Blythe seemed to have decided June was okay, after June didn't tell the others about her ex-husband, and they had lunch together almost every day, in the Senate Rose Garden, or in one of the cafés in Old Parliament House.

Harry added more detail to the wall. They were not there to assign blame, but it was impossible to avoid drawing conclusions. June had thought that it was the fossil-fuel companies and perhaps the politicians to blame, but of course, it was not that simple. No one could enact a global tax without a global tax collector, which meant an international treaty. Why should fossil-fuel companies take on a problem which governments were unwilling to legislate, one in which the effects were invisible—as they were at the time—and which to remedy would mean denying customers what they wanted and putting themselves out of business? And without an obvious, attainable solution, or widespread public support, no politician would try to enact policy that was doomed to fail.

June had the sense of an opportunity slipping away, as they argued over which small change could snowball into something big enough to divert the world from its disastrous course. They talked constantly, trying to figure out where a change would take them, how hard it would be to effect, and what chance it had of succeeding. They looked things up, and they ran ideas past Harry.

They brainstormed a lot more missions than they went on. Could they make Al Gore's greenhouse effect hearing in 1980 more interesting? It was ignored completely by the media, who reported on a baseball strike and the national surplus of butter instead.

"If we're going to gatecrash a hearing, we should do the Hansen hearing in 1982. At least there was some observable warming by then," Elijah said. He gestured to the whiteboard timeline with a piece of pizza, which flopped. "Hansen testified the surface temperature of the planet had already increased four-tenths of a degree Celsius, and the oceans had risen by four inches. Also, heatwaves and wildfires were sweeping the US at the time."

"And if we do gatecrash the hearing, then what?" Blythe asked in frustration. They'd been arguing for four hours by that point. The tree outside was covered in translucent leaves, brilliant green from where photons bounced around inside each leaf before continuing in through their window. When the wind gusted, the green canopy heaved, and the pattern of light and shadow on the table shifted.

"Don't forget, four days after the Hansen hearing was Woodstock for Climate Change. Which was a success—they created global diplomatic policy," Harry said. "Due, at least in part, to the Hansen hearing."

Phoenix nodded. "Let's not interfere with what's already working."

Phoenix seemed to worry less and less about whether they would change the past in unintended ways, because with every mission it seemed more impossible that they could change the past—in any meaningful way—at all. "What about 1979?" he asked, running his hand through his hair.

"From 1979 to 1983, the National Academy of Science was busy analysing the problem and preparing a report, and the Reagan administration answered any query about global warming by referring them to the upcoming report, *Changing Climate*," Harry said wearily.

"Can we alter the report?"

"The bigger question is whether we should. You see, the report was fine," Harry said. "It was better than fine—it was great. It noted that the world needed an accelerated transition to renewable fuels, warning that it would take thousands of years for the atmosphere to recover from the damage of the last century. It recommended a carbon tax. But then at the formal gala where the report was presented, the committee's chair, William Nierenberg, and the other members of the central committee, argued that action was premature. Nierenberg said . . ." Harry consulted his notes. "'If it goes the way we think, it will be manageable in the next hundred or so years.' He thought it was better to wait and see. Around the same time, a report came out from the EPA arguing that it was already too late to avoid the worst effects of climate change and that we should focus on adaptation. The *New York Times* published an article with the headline 'Haste on Global Warming Trend Is Opposed' and since no one was concerned, the American Petroleum Institute disbanded its CO_2 task force. It was a huge step back," Harry concluded.

"It sounds malevolent," June said into the silence. "Like someone has deliberately interfered with the event." She wound a strand of hair around her finger. The henna she had dyed her hair with had faded away over the past few months, leaving her hair comfortably brown again.

"Like other time-travellers?" Blythe said.

"Why would someone want climate change to go ahead?" Phoenix asked, looking confused.

"Maybe they know something we don't," Blythe said. "Maybe in the absence of climate change, something worse happens. Maybe it's our future selves trying to undo the fix we've made to climate change."

A moment of silence followed while they all thought about that.

June shook her head. "We can't second-guess ourselves."

"But we can find out," Elijah said. "Do you want to go, June? You haven't been on a mission yet."

June shook her head furiously.

"No? Okay, I'll go," Elijah said.

They sent Elijah back to the gala, but when he returned to brief them, he looked sheepish. "I tried to persuade Nierenberg to strongly emphasise the negative aspects of the report, and he got suspicious of me. I may, in fact, have pushed him into being positive about it," Elijah said. He put his head in his hands, exhaustion plain on his face.

Blythe laughed in a bitter way, but ended up snorting. Which was funny, so soon they were all laughing; more than the situation warranted, because the tension was getting to them.

Eventually, June wiped the tears from her face. Elijah was watching her with a fond smile, but when she noticed, he looked away and his smile vanished.

"Eh, Nierenberg sounds like he was an optimist by nature," Blythe said. "He was used to seeing problems crumble before him. He was probably going to be optimistic anyway."

Another day, another meeting. Blythe revealed the future to a *Save the Warming Planet* activist in 2015, who believed them, wrote it all in a book, and self-published it. With, as they discovered when Blythe returned, a particularly confusing blurb, terrible cover, and a lot of conspiracy theories woven in. It had no impact whatsoever, even though it outlined the events of 2015–2030 so accurately that only time travel could have produced it. It looked like the rantings of a crazy person and was published at a time e-books were being added to online bookstores at a rate of nine thousand per day. Harry bought a copy of it in 2030 and read it, but he wondered aloud whether he was the first.

Blythe suggested going back and accelerating the destruction of the Lislax gas platform, but was shot down; no one wanted to resort to violence.

Phoenix took books on manufacturing solar panels back to the past to try to speed up technological development and handed them out to companies in that space. It didn't seem to have an effect. Most battery information was proprietary, but Harry worked hard and found some information they could use, but with the same result.

"Right," Blythe said, entering the meeting room with a stack of paper as thick as several encyclopedias and thumping it down on the table. "This is every academic paper related to climate change ever published, or near enough. It's too consistent to be fabricated. I'm going to drop it on an academic in the seventies."

No bulldog or binder clips, and no staples. Blythe had tied various parts of the papers together with holes and string.

Her tone said the matter was settled, but her body language was aggressive, June noted. She waited for Phoenix to object. It wasn't a nudge, it was a shove, and one which would risk the integrity of the timeline. The academic would regard the papers with suspicion, ask questions about where they came from, especially given the big disconnect with the state of the art at that time. Also, how had Blythe figured out which papers would be relevant to the academic in question, and how did she know where to obtain them? Who would use the research?

But Phoenix just rubbed his temples and nodded wearily. The last two months had worn him down. Harry and Elijah didn't seem to care either, and June wasn't about to object.

So Blythe went, the weight of the papers compressing her chest in the MRI machine in a way that made June queasy.

"The past resists change," Phoenix said, after Blythe was detained by police, had the papers confiscated, and nearly didn't make it back to 2030. He sat at the control desk near June. Elijah sat in the chair on June's other side; June watched Elijah surreptitiously in the reflection on the glass partition, and with sideways glances.

Blythe had explained to them what had happened and had let the travel room door slam behind her as she left.

"You don't believe that," June said to Phoenix. She fanned

herself with her hand; the air-conditioning for the entire building was broken, and she was sweating. Although it was only mid-November, there were heatwaves already. Elijah drank from his water bottle.

Phoenix said nothing, but he pursed his lips and raised his eyebrows at June. Behind him, the waveform on the oscilloscope undulated smoothly.

The past resists change; it echoed in June's mind. The gleam in Harry's eyes was not healthy when he said that.

"No," June said. "Harry's not stupid, but he's not technical. You can't anthropomorphise the past."

"I'm beginning to wonder," Phoenix said. His voice was flat. "Maybe the resistance to change is in proportion to the size of the change."

"I don't believe it."

Phoenix pushed himself off the desk. "You're an engineer," he said. "Don't just tell me that. Prove it."

He left June alone in the dim room with Elijah. She stared fixedly at the screen in front of her.

"I still don't think it's the past resisting change," Elijah said. "The present resists change too. If we had come together to try to change the future, we'd be struggling too. But that doesn't mean it's impossible."

"Oh, yeah," June said dismissively. "Good changes are happening all the time."

"They are," Elijah said.

June knew people were trying, but she believed human greed would prevail. What good were small changes when the problem required drastic changes?

With knowledge about what was going to happen, it should be straightforward to travel to the past and nudge events into occurring differently. *It should be*. But it wasn't.

None of it made sense to June. Spring was drawing to a close, with hotter days of summer ready to descend. She couldn't believe how much time they had spent—that they had *wasted*—

with no results. When cycling home with storm clouds overhead, buffeted by winds, she had a fleeting sense of the Dark One at work in her world; a malevolent, furious force that was thwarting them every time. She gritted her teeth and cycled faster, full of determination.

CHAPTER 9

Two women stood in the Old Parliament House hall talking in hushed, scandalised voices. June recognised them as sales reps from the agricultural monitoring start-up next to MediSlice and nodded to them. Then the guy who she always saw with a phone in his hand and wearing earbuds appeared from the end of the hall. He always looked ludicrously futuristic in the quiet carpeted hall, which had light fittings from the last century. He passed June without acknowledging her, looking shaken. June slowed, but saw nothing that concerned her.

As she passed the House of Representatives, she paused, because there was a woman sitting in one of the seats, head in hands. It was Blythe. The House of Representatives was silent and empty, but for the woman; it was too early for tourists or school groups.

June made her way silently around the arc of the seats and sat on the green-upholstered leather bench next to Blythe. The library-quiet hush of the room and its rich wood panelling made it feel like a sacred space.

"Blythe?" June whispered.

Blythe raised her head. "Hey," she mumbled.

"Are you okay?"

Blythe sighed heavily. "Fight with my ex-husband. In the corridor. Verbal. But pretty intense."

That explained the gossiping sales reps and the disturbed earbuds guy. June sat quietly next to Blythe. Blythe's handbag was at June's feet, an expensive leather strap nudging her ankle.

"Have you ever heard of KestrelWare VR?" Blythe asked out of nowhere.

"Of course. It made me nauseated. Have you tried it?"

June had tried it out when she was at a trade fair with Elijah. He loved virtual reality and after shooting asteroids in a virtual spaceship, he wanted to buy it, but it was too expensive for them.

Blythe laughed bitterly. "I created that company when I was eighteen. We never quite solved the nausea problem."

June smiled, although she didn't quite get the joke, but Blythe just watched her, morose.

"Wait, are you *serious*?" June asked.

"I used gaze tracking to work out where the user's foveae were directed. KestrelWare renders only the area in the user's gaze in high resolution. People only see a tiny section of the world in high acuity, and don't even notice if the area out of their gaze is low resolution. The technique uses a fraction of the computational resources, allowing much more sophisticated graphics algorithms. Maximum realism, minimal cost."

June nodded, fascinated. She vaguely remembered reading about KestrelWare now; the small-town girl genius who turned an idea into a multi-billion-dollar company, but that couldn't possibly be Blythe, because Blythe was just a normal person.

"I'm not allowed to say that I'm brilliant, because no one wants to hear that from a woman, but I'm saying it anyway. I moved to Silicon Valley to manage the company and became a billionaire," Blythe said.

June stood up. "You're a *what*?" she hissed.

"Let me guess. You have a sick aunt who needs the money for

a life-saving operation. No? Or maybe you have a business venture that needs funding. And I'm your friend, right? So, my money is your money. Or at least it is when I have so much of it."

"Blythe!" June said, sitting down slowly again. They were in a quiet space, so it was an outraged yelp.

Blythe gave her a weary look. "Actually, since you're a doomer, it'd probably be about the planet for you. You'd want me to donate to *Save the Warming Planet* or something."

June wondered if Blythe was right. If given a billion dollars, June's first thought would be to use the money to solve the climate disaster, but if it was something solvable with a billion dollars, someone would have done it. But then June had always daydreamed about buying a beautiful house—with an underground swimming pool—or perhaps a castle. She felt like Galadriel from *Lord of the Rings*, tempted by the one ring; June would take the money and believe she would use it for the good of the world, but the world didn't need all of it, it wasn't her job to fix the world's problems. She would keep some for herself— perhaps more than a little—

And so, power corrupts.

"You don't *look* like a billionaire," June pointed out, still half-thinking that at any minute Blythe would crack and admit she was joking.

"Thanks. I've tried hard. No private jet anymore."

"You have a *private jet*?" June was sure she was being played.

"*Had*. I gave all my money away. I thought that would be enough to save us, but it hasn't worked." Blythe looked haunted. "I sold KestrelWare VR for about two billion dollars when I was twenty-one. Around that time, I also got married. I went back home to be closer to family and my husband's family. We had a daughter—Lucy. But everyone knew I was a billionaire, and my life went to hell. Poor me! I'm too rich," Blythe said.

June shook her head in consternation. It was impossible. She looked down, unintentionally looking into Blythe's bag. She tore her eyes away as soon as she'd done it, but not before she saw what looked like a heavy white torch, with "TASER" written on the side.

"It was insane. You have absolutely no idea what people are like once you have billions of dollars, and you can't imagine until it happens to you. The whole town knew who I was. Traffic cops harassed me. If I went into a café, people I didn't even know expected me to pay for their food. Friends came to me with business proposals or just asking for money until I didn't have friends anymore. People I barely knew brought frivolous lawsuits against me. A classmate I worked with on a different project, nothing related to KestrelWare VR, thought he was owed something. It was a disaster. And my marriage—"

Blythe shook her head, tears in her eyes. June nodded, wide-eyed, and patted her hand. Blythe wasn't joking. And June couldn't get Blythe's torch out of her head. She was pretty sure that if it was branded TASER it was, in fact, a weapon. Tasers were illegal in Australia.

"I tried to change the past, when I first joined MediSlice, going back and calling myself, but after I'd gone, I started to remember a weird phone call that I ignored, so of course that didn't work. Phoenix caught me and convinced me that climate change was more important, and that if we solved the climate crisis, it was possible my life would have been different. Anyway, after it all went to hell, I moved to New Zealand, bought a, well, a billionaire bunker, and married Lucy's science teacher. For about two years, things were okay. Good, even. Then we had a break-in attempt, which sparked a fire. We couldn't get out," Blythe said. Someone wandered past the open door to the House of Representatives and Blythe lowered her voice to a whisper.

"All the layers of security that were meant to keep people out kept us in. We eventually busted a skylight open and climbed out. Ollie cut his leg on it and will never be able to walk properly again. The whole incident was only thirty minutes, tops, but we both have PTSD from that night."

June realised she had been holding her breath and exhaled slowly. Blythe continued, face haggard. "At least my daughter was at a sleepover. I just kept thinking that we were targeted because we were rich; when I was growing up, we didn't even lock the door. We had nothing to steal. So, I donated most of my money to *End Abuse Australia* and to *Save the Warming Planet*. I thought by giving my money away I was ridding myself of bad karma. My husband and I changed our names, moved to Canberra, and tried to live like normal people. But my past is following me around. And now I don't have the money to deal with it."

———

Rain fell outside, not heavy, but blowy. They sat together in the break room eating Indian food. At 6:00pm, it wasn't dark yet, but the window let in nothing but grey. June wasn't in a hurry to ride her bike home. Blythe sat, legs dangling and a cup of tea in her hands, on the kitchenette benchtop that ran the length of the room. She seemed almost radiant; perhaps her confession to June had taken a weight off her shoulders. June sat cross-legged on the carpet near the window, her back against the cupboards below the benchtop. She wasn't sure what to make of Blythe, of her deliberate rejection of wealth. June couldn't help feeling that she would have used the money more productively, but even with her expertise in the climate crisis, she couldn't think of a way to use it that could have saved the world. Maybe the only way to save the world was by using the time machine.

A meeting had taken place on 6 November 1989, on the coast of the North Sea in the Dutch resort town of Noordwijk, which aimed to approve the framework for a global binding treaty. The Dutch minister proposed capping greenhouse gas emissions at 1990 levels by 2000, but the US delegate, at the bidding of John Sununu, Bush's chief of staff, sank it. The outcome was that "many" nations supported stabilising emissions, with no indication of which nations, what level of emissions, or by when.

Sununu didn't believe in climate change, and to be fair, there were many wild scientific theories circulating at that time that were wrong.

"Can we blackmail Sununu somehow?" Phoenix asked. He'd taken one of the chairs at the tiny table, and Harry had the other. Elijah was at the sink, washing a cup.

"I don't think it would have made a difference anyway," Harry said. "If one man managed to derail the treaty, the other delegates weren't trying very hard. The politicians were trying to make it look like they supported the policy without actually making painful commitments. Even if they had signed the treaty, do you really think they would have done anything about emissions?"

Blythe spilled her tea on the bench, but before she could even look around for something to wipe it up with, Elijah handed her a washcloth. She smiled gratefully.

"Maybe we could look into whether we could affect his behaviour in any way. Convince him earlier that he was wrong about climate change. Make friends with him. I don't know," Phoenix said.

Harry nodded, but he didn't look enthusiastic; uncharacteristically, his forehead was creased with a slight frown.

Elijah dried his hands on a tea towel. "I've got to go," he said with regret in his voice, looking at the fitness tracker he wore on his wrist.

"Don't want to keep her waiting," Blythe said, smiling at him. Elijah blushed a deep red, and Blythe laughed at him. Phoenix ignored the exchange, chasing the last of his curry with a bit of naan. June kept a pleasant smile on her face. It was painful, but she suspected it was another first date; he wasn't seeing someone properly, not yet.

Elijah slipped out. June went back to work to finish up, another fifteen minutes. The rain splattered against the window, driven by the wind. Duke Ellington's "Take the 'A' Train" sounded faintly from down the hall; Phoenix was still in the office.

June suspended her computer and went to see what Phoenix was doing. Blythe had gone back to work as well, June assumed, because she could hear the sound of drilling coming from the collider room.

Phoenix sat on the floor of his office, legs crossed at the ankle, scrolling on his phone. A half-empty bottle of ginger beer sat next to him. The corner lamp cast a warm glow in the darkness. Sensing June, Phoenix looked up.

"Hey," he said. "Come in, I'm not doing anything important."

June smiled and sat next to him on the carpet in the narrow office space. He looked like he was doomscrolling, but social media was all paid accounts these days, and because it was no longer ad-supported, it wasn't trying to maximise the time people spent scrolling through it. It no longer served up the most emotional and blood-pressure raising content; instead, it was mostly funny and informative, and you could adjust the settings for the amount of depressing material you were willing to tolerate. But June, like most people, still felt compelled to understand what was happening in the world, and so was exposed to all the bad news.

"Did you see the news about the Thwaites Ice Shelf?" Phoenix asked after a minute, breaking the companionable silence. He was a comfortable shadow beside her, not even trying to make eye contact. June was more relaxed than she'd been for a long time.

"Yeah," June said. "Terrible."

Yet it had barely made the news, among the steady pulse of natural disasters, growing political instability, worsening food shortages, and refugees fleeing all of the above. The ice shelf fracture didn't cause any loss of life. Also, June guessed, given that global warming was happening, of course ice shelves would disintegrate, so perhaps the media didn't think it was newsworthy. The International Thwaites Glacier Collaboration had predicted the ice shelf would fracture within five years back in

2021, so it was overdue. Even when the remaining icebergs from the ice shelf melted entirely, it wouldn't raise sea levels, because they were floating anyway. But it increased the rate at which the Thwaites Glacier was melting, by about twenty-five percent.

"If we do pass a tipping point and end up causing a mass extinction event, anyone who's investigating in the future will look at all these pieces and think it makes perfect sense," June said.

Phoenix sipped his ginger beer. "As the owner of a time machine, I have spent a lot of time wondering where we all went wrong. If there was a moment in time where we took the wrong path."

"And?"

"And, I think it was when we developed the scientific method," Phoenix said. "I see it as a discontinuity in history. The second discontinuity. The first discontinuity was culture. Evolution asks the question: how can you pass on what helps you to survive? And for many animals, it's in their genes—no one teaches a beaver to build a dam. But for us, we started passing on the ability to discover better ways to do things, to imitate others exactly, and to teach our children. Tradition, where every generation tweaks it, and keeps the parts that work."

Phoenix sighed. "And then comes science, the second discontinuity, which says that no piece of knowledge is true or useful until it's proven by multiple randomised double-blind placebo-controlled trials. Science encouraged us to throw away traditions that had been developed over centuries or longer. It gave us contempt for tradition; we now treat traditional knowledge as historically interesting, not as the life-preserving set of tools that it is."

June nodded, understanding. "Often the codebase for software becomes rotten over time. Too many quick fixes in the wrong places, too many bright ideas that never worked out. It gets brittle, hard to change things. A junior developer will want to throw it out and make a fresh start, but a senior developer will understand that there are solutions baked into the code, bugs fixed over the years, often for cases that were completely unexpected. If you throw the code out, you throw that out too."

"Okay, I didn't completely follow that, but sure," Phoenix said. He gave one of his rare smiles, which made him look ten years younger.

"Science has made our lives better, though," June said.

"Has it really? I wonder sometimes."

June was momentarily stumped, because she thought it was such an obvious statement there would be no refuting it.

"It's like this," Phoenix said. "We invented anaesthesia in 1846. Not that long ago. Before that, if you wanted to be operated on, you were awake. Maybe drugged with alcohol, but basically awake."

"You're proving my point for me here," June said.

"But that was the way things were. Before humans dreamed it was possible, were they unhappy with the way things were?"

"I'd have to say *absolutely yes*," June said, laughing. "Being operated on while awake is horror movie fodder."

"You think that because you've grown up knowing general anaesthesia is possible. What I'm saying," Phoenix said, gesticulating wildly, "is that we think poverty is synonymous with unhappiness. The whole aim of our society seems to be to eliminate suffering, but it's impossible, and it's costly. People in the past suffered more—women dying in childbirth, children dying of accidents or disease, and so on and so forth—but were they more unhappy? Because I think that's the important part."

"Well, we have a time machine. We could check," June said, and he laughed with her. "Worldwide, child mortality rates were almost fifty percent prior to the twentieth century," June said. "I don't know what they are now, but I'd guess less than five percent."

"Which sounds terrible to us, because we expect that all our children will live—all of the one or two children that we have. We fear what we don't understand, and we no longer understand suffering, or death, because we so rarely see it. If you grow up knowing that some will die, is it that tragic to lose some?"

"Yes, I think it is," June said. She tried to imagine a world where every second child would die, but couldn't. She guessed Phoenix didn't have any children in his life, or that would have been obvious to him.

Phoenix shook his head. "Our goal is to develop, to increase prosperity. As if you can eliminate suffering and happiness will fill the vacuum. But every scientific advance has a cost, and the cost isn't just the time you spend working to pay for all of it. The cost is a planet we can thrive on. The cost is hope."

Phoenix got up and went to his desk, picking up his tennis ball. "Modern life is inherently destructive, but it's also rubbish. Especially in Canberra. Open your eyes next time you're in Civic. Our buildings are so ugly we have to cover them with plants to hide them. Hide the lack of symmetry and proportion, hide the cheap anonymous materials that look terrible as they age, the hideous design. Pre-industrial revolution, we had better architecture, better urban design, fresher food, better art, and healthier people—apart from infectious diseases—and, most importantly, *happier* people. Not only are we destructively terraforming the Earth with the way we live, *it hasn't even been worth it.*"

"Have you actually visited the past, to see all these happy people and beautiful buildings?" June asked, because she suspected that watching movies could give one a rosy view of the past, since everything in the movie was created by artists.

"Well, no, but—"

"I see you're getting the 'the industrial revolution was a mistake' spiel," Blythe said, popping her head around the door with a wicked grin.

"Really?" Harry said, leaning into the doorway to address Phoenix. "But you're a physicist and an engineer. How can you be anti-science?"

Phoenix just shrugged, smiling. But June wasn't even a little bit surprised; most software engineers that she knew were staunchly against smart door locks or internet-enabled fridges or wi-fi-controlled lightbulbs. Some were obsessed with privacy and used obscure Linux distros to avoid common operating systems. To work with technology was to become intimately familiar with its downsides.

"Anyway, good night," Blythe said. "Harry's giving me a lift home."

"Awesome. Swell," Phoenix said in a fake American accent. Blythe laughed at him. "Bloody hell, I don't reckon I sound like that, mate," Harry said, in a not-convincing Aussie accent. Phoenix tipped his head back, long neck exposed, as he laughed freely.

Harry smiled and tipped a salute as he disappeared.

"June—I'm sorry about what I said earlier to Elijah," Blythe said quietly. "I forgot about you and him."

June mentally filled in the blanks. *Forgot they had been engaged. Sorry she said something about him dating.*

"It's fine," June said, which it was, because she was fully aware Elijah was dating, and Blythe had nothing to do with it. Blythe studied her face for a moment, nodded, then waved goodbye to both of them. Phoenix looked closely at his tennis ball.

Outside in the hall, the sliding door of MediSlice clicked closed.

"What did she mean about Elijah?" Phoenix asked.

"Um. Well, you know Elijah and I were together," June said, realising as she said it that perhaps he didn't know.

"What?" Phoenix said. He hooted with laughter. "What did he move on to, July?"

He obviously expected her to laugh, but she couldn't, because it hurt. She plastered on a smile. "Okay, well, good night," she said.

"Oh—good night," he called after her, as she headed out of MediSlice. June usually felt at home around technical people, perhaps because they were frequently uncomplicated, forthright people, but even she could see that Phoenix could have been more empathic. Although obviously he didn't know she dated Elijah for three years, that she had been his fiancé; perhaps he thought she only went on a few dates with him. She put Phoenix out of her mind.

Two futures whirled in her head as she rode home.

Elijah's rosy future, where eight point five billion people had produced a veritable wonderland of astonishing advances, creativity, and humour. A world that would decarbonise rapidly and run on more or less the same, but with renewable energy powering everything. One which would shortly develop space-flight and populate the solar system, and from there, other solar systems.

Contrast that with Phoenix's future, where rich humans were living a profligate, unhealthy lifestyle. Suffering had been all but eliminated, but people were more miserable than ever.

June didn't agree that every scientific advance was bad. Many were fantastic: vaccines, dental care, machine tools, access to music and movies. But as she rode down Northbourne Avenue, she looked at the city properly, as if she had never seen it before. Two lanes in each direction, with a bike lane adjacent to the road, and buses weaving in and out of the bike lane at bus stops. Tram in the middle of the road, surrounded by shrubs. And on either side, ugly monotone buildings rose into the sky, the colour and form of computer parts. Gigantic grey concrete panels. A black mesh covering a carpark on the lower floor of one building had strips of sheet metal arranged at random across the mesh, as if a preschooler had decorated it. Many of the buildings had floor-to-ceiling glass windows, but inside most of them had drawn curtains, because the Australian sun was harsh, and a massive window let in too much light.

A grocery delivery drone whined across the sky, its load swaying underneath, and vanished into a side street.

June rarely looked at people, but she did now, glancing at the faces of the pedestrians trying to cross. Harried, vigilant, inundated by the noise and petrol fumes, and frequently with earbuds as a kind of escape. Only about thirty percent of cars in Australia were electric, because government policies to encourage electric cars had only started relatively recently, but even electric cars wouldn't make this a pleasant place to walk or ride.

Yes, June thought. *What kind of world have we created?*

CHAPTER 10

The row of flags in Old Parliament House carpark shifted half-heartedly in the breeze. Past the metal letters spelling out "SOVEREIGNTY" and the gum trees, was the gentle tree-covered rise of Mount Ainslie, towering over the War Memorial. There used to be grass between the lake and Old Parliament House, June remembered, but now there was just a narrow strip left near the road, and the drought had turned it beige. To counter urban heat island effects and increase shade, native trees had been planted all over the city.

Hannah had been reading the autobiography of a police-woman, Tracey Turner, and June happened to pick it up. She talked to Harry and Phoenix about it as they walked up the stairs of Old Parliament House together. From the sting of the sun, it would be a baking hot day. They paused at the top, Harry's serious eyes watching her as June tried to explain why she thought the policewoman might be important. The campfire at the Aboriginal Tent Embassy across the road was out, probably because of the Total Fire Ban.

Policewoman Tracey Turner wrote about how, in 2017 when shifting demonstrators off Commonwealth Avenue Bridge, she could have made a difference by standing with the Extinction

Rebellion protesters rather than arresting them. That she could have ordered the other police to leave them alone. That would have made a difference, June argued.

"Frequently in ancient Rome, the Emperor would fall after his guard, the Praetorians, turned against him," Harry pointed out. "There's historical precedent."

Phoenix snorted. "Very different situation."

"It could be enough to shock people into realising it was important," Harry said thoughtfully. "Police are authority figures."

Phoenix looked sceptical. They walked past King's Hall towards the start-up space together, then into MediSlice.

At the meeting, Phoenix introduced June's proposal. Someone had put a stand-up fan in the corner, which whirred and turned its head from one side to the other, blasting June with a moment of blessedly cool air every few seconds. Elijah glanced at June as Phoenix spoke; she had no idea what he was thinking.

Since there weren't any objections, Phoenix rubbed his mouth. "All right," he said finally. "I guess it's a small nudge, too. Worth a try. Your first mission, June."

June sat up straight. "No—I didn't mean—"

The breeze from the fan passed over her, and the sensation of her hair playing in the breeze and tugging at her scalp raised goosebumps on her arms and neck.

"You don't want to go?" Phoenix said.

"No," June said. "I think someone else should go."

God, especially this mission. A noisy, crowded bridge in the hot sun. Physical handling by police.

"Are you sure? It'd be good for you," Phoenix said. This was a common theme in her life. People telling her to do things because it would be *good for her*. See also: *getting her out of her comfort zone.*

Harry looked sympathetic.

Elijah cleared his throat. "She said no," he said. "Leave her alone."

Phoenix frowned.

But she didn't want Elijah's help. She didn't want to show weakness in front of him. The fan passed back June's way and she shivered, suddenly clammy.

"Is that too cold?" Blythe said, "I can turn it down."

June nodded, and Blythe reached over and turned it down a notch.

"I'll go," Blythe said. "It sounds fun."

"Fun? Are you mad?" Harry said playfully, but his attempt to defuse the situation failed.

June noticed Elijah watching her with a faint expression of worry. She watched him in the glass tabletop reflection. Same expression he got when they ended up in a crowd. Or at a party. *Are you all right with this? Want to leave, go somewhere quieter?* He handled her so well.

Straight from university in the time of Covid-19—no classes, just masks and solitude—she'd joined Deep Scan, and that was a bad time, because anxiety and depression had overwhelmed her, as if every cell in her grey leaden body was filled with terrified misery.

Her parents paid for her to visit a psychologist. The psychologist said many of her peers were struggling too. Her generation thought the chaos caused by endless climate disasters was normal, and that was causing psychological problems, he said, but in the end, he referred her to someone who would assess her for autism.

But then Elijah showed up, like a cloud passing over the scorching sun. She relaxed into the soothing cool shadow he provided, and everything was easier.

She read about autistic traits and found many of them relatable, so perhaps she was autistic. Growing up, she felt like an alien from a distant star trying to pass as a human. At twenty-nine, she was finally competent at a whole plethora of social situations, having painstakingly learnt the patterns, but it never stopped being exhausting.

The only way she coped was to control the situations she was in. Work was usually fine. Riding was fine. Dating was not fine because she and Elijah had gotten together without dating, so it was an activity she knew nothing about.

This mission was not fine. But in turning it down, she had to face her shortcomings all over again—and have them displayed in front of her colleagues, who were now her friends—and that was mortifying. But Phoenix had agreed that Blythe should go, and the others were planning the mission. June listened unhappily, twirling a frond of hair around her fingers. Outside, the plane tree moved in a sudden gust of wind, and the sound of a thousand leaves brushing past each other was like a rain stick being turned upside down.

———

June ate her honey sandwich in the break room. The blinds were drawn over the window to keep the sun out, and when they shifted in the breeze with a clank, the light coming around the sides changed, sending light beams dancing around the room. She was trying to stay off her phone, because the news was all about the growing international crises. Closer to home, bushfires were breaking out across the country. Australia had been baked dry by heatwaves and was ready to burn.

Blythe went past, back from her mission. June jumped up and went out into the hall, but Blythe was dishevelled and looked sun-struck, and didn't seem to notice her as she left MediSlice and went into the corridor, probably heading to the shared showers. June finished her sandwich slowly, guilt and relief mixing to form a taste that made her sandwich unpalatable. *It should have been her.* But also: *thank God she was back safely.*

Phoenix and Blythe were looking over Harry's shoulder in the dim computer lab when June entered the room. Blythe's hair was wet from the shower. Seeing Phoenix's expression through the glass told June everything, as if she hadn't guessed already, just from Blythe re-materialising in a world June recognised.

"I wasn't persuasive enough," Blythe said, as June slid the door open.

"Tracey never attempted to join the protesters, as far as we could tell," Phoenix said to June. "I guess it was easier to write about wanting to do it, than actually doing it."

"Tracey didn't even believe in climate change," Blythe said.

"But . . . she said she did, in her autobiography," June said.

"I bet. But she wrote that in 2029, when it was obvious climate change was real. She didn't want to look stupid," Harry said. "To be fair, public opinion has changed drastically over the years. When the Earth started warming, we believed we weren't warming it. Or maybe the pollutants we emitted would actually plunge Earth into another ice age. Or a warmer Earth would be nice."

June laughed, but no one else did. "Nice! Having fires rage through your country year after year," she said.

Harry smiled. "It's funny that our picture of hell is fire and brimstone. Sometimes I wonder if somewhere in our mammalian brains, we remember the mass extinction events our ancestors survived. Whether some primitive part of our brain remembers the world on fire, again and again."

June shifted uncomfortably. She dreamed of fires sometimes— not often, perhaps once or twice a year—great walls of flame, channelling a force beyond her understanding. The crackling roar overwhelmed her, and the radiant heat dried out her eyes and raised blisters on her skin; she couldn't draw her breath in to scream—until she'd wake up gasping and soaked with sweat.

Blythe sighed and left the room. June thought about following her, to apologise for sending her on a mission that had no hope of success, but instead she sat in the chair next to Harry. The closed blinds kept the glare off his screen. He had a *Canberra Times* article open.

"The past resists change," June said quietly.

"So it would seem," Phoenix said.

"Maybe we *can't* make big changes to the past," June said. She pushed off the floor to make the office chair rotate, causing the room to spin gracefully. "Maybe Phoenix is right, that only small changes are possible."

"But small changes can turn into big changes. We've seen it. A schoolgirl in Sweden goes on strike and sparks a global movement." Phoenix shook his head. "We just have to find the right change."

June stopped the chair.

"What do you think?" June asked Harry. He seemed to slide sideways and catch, slide sideways and catch, because she was still dizzy. Behind his earnest yet goofy manner was a tiny ball of stress; he might not be jumpy like Blythe, but June was starting to realise that he was every bit as much on edge. Blythe had noticed it too and had said Harry seemed particularly starstruck around June, as if June were a celebrity, although Blythe didn't have any theories as to why.

Harry gazed into space for a bit before answering slowly. "I'm not sure."

June rested her elbow against the back of the chair and stared at him.

Harry coughed and gave her a small smile. "Excuse me," he said. He locked his computer screen, got up and walked out, glancing over his shoulder at June, but then startled when he found she was still watching him.

Phoenix stood in the dim room as if frozen in time.

"There's something strange about Harry," June said, looking up at him. "Right? Or is it just me?"

"Yeah," Phoenix said. He straddled the chair next to hers, within arm's reach, a distance that was almost intimate. "But there's a lot of that going around." He gave a teasing smile, and June laughed and punched his arm playfully.

Phoenix folded his hands on the back of the chair. The room rang with silence as his smile faded.

"Do you really think it's impossible?" he asked.

"I'm starting to," June admitted.

They said nothing for a few seconds.

"I think I offended you the other day, after you told me that you had dated Elijah," Phoenix said. The anxious way he spoke made it an apology; he cared about her feelings. It was the first time June had been alone with him since Friday, June realised.

"Don't worry about it," June said gratefully.

"Was it—the engagement ring you wore when you first started here, was that—"

"Yeah, we were engaged," June said.

Phoenix winced. Then nodded. "On reflection, he should have told me about your relationship when I asked him whether he could recommend you for the job. Not that he was wrong about you."

Phoenix reached out for a pen that sat on the table, and the back of his hand brushed against June's arm. His touch made June realise just how much she had been craving physical contact since she broke up with Elijah.

"What happened to your arm?" Phoenix asked. It took June a moment to realise he was talking about her burn scar.

"When I was one, and my sister was four, we were caught in the 2003 Canberra bushfires. We lived in Duffy, on the outskirts of Canberra. My mum was home with my sister and me and only had fifteen minutes' warning to evacuate. She got us into the car, but by the time she drove out, the fire front had arrived. She stopped the car as the fire went over us, sheltered us under wool blankets. My arm was burnt, but no one was sure how. No one realised for a while, because, you know, babies cry, so it was worse than it would have been if they'd run cold water over it. I was too young to explain."

Phoenix, who had been holding his breath, exhaled. "I'm sorry," he said. He spun the pen in one hand in an almost acrobatic fashion. It was so still in the computer lab that June pictured them as underwater, Phoenix's pen acrobatics setting currents whirling.

June shrugged. "It was a long time ago."

Her heart was beating faster. Phoenix nodded grimly. "I was a volunteer firefighter during Black Summer, when I was twenty-one. I still hear the koalas screaming sometimes in my dreams. And . . . I hear them whenever I think I should give up on the time machine. Which has been several times, over the past few years."

June nodded. The Black Summer fires burnt twenty-four million hectares, but didn't reach Canberra, although the fine particulate levels in the smoke made Canberra the most polluted place on Earth for weeks on end. She spent that time with a tightness in her chest, muscles locked solid in her belly, forehead aching from frowning, as she watched the news, the videos and pictures, come in. Houses burnt out, lives lost, people piling into boats forced into the sea to escape, flames and smoke on a scale too large for her to grasp.

"We're terraforming the planet so that it doesn't support us anymore," Phoenix said. He looked at her beseechingly, and June was struck by how lovely his eyes were, beneath his thick dark eyebrows; the brown like a lagoon dyed with tannins.

"June, I was wondering . . ." Phoenix said.

"What?"

Phoenix shook his head, looking away. "These past months, working with you . . . if you weren't . . ." he said.

June looked at him inquiringly. Phoenix didn't meet her gaze, instead looking at the computer monitor.

"You're going to have to spell it out for me," June said. "I can't do subtext. I'm bad at hints. Help me out here."

"Yeah. You're a bit like Data, you know," Phoenix said. "From *Star Trek*," he added, completely unnecessarily.

June didn't know how to respond to that. This whole conversation was off-script; she knew Phoenix well enough to not be nervous, but a certain amount of confusion was inevitable.

"Anyway. It's wrong," he said; to himself, June thought.

He stood up abruptly.

"Phoenix," June said, and he looked down at her. "What did Elijah say about me?"

"He said you were technically brilliant and hardworking," Phoenix said, but he said it in a tone of voice that made June certain she had made a faux pas, but she didn't know how. He walked to the door, slid it open, but then hesitated.

"He also said you were very kind," Phoenix added. He slid the door shut, leaving June staring, baffled, after him.

June worked at her computer until the light coming through the cracks in the blinds changed to gold. Then she wandered down the darkened hall of MediSlice. As she passed Phoenix's office, she saw the shadowy form of Harry standing there in the dark, a book in his hands. No sign of Phoenix.

"What are you doing?" June asked, standing in the doorway.

Harry started. The book fell from his hands onto the desk.

"Oh, nothing, I just saw this book as I passed. Always been interested in fungi," Harry said. *Mycoremediation and Other World-Saving Uses of Mycelium*, June read off the spine.

Harry put the book on top of a stack. He gave a polite smile—such perfect teeth he had—and tried to get past her; June moved aside to let him pass.

"I see you're still having trouble finding light switches," June said.

Harry laughed, but the panic in his eyes was unmistakable as he fled up the hall.

June breathed in, letting the comforting scent of books fill her lungs. She turned the light on and picked up the book Harry had placed on top of a stack of five others. It was published in 2004 by the University of Chicago, with chapters from different researchers. The thin pages were bound into a volume covered with maroon cloth.

According to the contents, Chapter Six was about using fungal networks to increase carbon dioxide sequestration. June leafed through to Chapter Six. What Phoenix had said about terraforming had stuck with her; they needed to terraform the Earth back to a state that would support life.

The author of Chapter Six was Richard Simpson. June tilted

her head to the side when she saw the author picture at the start of the chapter. A man, about sixty years old, stared at the camera with a slight smile and wide eyes, as if he'd just told a joke to the photographer. His hair and eyebrows were white with age, but the long neck was the same, the penetrating dark eyes, the full lips.

It was printed in black and white, but the resemblance was clear: he looked a lot like Phoenix.

Phoenix hadn't mentioned he had a relative working on carbon sequestration, which was strange, because the research was relevant to the climate crisis. Maybe they could take the book back in time and give it to him.

Then again, maybe that would have exactly as much impact as the previous attempts to take information back in time, which is to say, none.

June sighed and put the book down. Time to go home.

CHAPTER 11

Pranav was out in the garden with Amy when June came out the back door that evening, carrying a basket of wet washing. Pranav raised a hand in greeting and gave June the flash of a grin. The dried-out beige lawn was a wilderness of weeds. The yard was bordered on three sides by faded grey fence planks. The smoke smell in the air sent a stab of fear through June.

June put her basket down by the Hills hoist and started pegging her washing out. She had been reading the news on her phone: the firefighters who had been killed in Victoria; the fire in Bega that destroyed over seventy homes and killed nine; and the fire that started in Namadgi National Park near Canberra, but had been extinguished.

She realised she was breathing shallowly and tried to take some deep breaths. The fire season in Australia started a full two months earlier than it had a decade ago, but now, in November, was when it really intensified. And this year, everyone was talking about perfect-storm conditions. Despite the floods in Queensland earlier that year, most of the east coast of Australia had a Keetch-Byram Drought Index of over one hundred. Which was crazy, yet typical; Australia was a big enough continent to be several large countries.

The international news was even worse. The tactical nukes that Pakistan had launched against India, and the rush of nations tripping over each other to try to de-escalate the situation. Growing food scarcity, especially in south-east Asia, exacerbated conflicts. Conflicts which created more food scarcity.

Pranav held his phone in one hand, hold music emanating from it, and danced in a completely uncoordinated fashion. Amy, lying on a mat on the grass, giggled at her father.

"Oh, hello, yes," Pranav said into the phone, as the hold music cut out suddenly. Amy realised she wasn't the centre of attention and started crying.

June left the washing she was hanging out and sat down on the picnic mat with Amy, scooping her up. Even her onesie had the scent of smoke on it. Pranav mouthed "thank you" at her as he listened to the phone, then walked towards the house while answering questions. The door banged closed behind him. He'd been on the phone for what seemed like days, on hold more often than not, trying to organise visas for his family to come to Australia. Hannah and Pranav were terrified, watching the weather forecasts and hoping that no more heatwaves would occur before they could get them out of there. Construction on the Oceania grid suffered delay after delay, with the cost more than doubling at last count.

Amy calmed down in June's lap, and June stroked her hair absently. June felt as if she'd been hollowed out, leaving a tense shell. The bright overcast sky pressed down on her. Soon June was shaking with sobs, great wet tears splashing onto her hands and Amy's head. Amy flopped around until she was staring up at June. She watched June with an uncomprehending expression, devoid of distress.

Beyond the edge of the plaid picnic mat where June sat crying, giant plates of three-leaf clover emerged, each of the leaves dotted with an irregular brown blotch like a blood stain. A breeze, not strong enough to be felt, made some grass blades fidget.

"Oh hey, I'm sorry," Pranav said, appearing out of nowhere to sit beside June. He put his large, warm hand on her shoulder, his face creasing with sympathy. "I shouldn't have dumped Amy on you. Are you okay?"

June, humiliated, tried to tell him that it wasn't fair for him to comfort her; he was the one who had lost his father and his niece —and how would she cope if Hannah died? Losing Elijah had nearly broken her—but it came out as *urk* and her nose was dripping, so she half-laughed and half-cried while she fumbled for a tissue in her pocket.

Nose blown, she tried to explain in hiccupping packets of words that it was all a bit much, but she was incoherent. Her eyes darted around the lawn, looking everywhere but at Pranav. He just patted her shoulder and waited. Amy babbled, grabbing at June's shoe.

A single bright yellow dandelion stood alone in the dried-out lawn a metre away, and that upset her for some reason. That right here there was just an ordinary lawn, not perfect—not even very good—but comfortingly mundane.

But also right now, people were dying; were holding on to trees in floods, scorching in fires, being shot at and stabbed and blown up, and gnawed away on the inside by hunger. They were losing the people they loved, and June knew how much that hurt. The debt humans had incurred by burning fossil fuels was due. The grim future was *here*, not a single apocalyptic war or an alien invasion or anything you could point to and say "this is *it*, this is the end"; just a gradual slide into hell, where even while you were safe on your ordinary lawn, your fellow humans suffered and died by the thousands, day by day.

———

June hadn't slept properly since she turned down the Extinction Rebellion trip, and the morning's tears in the backyard had depleted her reserves. The world was becoming two-dimensional and harsh as she became more exhausted. The more tired she was, the more overwhelming the world became. Too hot or too cold, too bright, too loud. Even her constant urge to fiddle became annoying to her.

She hadn't been able to make eye contact with anyone; not Hannah, not the bus driver, not even the people who made way for her as she exited the bus. Trying to make eye contact was like trying to stare into the sun.

When Blythe entered the room, her face was stony; her bottom lip on the right was split.

"Hey," Blythe said. Her blond hair was pulled back in a pony-tail, and she wore no makeup that June could see, which was uncharacteristic for her.

"Blythe, what happened to you?" June said hoarsely, avoiding her gaze. She cleared her throat.

"I ran into the door of the shower," Blythe said. Her lip was swollen around the split.

June absorbed this silently, worrying about Blythe's ex-husband.

The others came into the meeting room one by one. Light spilled around the cracks in the drawn blinds, making the room simultaneously too bright and too dim. Blythe dodged their questions about her lip. Everyone was tired, June realised, when Elijah came in and sat with his eyes closed for a minute. It was Friday. They were running out of ideas, and nothing had worked so far.

As soon as Phoenix wandered in, holding his coffee mug, Blythe stood up.

"We need to do more," Blythe said. "We need to move on to sabotage."

She had suggested it a month ago, June remembered, in a Save-the-World meeting, but they had all agreed on a non-violence policy for missions.

"People will get hurt," June said, an obvious yet important point.

June expected Blythe to protest, to tell them that they could do it without hurting anyone. But Blythe said nothing, just bit her fingernail and waited. That was fair. They couldn't guarantee no one would be hurt. They would risk capture or death if they tried; none of them were trained to do anything remotely like sabotage.

"The Lislax gas platform?" Phoenix asked, drinking his coffee. It was the target Blythe suggested last time.

"It's the biggest one in Australia," Blythe said. "When it exploded, it had a massive impact on policy. All we need to do is bring the date of its explosion backward. Like I said, everyone is waiting for someone to act. Australia needs to keep ninety-five percent of coal in the ground to meet the one-point-five target. Do you think we're likely to?"

Elijah started shaking his head, and once she finished, Phoenix groaned.

"We have advantages," Blythe said. "We disappear back into the future. We're not going to get caught."

"Say you go back to 2022 and blow up a gas platform. You scrape your knee at the scene and they pick up your DNA. They get a clear image of you on CCTV. Who will they arrest? Your past self, a clueless thirty-year-old," Phoenix said.

"I wasn't thirty in 2022, but thank you," Blythe said, amusement softening the tightness around her eyes. "And my past self probably has an airtight alibi. She should, she's in New Zealand in 2022, thirty-five years old and pregnant. Looking nothing like what I look like now, should they get a picture. A gas platform explodes off the west coast of Australia, and you think they'll blame a pregnant woman in New Zealand? They'll think I have a lost twin if they do DNA tracing."

"We should be able to use our knowledge of the future to prevent getting caught," Harry said; his first contribution. His normal enthusiasm was noticeably muted today. The collage of articles and pictures on the whiteboard behind him was annotated with thick black arrows and neat handwriting, and it struck June that it resembled the murder investigations that she'd seen in a streaming series.

"You think we should do this?" Phoenix said to him incredulously.

"Not necessarily," Harry said. "Just exploring the idea."

"Anything is allowed under capitalism," Blythe said. "Provided it doesn't kill people instantly. Anyone who is causing harm slowly is allowed to continue, and all we can do is protest, non-violently. Surely protests in history were effective because they threatened violence."

"It's true," Harry confirmed.

"That doesn't make it right," Phoenix said. He stood up and walked over to the window, opening the blinds.

June blinked in the glare. Phoenix stood with his arms crossed, looking out at the tree and at the tall hedges on the other side of the road.

"Oh, come on. We're going to pass one-point-five degrees," Blythe said, "and we're not even willing to sabotage a gas platform to stop it?"

"No wonder the world is screwed," June said quietly. Elijah looked at her, but she couldn't maintain eye contact; her gaze skittered around like the visual equivalent of not knowing what to do with her hands.

"The world is not screwed," Elijah said wearily. "One-point-five is not a tipping point, it's just an arbitrary target. Yes, there's a lot of damage to the ecosystem at one-point-five, and more at one-point-six, and the risks increase the higher you go. But can we stop pretending that we're doomed? The chances of climate change being a world-ending event is slim, given the action that's taking place now to curb emissions. It's dismissive of the thousands of people who have spent their lives on this problem, quietly doing the work to make it possible for us to survive."

Blythe started to reply, but June had heard them argue before. June turned to Harry.

"What do you think, Harry?" June asked him quietly. And somehow, this calmed her down.

He hesitated, flustered. Blythe and Elijah stopped arguing and listened.

"I think we should do it," he said into the silence.

"Why?" Phoenix asked, turning. He laid his hand on the windowsill, looking at Harry searchingly.

Harry exhaled slowly. A crescent of sweat was forming under his arms, soaking his white shirt. "Because we're at such a critical point now. I'm sure you know that the lower temperature target of the Paris Agreement, one-point-five degrees Celsius, is enough to drive the West Arctic ice sheet into retreat. Worldwide, reefs are zombie ecosystems; the vast majority will be lifeless limestone by 2050, and they won't reappear for millions of years. The AMOC has shut down. The other tipping points are a heartbeat away from falling, dominos toppling one after the other. If we say no, we won't cross that line and perform violent actions, it might be a death sentence for billions. I think the time for bold action is here."

He glanced at June as he said the last. Even though Harry made less eye contact with her than the others during his speech, something about the glance made June feel like the whole speech was aimed at her; that he was entreating her alone.

June would have thought she imagined it—perhaps because she felt guilty about passing up the last mission—except that she paid a lot of attention to body language. It wasn't intuitive to her, so she had painstakingly studied it, and she felt she had a good grasp of it now. Yet sometimes she couldn't understand it, because she just couldn't make the leap to the other person's head, and now was one of those times.

Harry was feeling something about June, she was sure, but she didn't know what.

Phoenix and Elijah looked at each other, clearly confused. Blythe stared at the table in front of her, a dissatisfied expression on her face.

"The AMOC has shut down? That's news to me," Elijah said. June had been focusing on Harry's body language, so had missed that detail. Of course the AMOC hadn't shut down . . . had it? The AMOC, or Atlantic Meridian Oceanic Current, regulated climate. It was one of the biggest current systems in the ocean, one that scientists had been watching with concern because of the drastic consequences if it stopped operating.

"Yeah, that didn't happen," Phoenix said.

Harry looked taken aback. "Oh . . . didn't it?"

"A collapse is meant to be unlikely," Elijah said.

"It's weakened," Phoenix interrupted, looking at his phone. "It's at its weakest state in a thousand years. It's slowed fifteen percent since the fifties."

June saw he had an article on the AMOC open. Phoenix scrolled down on his phone. "No, the AMOC has definitely not stopped."

"My mistake," Harry said. He gave a nervous smile. "I must have confused myself. Scientists are always talking about how it might happen."

A moment of silence, and then they started talking about whether they could sabotage something else, something easy, to make a difference. June sank into gloom listening to them bicker. If there was just one factory on Earth producing greenhouse gas, this would be easy. If only there was one boss they could fight.

"It needs to be Lislax," Blythe said; it silenced the others, because she hadn't said anything for a while.

The Lislax gas platform, one of the largest offshore platforms, had had a technical flaw that had caused the platform to explode in 2028. If they went back to 2022, right after it was built, they could exploit the flaw. The O-ring on a critical part had been replaced in 2028 with an inferior one, and through a complicated series of cause-and-effect that took less than eight hours, the whole platform was destroyed.

"It needs to be Lislax, because we could replace the O-ring with the defective part years earlier. We could warn the company and the public that it would explode. Then when it happens, it'll be clear it was deliberate. And the O-ring is such a tiny part. Even if they're alert to the idea of someone sabotaging the platform, they won't be looking for someone with a spare O-ring. Once the platform explodes, the threat of sabotage will change the way businesses think of risk," Blythe said.

"I still think it's a bad idea," Phoenix said.

Elijah looked down. "It'll save lives," he said. "Twelve people died in the accident. If we're going to cause it, we can warn them, and they can evacuate."

Although their job wasn't to save lives, it somehow made the mission more appealing. June listened to them argue about who was going to go back for a reconnaissance mission to find out how hard it would be to carry out the sabotage.

"I'll do it," she announced. She gave a watery smile. Elijah had one foot up on his chair, so he was hugging his knee to his chest. For an instant a current ran through her, a skin-memory of their intimacy. June looked away, confused, and when she glanced at him again, she noticed he was blushing.

Blythe sat forward, surprised.

"You're not serious," Phoenix said to June.

"I am."

"You don't have to do this," Elijah murmured. June wondered if he thought she was trying to impress him.

"Yeah, June," Blythe said. "I can go. I don't mind."

"I know," June said to them. To Elijah. She did have to do this, even though she didn't want to. What kind of chance did humanity have if she was unwilling to risk anything for what she believed in? Wasn't the crux of the problem with the climate crisis that everyone was waiting for someone else to step up and solve it?

She knew it was stupid, and that it was her sleep-crazed brain speaking, or the buzzing fear in the back of her mind because of the fires raging, but she was taking their lack of progress personally. *The past resists change*, she thought, but maybe it resisted because she wasn't willing to change it. Because she was letting others risk themselves rather than face her fears. Yeah, she'd read too many fantasy novels. But the idea wouldn't go away.

"—June?" Phoenix said. The others were staring at her, waiting.

She had no idea what he had said.

"I'm going to 2022," June said. She stood up and left the room. She made it to the bathroom before something inside her cracked. "Crazy," she whispered and splashed water on her face. The word didn't echo in the bathroom, but it echoed in her imagination. *Crazy*, she said over and over again, the soothing sound soft like a teddy bear. *Crazy crazy crazy crazy crazy.* The syllables ceased to mean anything.

———

"Are you ready?" Blythe asked June as she entered the travel room. Blythe's lip was still swollen, but her eyes were clear.

"No," June said. The MRI was making chirp-THUMP noises as it calibrated.

Blythe laughed, even though June had been answering truthfully, not joking. June kept her elbows tight by her sides. She felt a dribble of sweat leak out of her armpit.

It smelled like plastic, but without the disinfectant odour she associated with hospitals. That morning when she came in, she fancied there was smoke inside, but she probably imagined it, or perhaps it was just the smell of Old Parliament House. A fire had been set by protesters in 2022, destroying the front entrance and leaving soot on every surface on the main level, and June often caught a faint whiff of smoke under the old-building smell.

She pictured herself in the MRI, trapped and flailing at the walls as the noise of the magnets assaulted her, and she shuddered. Everything seemed to be happening too fast, and she couldn't breathe properly.

She took the earplugs Blythe offered her and put them in with trembling fingers, then sat on the flatbed, far too hot in her puffer jacket, yet shivering. It would be colder where she was going. On the ceiling behind the MRI was a wide titanium—presumably non-magnetic—pipe that fed into the ceiling. June wondered if it were part of the time machine, before remembering that MRIs had to have a cryogen discharge vent for when the cryogens had to be discharged.

This is stupid.

Through the glass, Elijah watched her from behind the control desk. Phoenix came in and looked over the array of machinery in the corner. He said something to Elijah about tritium levels; June couldn't hear him properly with the earplugs in. The sound of his voice was comforting, though.

Her jacket rustled as she lay down, holding a squishy air-bulb attached to a tube in one hand that could abort the trip. The downlight above the bed was blinding, so she shut her eyes. *I'm in control,* she told herself firmly. She was trembling quite badly now, and she wondered whether that would affect the MRI.

The ceiling slid smoothly past as the flatbed rolled into the scanner, headfirst, then continuing down her body. Something about the sensation made June aware of the wheels beneath her that were feeding the bed in. An orange power cord hung from the ceiling above her, cable-tied to an aluminium chain, terminating in a power point. A printed sticky label on it read "Power Available."

The MRI clanked, then emitted loud morse-signal tones. Louder and louder, a throbbing hum. *It's impossible, time travel isn't real. I don't have to do this.* Stop now? *No, keep going.* She should have asked whether it was going to hurt—

CHAPTER 12

TUESDAY 13 OCTOBER 1987 AT 12:00PM, 349 PPM CO$_2$

As soon as June materialised in the past, she knew something had gone wrong. She was expecting to see the Algastic start-up display room that she'd seen photos of, but she appeared to be in a small wood-panelled booth. After a moment, and with a rising sense of horror, she realised it was a phone booth, used for making private calls. This wasn't 2022.

Her armpits were wet and cold. The thought that the MRI had faithfully re-materialised even her clammy armpits amused her.

A small wooden desk was built into the end of the room, where in her time the Ikea cube storage unit was, with one of the chairs June recognised from the meeting room.

According to a newspaper on the desk next to the phone, it was Tuesday 13 October 1987. Or, she supposed, it could be an old newspaper. But it looked new; it had an inky scent. She cautiously opened the door and poked her head out.

The room was empty. MediSlice's partitions had been completely removed. This was Parliament House, a Ministerial

Party room. Not a museum or a start-up space, but the home of the Australian government.

Fabric sofas were arranged in a small circle. Across the other side of the room, their meeting room table, with the same chairs that June had sat in many times. A small cathode-ray tube TV sat in one corner.

The clock set into a wooden box read 12:00pm, and one of the buttons below it was flashing red, signalling that a division of the Senate was taking place.

June retreated to the phone booth and sat up with her back against the wall. The diamond-pattern green-and-cream carpet hadn't changed since they built the place, but it looked newer now. The room stank of cigarette smoke. At the desk, a man's suede suit jacket hung on the back of a chair.

She stayed where she was for a long time, processing her feelings. The time machine would wait twenty minutes after transporting someone before attempting to bring them back, so that they weren't snatched back accidentally. But it had been longer than twenty minutes already.

The shock had brought everything into sharp focus. A sick feeling gnawed in the pit of her stomach, threatening to turn into panic. She was lost. Why did she agree to this? How could Phoenix let her use the machine when it was obviously unsafe? How the hell was she going to get back?

After a few hours, her backside hurt and she needed to pee. She wasn't dematerialised by the time machine, so she would have to do something. Send a message. Perhaps they didn't know what time period they'd sent her to. Why hadn't they set up a system for sending messages?

Her clothes had been carefully chosen to fit in with 2022, so here she would look ridiculous. She was wearing jeans and a plain green T-shirt. And, because it was supposed to be winter here—even though she came from early summer—she was wearing a green Kathmandu puffer jacket, with black lining. Although fashion had never been one of her interests, she was beginning to understand it, because of the research she had done for time travelling. The denim fabric of her jeans was okay, but they sat far too low; they were just under her bellybutton, rather than at the narrow part of her waist. And her T-shirt was nowhere near baggy enough. But maybe it would pass.

The jacket wouldn't, though, so she stuffed that in a cupboard in the party room. She left her 2022 money there too, colourful plastic twenties and a fifty, pushed right to the back on the bottom shelf where hopefully no one would see it until she returned.

Guiltily, she checked the pockets of the jacket that was slung over the chair in the phone booth and extracted the banknotes from the leather wallet she found in there, tucking them into her pocket. It helped slightly that the money in the wallet looked nothing like money to her; instead of bright plastic notes, the paper was dull and smooth. She had seen the notes, or pictures of them, in 2030, but the difference was that these weren't brown with age, but white and crisp.

Opening the door as quietly as she could, she walked down the corridor.

Two men stood in the hallway, smoking and talking. They shut up and looked her up and down in a curious way as she passed.

On a small table beside the men sat a pack of cigarettes, with a warning "SMOKING REDUCES YOUR FITNESS," in white text. Next to the cigarettes was a square amber glass ashtray filled with ashes.

Smoking reduces your fitness? She reeled with culture shock.

"You lost, darl?" one of the men said. "What are you here for?"

June shook her head and walked quickly away. She heard them laughing behind her. *Journalists*, she realised. As she passed the House of Representatives on her left, she heard raised voices, heckling.

With great relief, she found a toilet near the Senate; she remembered a sign in her time noting that they hadn't installed women's toilets when they built the place in 1918, and she couldn't remember when they had retrofitted some.

They had boxed off one of the urinals from the men's toilet and painted *Ladies Toilet* on the front of the frosted glass door. She struggled with the lack of flush button before she spotted the chain dangling from a cistern up high.

She exited the toilet. Now to find food.

———

She left Old Parliament House, except that it was 1987, so it wasn't that old, and it was called the Provisional Parliament House. She tried to grab the railing as she went down the front steps and nearly fell, because it was missing. The Aboriginal Tent Embassy was gone too, even though June was certain it had been around well before 1987. But there stood the pinnacle of Telstra Tower pointing to the clouds from the top of Black Mountain. Canberra's sentinel on duty already.

She walked to the National Gallery near the lake's edge. The buildings she remembered were all there, but the trees had been replaced with vast expanses of grass. It was so strangely empty that it felt post-apocalyptic, but that was due to the sudden absence of what June knew should be there. Also, Canberra was always a bit odd, because it didn't grow organically; it was a 1960s idea of utopia. One of the reasons it was hard to get around without a car was because Canberra was so sparsely populated, unlike older cities in Australia such as Sydney and Melbourne.

Walking around was like watching a period drama, except that the cinematography was poor. People weren't as good-looking as in the movies. The cars were dirtier.

The brutalist National Gallery loomed above her, much brighter than she remembered. The café was open.

She stepped inside, where the aroma of toasted bread and the babel of conversation filled the space. The velvety red carpet was lit pink where the sun hit it. Solid concrete walls covered in tall posters soared upward, creating a space three times the height of an ordinary ceiling. Light filtered in through high rectangular windows behind the counter and along the opposite wall.

The café was crowded with mothers and their squirming children, businessmen, and silver-haired seniors. A young man at a table near the door stared at her as she entered, probably because of her clothes. She ignored him.

She paid for a grilled cheese sandwich—the only savoury vegetarian option in 1987—and a cup of Earl Grey tea, trying not to look shocked at the minuscule amount they charged her. The money she had taken from the jacket took on new value as she realised just how far it would stretch.

Sitting at a table by the window, she ate her hot sandwich, her elbows on the sun-warmed blonde wood table. The windows above her slanted in like a greenhouse. The Sculpture Gallery she overlooked was dotted with newly planted shrubs and dominated by a gas-fired barbecue.

After a while, a bevy of business-suited men—some with tan pants, as was the fashion—entered and claimed a table near the counter, far from June. With great surprise, she recognised one as Bob Hawke, with his bushy eyebrows and larrikin grin, from a portrait hanging in Old Parliament House. Given that it was 1987, he was probably the prime minister. What were the chances of running into him? She didn't know what Canberra's population was now, but it wasn't a tiny town. Still, Hawke could come to this café every day, for all she knew.

June sipped her tea, listening to the sound of cutlery clinking on porcelain plates and the soothing murmur of conversation where she couldn't make out the words, feeling, for the first time since she'd arrived, quite relaxed.

Then she spat her tea back into her cup involuntarily, because in walked June.

It was clearly her and not someone who looked like her. A flash of confusion: *I don't remember wearing that outfit.* It was a skirt to the knees and a floral blouse, and June was sure she had never worn it before. Future June? But it was impossible! Seeing her past self should be possible, but not her future self, because that trip hadn't happened yet.

And yet, here she was.

Her future self looked at the man near the door with something like shock, although June couldn't understand why. Then she looked at the floor, as if crestfallen. Slowly, her eyes lifted until she met June's gaze. June shivered; eye contact was intense at the best of times. She had never pictured eye contact with *herself*, outside of a mirror.

Her future self crossed the sea of red carpet and sat opposite June, smoothing her skirt. She didn't appear significantly older than June; June found herself updating the mental image she had of herself. Her hair was prettier than she realised, but her mouth was a bit asymmetrical, how had she never spotted that?

"So," her future self said. Her voice sounded far rougher and lower-pitched than June had imagined her voice to be.

"So," June said, then realised she'd unintentionally lowered the pitch of her voice to match the other woman's and cleared her throat, embarrassed.

"Our model of time travel is wrong," June said, realising, as she said it, the full implications. Zikshita, Pranav's three-year-old niece, was lost forever. Human civilisation would be destroyed. Humans might even become extinct. June dropped her head in her hands, covering her eyes with her palms.

The boulder that Phoenix carved was among hundreds. It would have been so easy for him to check the wrong boulder. She pictured him choosing a boulder, in the present, deciding that was the boulder to graffiti and ensuring it didn't already have the date he intended to carve on it. Then walking away, not knowing that just a few metres to the left was a boulder with the date he intended to carve on it, already there . . .

"The past doesn't resist change. The past just *seems* to resist being changed because the efforts to change it failed," her future self said. "Everything that you do here was always done."

"Which means we can't prevent the climate crisis," June said.

"Right."

June never swore, but she did so now. She thought suddenly of holding Amy, her uncomplicated smile that contained more joy than was reasonable in this doomed and crazy world.

"Yeah," the other June said.

Here June was, in the past, no one knowing *when* she was. Was there some artefact in the future showing she lived out her life in the past? Because if there was, she wouldn't be—couldn't be—rescued.

"I have to go," June said, horrified.

Her future self reached out for June's unfinished tea. "Yes, you do," she said in a singsong voice. She knew more than June; June could see she was holding things back, but so what? Of course she knew more: she was from the future.

But that her future self had visited this era meant that June must be rescued, because otherwise she couldn't visit from the future. Her chest loosened.

She left. She glanced back through the window of the café before she walked away and saw that the young man from beside the counter had gone to join her future self, sitting in the seat June had just vacated. June shook her head.

CHAPTER 13

TUESDAY 13 OCTOBER 1987 AT 4:12PM, 349 PPM CO_2

Outside, the lake glittered. Two ducks shepherded their ducklings across the path in front of June. Flags didn't whip in the breeze from the International Flag Display at Commonwealth Place, because that must have been built later; right now, it was a muddy patch of grass.

Although June was tempted to wait around in the phone booth at Provisional Parliament House, she knew it was pointless. If they knew when she was, they would have scanned the room within minutes after she left. The hours she spent there not dematerialising proved they had no idea. As soon as she managed to send a message, they could pick her up from her long wait, but she had to list a time after she sent the message, or she wouldn't have sent one.

She walked to the Hyatt Hotel Canberra, not too far from Parliament House, knowing that it was one of the first hotels built in Canberra and would certainly be there, although when she arrived, she discovered it had apparently only just opened after a multi-year refurbishment.

"Can I help you?" asked the man behind the counter; white, middle-aged, wearing large square-rimmed glasses. Even the accents were different. Everyone who had spoken to her had sounded strange. Visiting 1987 Canberra was like visiting New Zealand, where things were almost the same as Australia, but not quite.

I'm June, and I care about the climate crisis, June thought and suppressed a laugh at the thought of the man's expression had she said it out loud. "Could I get a room, please?" June asked instead.

"Certainly. And will your husband be joining you?"

"What? No. Just me. A room for one," June said.

The man nodded, giving her an odd look. But once June had filled in the paperwork and paid cash, he gave her a key. She used her real name on the paperwork. She was nobody. No one would notice. It was unlikely the records were kept past a couple of years, anyway.

Her room didn't look that different from other hotels she'd stayed at. Even the television, a wood-panelled cube, was familiar from her childhood memories, from hotels that were slow to upgrade. Beige carpet, single bed, dark heavy curtains. It was reassuringly familiar.

She sat on the single bed. The wall-mounted lamp shone on the telephone. A curly cord attached the handset to the telephone, but it had buttons for numbers rather than a dial as June had expected.

They'd given her a copy of the paper: the *Canberra Times*. To serve the National City and Through it the Nation, it said. She scanned the headlines, which were refreshingly free of climate-change related disasters. *Nature springs a wintry surprise. PM jumps the gun on Fiji speech. Hawke under fire over trade dispute with the US. Stuart to join tour.*

June had been vaguely aware of Bob Hawke, who had been prime minister at some point in the past, but it seemed like a long time ago, except that as the newspaper showed, it was suddenly and shockingly *now*.

She stood up and paced around. *What am I going to do?* Perhaps she should just stay and wait for rescue. If she could compose an email, setting it to send at a future time, that would work. But there were no scheduled emails here . . . were there? An ad on the front page of the *Canberra Times*, read "Cleveland, the Australian Computer from Tomorrowland. A range of PCs made in Australia—now purchased by government in significant quantities. RING 811977 or FAX your needs for an instant quotation on 813719."

June didn't even recognise the numbers as phone numbers to start with, as they didn't have enough digits. So PCs, and apparently modems, were for sale. But email? She didn't know for sure. She guessed if email existed it was between a handful of academics at universities and probably still called Electronic Mail. And an unsent email was unlikely to survive on a server for decades, even if the system permitted her to set the send time to such a faraway date.

A handwritten letter would be chancy. Even if she painted in big red letters on the front door of MediSlice, "JUNE IS STUCK IN 1987," assuming no one erased it, that wouldn't work, because Phoenix clearly didn't know already where she was going to be stuck, and didn't know that he couldn't change the past. It had to be a message he would get *after* Friday 22 November 2030 at 1:00pm, when she dematerialised there and re-materialised in 1987, because *she couldn't change the future*. What happens stays happened.

It wasn't even enough to shout out her presence to the world here. To take out a paid ad in the paper, for example, or to do something so newsworthy that she was included in an article. Why would the team read through a random paper printed in 1987? Some foreknowledge about what happened in 1987 and what was about to happen would have made her task much easier, but it was too late now.

It seemed too hard to change the future, but she had to. Just a tiny change, something small enough to be unnoticeable to nearly everybody, and large enough to bring her home.

She would have despaired, but she knew it could be done, because she had done it already.

To an observer, June knew it would appear that she was doing nothing. She sat in the leather chair by the window and stared out over Lake Burley Griffin. She paced the hotel room from one end to the other. She lay on the quilted bed and stared at the ceiling. Inside, though, her mind ticked over.

June tried to picture what would happen at MediSlice after they worked out she was missing. Blythe would be near the collider holding—a multimeter? June didn't know much about electronics—doing diagnostics. Elijah would be at the control desk, checking mission logs. Or maybe since it was after 5:00pm, he would have knocked off and gone on a date.

Harry was probably at his computer searching the past for her; trying to find a message from 2022 and wondering why she didn't just send them a scheduled email.

In Phoenix's office, the door would be open, and Phoenix would be sitting on his chair throwing the tennis ball against the wall—thud, smack, pause—staring unblinkingly as he thought about how to rescue her. Could she alter the wall in some way, where Phoenix threw his tennis ball?

June pictured a chunk of wall falling off, revealing a compartment with an aged scrap of paper, and Phoenix lifting it out with puzzlement and increasing excitement. But that was stupid, because there was no way to make sure the compartment was found then rather than years before, or years afterward.

What about scheduled email, 1987 style; a posted letter, like in *Back to the Future II*? June did the math and her heart sank. Get someone to post a letter forty-three years from now? What were the chances they would succeed; that they wouldn't lose it, die before then—like in *Star Trek: Voyager* "Eye of the Needle"—or forget?

Something worked, June reminded herself. Maybe the best approach was to have lots of messages. Spend a day, or a few days, putting out messages, then go to the room and see if she dematerialised.

But how could she get a message in front of Phoenix's eyes? She pictured him waking up in his bedroom. By himself, because he'd been working non-stop on the time machine for years and didn't have a girlfriend. Also, his social skills were terrible. He could be arrogant and generally offensive, but that didn't bother her; on the contrary, she liked him for it. Politeness was a false face. Most people—the socially adept—danced around, never saying what they meant, leaving her to make futile guesses, and getting angry when she didn't guess right. Phoenix was delightfully uncomplicated. Delightful full stop, actually.

Lying there on the bed in her hotel room, forty-three years in the past, June had a revelation that hit her with a great wave of embarrassment, because she was very bad with people. *Working with you these past few months. It's wrong.* Phoenix touching her arm. His head close to hers.

Painfully obvious to anyone but June. *Phoenix wanted her.*

She hadn't considered him in that light, mostly because Elijah was in her thoughts so much. Phoenix was her friend.

He was extremely attractive. If she wasn't in love with Elijah—

But she *was* in love with Elijah, so she wasn't remotely ready for another relationship. Anyway, all this was academic. First, she would have to make it back.

———

June engaged a law firm, Bennett and Sons, to pass on a message. They asked no questions and took her money. She vaguely remembered their office in Civic, off London Circuit, so at least they would be around in her time.

It was with optimism that she went back to the Provisional Parliament House on the morning of Thursday 15 October 1987.

She checked out of her hotel room, in her sweat-stained and rumpled clothes that she hadn't changed out of in two days. Some money remained. If they didn't pick her up now, she wouldn't have much to live on. Her stomach turned at the thought.

Just one security guard attended the entrance, and he barely looked at her. In 2030 at New Parliament House, she would have had to go through a full-body scanner and have her possessions searched. New Parliament House sat under a grassy hill; architect-designed so that people could walk over it, to remind politicians who they served, but ironically fenced off due to security concerns.

As June walked down the corridor, the woman she was passing cried out. June didn't look at people by default, so was constantly surprised when someone she knew appeared out of nowhere. Frequently, they seemed to think June was ignoring them on purpose, which was another tedious facet of June's existence.

It was Blythe, with no jewellery, wearing a knitted sweater, pants, and sneakers, all appropriate for 1987. Her eyes looked huge with blue powder top and bottom, and the lipstick she wore disguised her split lip extremely well. Her loose blond hair was somehow fluffier and wavier.

"Blythe," June said, with tremendous relief. A waiter passed them, carrying a metal tray with plates and glasses on it, and then went into the function room on their left. A babble of conversation spilled out into the hallway with a clinking of glassware and cutlery.

On closer examination, Blythe's split lip wasn't concealed by lipstick—it had nearly healed. She must be from after June had left, but not far enough in the future for it to have healed entirely.

"What are you doing here?" June asked.

"Preventing plastic from being invented," Blythe said.

"But plastic was invented—" June said, then spotted the sarcasm. "You're here to rescue me."

Blythe nodded. She seemed to be suppressing a smile, June

noticed, which was another thing people frequently did around her. June knew her ways were strange, but she could tell when people were making fun of her; sometimes she thought they didn't know that.

"Actually, plastic was invented in 1869," June said, it being an interest of hers. "Did you know it was considered environmentally friendly? Because it replaced materials like ivory, tortoiseshell, and horn, saving lots of animals. I guess they didn't consider the whole life cycle, or—"

Inside the function room on the left, a crash sounded.

June jerked. Blythe twisted around to the source of the noise, her breath coming in short, panicked gasps. June stared at Blythe, hearing the laughter and half-hearted applause from within the room.

Blythe turned back around. Her white face flushed deep red as she struggled to get her emotions under control. Normal sounds resumed in the conference room.

"It's okay," June said gently. "We're safe here."

Blythe blinked and looked at her. "Yes. Yes, we are, aren't we?"

After a moment, her breathing evened out.

"Why send you? I said in the message to scan from today at midday, and it's not midday yet," June said.

"What message? We didn't get any messages. We worked out from the log data, eventually, where you had gone. The selected wormhole was the wrong length for some reason. But of all the missions we've been on, none of them have been closer in time to our own than the year we tried to send you to—2022. Perhaps there are fewer wormholes with ends in the near-past than in the far-past. We're not sure, though. We're speculating."

June nodded, and Blythe exhaled. "It's been a week for us. Phoenix has been out of his mind, Elijah's grumpy, and Harry just looks terrified. We fixed the bug by reducing the wormhole length tolerance, we thought, then we had to run a bunch of tests to make sure it was working, and then we also had to find you. I've been here for days looking for you . . . you've been here for days, right? Or did I get the wrong time?"

"Almost two days. I stayed at a hotel. I've been gone *a week*?"

Blythe nodded. "Your sister texted you, and I took the liberty of pretending to be you when I texted back. I said we were doing a coding sprint, which Elijah said your sister might find plausible."

June nodded, amused.

Blythe swept a hand through her hair. "I've been mostly wandering around Parliament House asking questions and going to nearby shops. This is my second jump, because I didn't find anything the first day. Anyway, let's go."

They walked side by side to the phone booth, which would later become the MediSlice travel room. But as June opened the door, she surprised a bald man sitting at the desk, phone to his ear.

He stared at her and Blythe.

"Hello," Blythe said, entering the phone booth. June followed her reluctantly; she was tired and clammy, but she still would have stayed out until he had gone, not confronted him.

"You can't be in here," the man said aggressively. "Sorry, Dick," he said into the phone. "Some sheilas wandered in." He had the stout and rosy demeanour of someone who drank too much.

"When will the room be free?" Blythe said.

"Sorry, who the hell are you?" the man said, but June didn't think he sounded very sorry.

"No one important," Blythe said. "When will the room be available?"

June longed to tug on Blythe's arm to pull her away, but didn't dare. "Blythe, maybe we should—"

"Now see here," the man said, bristling—

June was flat on her back, noisy clanging above her head beginning to subside as the MRI shut down. A hint of smoke lingered in the air; June wondered if it was from the Aboriginal

Tent Embassy out the front of Old Parliament House, because they often had a campfire going, but she didn't remember smelling it inside the travel room before.

"Do we have Blythe?" June said, struggling to get up as the flatbed rolled out of the tube. Elijah gave June a thumbs up. Phoenix and Elijah sat in the control desk behind the glass partition, relief plain on their faces. Given June had realised that Phoenix liked her, she found it hard to meet his eyes; she flushed in confusion. But she thrust that to the back of her mind.

The flatbed slid back in, and the machine noise increased. June exhaled and left the room. She realised she had left her puffer jacket and some future money in the back of a cupboard in 1987 and shook her head ruefully. That would be a historical curiosity, no doubt.

She stopped dead in the hall, adrenaline spiking through her, the bitter taste of fear in her dry mouth. The light coming through the closed window at the end of the hall was orange-brown. Acrid smoke burnt her nose.

"The bushfires got worse, as you can see," Blythe said from behind her. June jumped. "New South Wales has declared a State of Emergency. Victoria will probably follow. They're bringing in firefighters from Canada and the US, although not many, because their fire season is still going."

Another Black Summer, June thought numbly. Every year she wondered if it would be repeated, but they had been lucky since 2019, and had had only minor fires. Or perhaps they weren't lucky, because the years of wet weather had built up an enormous fuel load, leaving Australia in danger of a fire season worse than Black Summer, especially given the hot, dry conditions forecast for the next few months. She crossed her arms over herself.

CHAPTER 14

They crowded into the break room, instead of the meeting room, because June was shaking and they decided she needed food. The blinds were drawn, but the quality of light coming through the cracks was subtly wrong, filtered as it was through the smoke haze.

June sat at the table, Blythe in the only other chair opposite her. Phoenix sat on the kitchenette bench, and Harry stood next to him. The printer beeped, telling her that her blueberry protein bar was ready. Her phone buzzed in her pocket, but she ignored it.

She took a deep breath. "So, about what happened to me . . ."

Elijah came in and sat on the beanbag by the window, with a cola bag in his hand, drinking from a metal straw. They listened as June explained that she met her future self. Because June was talking, they were all watching her, but according to the eye-contact ballet, it was customary for June not to stare at them. Her eyes had to dart around and only make fleeting eye contact to make sure they were still listening. A longer period of eye contact could follow to indicate she was finished talking.

The others listened to her talk. Blythe still wore her eighties outfit: diamond-patterned sweater, fluffy hair and blue eyeshadow. Old Parliament House had been vacated a year after June was there—in 1988—the interior design had remained frozen from that time period, so the museum spaces and the start-ups were all decorated in the style of 1988. Blythe fit in; it was the rest of them who looked incongruous.

"Could you have checked the wrong boulder, Phoenix?" Elijah asked.

"It's possible," Phoenix conceded.

"That doesn't make any sense," Harry said. "Even if Phoenix missed seeing his graffiti before he went back in time to make the graffiti, we've been on a bunch of missions since then, changing the past."

"Have we, though?" June said. She held up her hand, counting off their missions. "One. Maybe your angel investor—"

"Ted McNamara," Phoenix supplied.

"—maybe Ted was already in the Battle of Helm's Deep, but he'd never freeze-framed and searched for himself. Even after he went back in time, he was hard to see in the footage that remained in the movie."

Blythe's face was drawn as she listened, but Harry and Elijah seemed more interested than upset. Phoenix was shaking his head, stricken, although she thought he believed her.

Phoenix's phone rang, a holo of a grim-faced man appearing above the screen. "Excuse me," Phoenix said, sliding off the kitchen bench and disappearing into the hall as he answered.

"Two. The Pink Palace climate meeting that Phoenix attended. As he noted, his presence made no effective difference. Three—the clambake Charney report, which Elijah said was a wash. Four. The *Changing Climate* gala, where Elijah's attempt to help caused the very event we were hoping to avoid, because he made Nierenberg suspicious, causing him to urge caution before urgency."

The muted sound of Phoenix's voice travelled in from the hall. He sounded agitated.

"Five," June continued. "The reveal to the *Save the Warming Planet* activist. We didn't check whether the activist had written a book before going back, because it didn't occur to us that she could have. Six. Books on manufacturing solar panels. Maybe they did help—maybe they're the reason solar panel efficiency has increased so drastically within a short window of time—but they didn't change the present. Seven. Batteries, same. Eight. Academic papers, which probably ended up in the bin at a police station, so no impact on the future there. Nine. Tracy Lismore, the police officer Blythe tried to talk to. She apparently didn't try to change the future. And lastly, then my 2022 mission to the Lislax gas field, which I never made it to, because I got stuck in 1987. But the strongest evidence is that I met myself in the café. I couldn't have met myself under Phoenix's model, because I haven't travelled from the future yet."

June stood up. Her phone buzzed again, vibrating against her thigh. "All changes we made to the past have already happened in our timeline. The past doesn't *resist* change; it *has already been* changed. The cold hard truth is that what we have now is what we're stuck with."

Phoenix appeared in the doorway of the break room. June stared at him uneasily because he seemed to be close to tears.

Elijah's mouth set in a grim line, and he didn't look at anyone. He stood up and rinsed his straw, leaving it in the drainer, and put his empty cola bag in the compost caddy. Blythe's phone rang, but she glanced at the screen and silenced it. Elijah's phone made a series of tones which indicated a message from his dad had arrived.

June sat down slowly. This was one of those moments, wasn't it, when years later people would say, "Where were you when it happened?"

"What is it?" Harry said. He didn't seem concerned at Phoenix's demeanour. As Phoenix started speaking, June suddenly wondered if Phoenix was going to announce that the AMOC had shut down, like Harry had said in one of their Save-the-World meetings. She looked sharply at Harry, who raised his eyebrows at her as if to say *what?*

"Thwaites Glacier is collapsing," Phoenix said. Elijah glanced at June, compassion in his eyes. How many times had she fretted about Thwaites Glacier disintegrating? A glacier the size of Florida that formed the cork holding back the West Antarctic ice sheet. Late at night, sitting on the sofa with her feet in his lap, a back-and-forth discussion about what the worst thing was that could happen.

"But it'll take centuries for it to melt," June said, aware that she was echoing what Elijah used to say to her.

"Actually," Phoenix said in a tight voice, "they think it will take decades. At most."

"Oh God," Blythe said, breathing too fast. "Oh no."

June shivered.

"What does that mean, exactly?" Harry asked. June was sure he knew what it meant and felt like he was asking to find out if *they* knew, but she didn't know why he would do that. Harry had a liberal-arts background; perhaps that was what made him harder for her to understand. Engineers were an open book, but artsy people were strange.

"It means sixty-five centimetres of sea level rise by 2050," Phoenix said. He hesitated. "And scientists are now predicting the entire West Antarctic ice sheet will follow within the century," he added.

"Three metres by 2100?" June said incredulously. The others groaned, all except Harry. June had feared this, usually in the depths of the night when her mind went to dark places. But it didn't seem real in daylight.

"What's that in American?" Blythe asked, probably because Harry seemed so unconcerned.

"Um. Sixty-five centimetres is twenty-five inches. Three metres is what, ten feet?" Phoenix said.

"Ten feet? That can't be right," Harry said, laughing, but he sobered when no one else laughed. Elijah checked Phoenix's calculations and nodded to the group. Harry's face fell, but again, June felt this was an act. He was playing dumb for reasons she didn't understand.

Phoenix sighed heavily.

Blythe got up, went to the window and back to her seat, a caged bird. She left the room, then came back in and said, "I have to call my mum," before disappearing.

"Are you going to be okay?" June asked Elijah, knowing his dad, a climate doomer worse than June, would require a lot of emotional support after the news. His dad wasn't the easiest person to manage. *Was it appropriate?* She and Elijah were friends. June didn't know where the line was, but right now, she didn't care.

"Yeah," Elijah said softly. "Thanks, June."

June dug her phone out of her pocket, flipping it open to check it. Messages from Hannah in the family group chat they had with them and their dad, who lived in Canada. Hannah's messages were about the news and peppered with anguished face emojis. No reply from their dad yet, but it was probably around 4:00am in Ottawa.

Elijah and Harry left, then there was just Phoenix. June couldn't meet his eyes; she was spent and needed to be somewhere where there were no people. Eye contact had become painful. Nonetheless, in the stiffness of his frame, she sensed silent anguish.

June swallowed. As she passed him, she grabbed his hand and squeezed it. He squeezed back with warm dry strength, then let her go.

———

The bushfire smoke was thicker than June expected. She managed to catch the wrong bus, in all the confusion, and ended up in

Civic, the middle of Canberra. PM 2.5 masks were on sale in the convenience store nearby. Planter boxes of flowers sat on urine-stained and bubble-gum-marked concrete. A man wearing an unbuttoned business shirt asked June for fifty dollars and swore at her when she shook her head. Two bodies in sleeping bags were tucked away at the base of a plane tree, near bronze statues of a pack of wild dogs racing forward.

A young couple were having an argument in the Interchange, next to the refugee centre.

"—just saying that you don't approve new fracking projects if you're serious about climate change," hissed the woman. "They're in bed with the fossil-fuel companies! It's so obvious, and no one seems to care."

"I didn't say that, just that—"

The next part was inaudible to June as a bus rolled past.

"You drove here! Burning fossil fuel! It's the very definition of fiddling while Rome burns! But sure, let's talk about the accent colours for your autumn wardrobe. That's *so important*."

A mother pushing a stroller crossed over to the other side of the street to avoid them. Nonetheless, the woman directed her rage to those around her.

"Wake up! WAKE UP! You're sheep, all of you. Sheep! BAAA!"

June walked quickly away, but the shouts of the woman echoed behind her, even as she boarded the bus. The thing that depressed her most about the climate crisis was not the crisis itself, but that it was happening to humanity, perhaps the first sentient species ever to exist, aware enough to know exactly what was happening but apparently not organised enough to stop it. She sat with her hands in her lap and stared out the window as bushland reserves slid past, gums and undergrowth looming out of the yellow-orange smoke either side of the wide black road.

When she opened the door to Hannah's house, Pranav, still in his scrubs, was holding Hannah. They disentangled, and Hannah looked at June uncomprehendingly.

"June, thank goodness," Hannah said. "If you're going to be

away for a week, you have to *tell* me first, okay? I was really worried!"

"Okay, sorry," June muttered. She'd read over the messages Blythe had sent to Hannah while pretending to be June, claiming June was staying with Blythe and coding. Even June found them convincing.

But June being away had been overshadowed by the news about Thwaites Glacier, June could tell, because Hannah wasn't nearly as angry as June had expected her to be.

"Mum! I can't sleep." Rahul came out of the hall, hair tousled, holding his dinosaur soft toy.

"Go back to bed, Rahul," Pranav said.

Instead, Rahul rolled his eyes and flounced to the living room. "TV, on."

The sound of the TV filled the room.

"Rahul! TV, off," Hannah said, and silence returned.

"But I need another story!" Rahul complained.

"I'll read him a story," June said.

Hannah nodded gratefully. "And tomorrow maybe we could talk," she said, her tone of voice making it clear that it wasn't a request.

June followed Rahul back to his room and sat on the floor next to his bed, surrounded by Lego bits. Rahul climbed into her lap with a book. June just wanted to be alone, to process what had happened without anyone observing her and to find out how the world was reacting.

"This one," Rahul said. Compared to Amy, he was incredibly heavy and bony, but he had the same soft child-warmth to him, the same smooth skin. The weight of him was comforting.

June mechanically read the words without listening for the meaning, but the story eventually broke through.

The long-tailed planigale
Zero on the Richter scale
Stepped up when nobody spoke

"I'll save him," she said
As the possums all fled
"Though I cannot see through the smoke"

June's voice cracked as she turned the page and kept reading. Caught in a bushfire with larger animals, the tiny planigale saved the kangaroo, because even the smallest creature can make a difference. June tried to blink her tears away, but her eyes were full, leaving nowhere for the liquid to go but down her cheeks.

Rahul looked at her with sharp worry. "What are you feeling?" he said.

"I'm feeling sad."

"It's okay. I'll make you feel better," he said. He got off her lap and left the room at a run. June took a deep, wobbly breath and wiped her tears away, smearing them across her cheeks until her face was dry.

Rahul came back and dumped a chocolate bar in her lap. He gave her a hug, although it felt like something he had been taught to do rather than a genuine impulse. "Are you better now?" he said.

"Yes, thank you," June said, and Rahul dropped his arms immediately. She put him to bed.

Pranav was putting rolled up towels under their doors to try to keep the smoke out and taping up the exhaust fan vents in the bathrooms. In the living room, Hannah was on the sofa watching TV, the Prime Minister, Peter Larden, was being interviewed. June sat in the armchair next to her.

"Two degrees doesn't seem like that much," Hannah said, in response to the PM talking about how the world was on track for two-point-two degrees, and that two degrees Celsius was unavoidable.

June wasn't sure what to say. Hannah probably knew as much as most people about climate change, which was to say that she avoided it where she could.

"Well . . ." June said. "Four degrees would probably mean the end of civilisation, a world we couldn't adapt to, so two degrees is actually incredibly dangerous. I mean, look at the chaos that's going on now, and that's with just over one degree of warming."

Hannah looked at her in shock.

"And you know it's an average, right?" June continued. "Temperatures are lower over the sea. So, say a global warming of four degrees Celsius might mean six to eight degrees of warming in Canberra, because we're mid-latitude. That could add ten degrees to the summer average, or maybe twelve in heatwaves. Canberra's hottest recorded temperature was forty-four, but western Sydney has a record of forty-eight. If you add twelve to that, you get summer heatwaves of sixty degrees."

"Jesus," Hannah said. June knew Hannah didn't have the capacity to even know the details; she was chronically sleep deprived and overworked. And why should she? How did it make sense that everyone had to become a climate activist in order to bring about change?

June left Hannah watching TV and got ready for bed.

When she finally reached her bedroom and shut the door on the world, she scrolled for hours on her phone.

On Thwaites Glacier, people in beanies, sunglasses, and orange coats erected a silver tripod twice their height. Behind them, round red tents were pitched in the snow, like a field of boulders. Beside the tents were barrels, vehicles, and a sled. Tiny flags at the perimeter of the camp flapped wildly, and the audio blasted static as the wind gusted.

In the background of the interview, a tinny voice was talking, perhaps from a radio transmission. Ice loss in the Arctic barely affects sea levels because the ice forms at sea, explained the researcher they were interviewing. Antarctic ice, however, was mostly on land, so any melting added to sea levels. Thwaites was particularly vulnerable because the bottom of the glacier was below sea level, so the warm water in the sea circulated underneath.

On social media, there was shock, anger, and frustration. Lots of people saying the world shouldn't be how it was, which was undeniable.

The Thwaites was cracking up even now, a process that would continue for perhaps decades, but the effects wouldn't be felt for a while. Already it was starting to be swept away in the news cycle, making room for something sexist the director of the latest season of *Hollow Planet* had said. The most shared article on the *Guardian* website was a recipe for baklava, which looked so delicious even June was tempted to save it. And why not? If you can't do anything about the climate, why pay attention?

June folded her phone, tossed it onto the bed, and rolled over, burying her face in her pillow. Sleep didn't come. She probably didn't have a job anymore. MediSlice's mission was impossible.

Eventually, in a half-asleep state, her mind was full of stormy waves crashing on jagged rocks; each wave leaving a confusion of milky white foam as it was sucked back to sea, only to be dashed violently against the rocks again. In the black, formless darkness, her skin was clammy; as soon as she threw off the blanket, she was cold again, but the blanket suffocated her. It didn't seem to matter how deeply or hard she breathed, there was not enough air to satisfy her, and besides, it reeked of smoke.

She sat up. *I have free will*, she thought. *I can travel back in time, and I have free will. I'm not giving up.*

CHAPTER 15

I t was midnight by the time she left the house, closing doors as silently as she could and mounting her bike in the darkness. The wide asphalt roads were brightly lit and completely empty. Every so often she heard a car in the distance, but never near her. She shot through the night on the cycle path at unsafe speeds, out of breath as she reached Old Parliament House.

Her key card wasn't meant to let her into Old Parliament House after hours—none of the start-up key cards were—but Blythe had mentioned once that they worked on the lower ground floor disabled access door, and fortunately she was correct. June swiped herself into the lower entrance and made her way up the internal stairs and through the dark halls to MediSlice, using the flashlight on her phone.

She used her computer for half an hour, checking through past editions of the *Canberra Times* and national news for 1987, as well as skim-reading everything she could about former Prime Minister Bob Hawke, until she was grimly satisfied that she hadn't affected his life in any way.

June raided the Ikea cube storage in the travel room. The clothes her future self wore in 1987, the floral skirt and blouse, were sitting there for her to use, which made her pause. But they were the only period-appropriate clothes that would fit her, so she changed into them.

She set the machine to 11:00am on Tuesday 13 October 1987, aware that she could potentially close the time loop by doing so, except that she would not. She was going to the café where she had met her future self, but she wasn't going to talk to her past self. Instead, she would tell Prime Minister Bob Hawke that Australia was in danger, with enough details about the future that he had to believe her. She had a detailed history of climate change in her head already, and now she had some events from 1987 that would have been impossible to predict. And she would take her phone, which would display an animated Fantinia holo above the screen when rebooted; that in itself would be proof enough. Even though newer phones were safe to use with the MRI, being non-ferrous, they hadn't dared to take them back before, for fear of changing the past in the wrong way. The café was crowded, and June had every intention of making a scene, so someone would tell the press. And June had seen with her own eyes that her future self wasn't coerced in any way to come to her table.

Nothing could induce her to act that way, so she was going to change the past, rules of physics be damned. What could possibly stop her? She'd seen that June didn't even attempt to see Hawke, so if she tried and was stopped, even that would be a difference, one that would prove she could alter the past.

At the control desk, June activated the time machine and switched on the lamp. The MRI made a series of bird-like chirping noises and thumps as it went through the initial calibration. She set the time carefully to one hour before she knew her past self would materialise, so she could be sure to avoid her. *Something's going to stop me,* she thought, but everything seemed to be working.

She lay on the MRI with her heart racing, and the flatbed slid into the scanner. It wasn't nearly as bad as the first time, mostly because she knew she could do it, but still her stomach was tight. The clanks as the MRI started the trip sequence were loud enough to wake anyone within a few kilometres, but no one lived nearby, so it didn't matter.

TUESDAY 13 OCTOBER 1987 AT 1:35PM, 349 PPM CO_2

As June approached the entrance to the café, her heart pounded, but she forced herself to continue.

There she was. Her past self sat near the windows, staring out over the Sculpture Garden, dappled light falling onto her face from the slanted windows above her. The pensive look on her face was completely unfamiliar to June; not something she'd ever seen in a mirror or photo before.

Her past self hadn't seen her yet.

Bob Hawke sat at a table of white men in business suits. Hawke, at the head of the table, laughed at a joke the young man on his left had made.

June ran her tongue over her teeth and steeled herself to confront a table full of Australian politicians, which would not be easy in 2030, let alone a time in Australia when women were still fighting against the belief that they belonged in the kitchen.

Then the young man who was seated by the door glanced at June, and she realised who he was.

Add forty-five years to his age, a thick salt-and-pepper beard and moustache, and some wrinkles around the eyes. It was him; it was Alejandro Gomez, the US Democratic Senator everyone said would be the next president. Here, in this lofty brutalist café in Canberra.

This was the man—or boy, as he was now—that June had seen talking to her future self the last time she had been in the café.

There was nothing stopping June from going over to Hawke's table. She could do it right now, if she wanted. But her future self had presumably talked to Alejandro Gomez and, in doing so, altered who he became. What would yelling at politicians achieve? Not much, she suspected. Yes, she had a chance to change the past, but to make it inescapably worse. Imagine a world where Gomez doesn't become a politician.

Her past self, sitting by the window with her grilled cheese sandwich and her Earl Grey tea, stared at her with horror.

June walked over to the other June's table and sat down with her back to the window, smoothing her skirt. Her past self was only a week younger than her, but it seemed like more; she didn't know she couldn't change the past. She didn't know about the Thwaites Glacier, or the fires raging out of control across Australia.

"So," June said, her voice gravelly as she tried to keep her grief out of it.

"So," her past self echoed in a low-pitched voice. The other woman put her head in her hands and covered her eyes. "Our model of time travel is wrong. The past doesn't resist change. The past just *seems* to resist being changed because the efforts to change it failed."

"Everything that you do here was always done," June said wearily.

"Which means we can't prevent the climate crisis," her past self said.

"Right," June said, thinking *you have no idea*.

The other June swore in a heartfelt way.

"Yeah," June said. Through the row of tall rectangular windows above the counter, the concrete ceiling continued, patterned with sunken triangles. The room felt solid, like a bunker, despite the rows of windows on either side; she didn't know how thick the walls and ceiling were, but she felt they must be metres deep.

"I have to go," her past self said.

June was suddenly thirsty and reached across the table for other June's cup of tea. "Yes, you do," she said, waiting for her past self to leave so she could talk to Alejandro. The other June left, only glancing back once she was outside the shop. By which time Alejandro had come to join June. She wondered what she was supposed to tell him, but whatever she had said was right, because she had already said it.

She stopped trying to script the conversation up front and let it unfold. As it happened, she info-dumped the history of climate change all over him, the history she had prepared for Bob Hawke. When she left the café, she took one last look to see him sitting there, sweaty and ill, with his head in his hands.

———

As soon as June slipped into the phone booth, she found herself lying on her back listening to the MRI power down. The smoke made her cough. Being away from it had been a relief, which she hadn't appreciated until now. She caught a glimpse of a figure behind the control desk, but couldn't make out who it was.

June guessed it was probably 2:22am, twenty minutes after the machine had sent her. That was the minimum time for the machine to change modes and start scanning the past for a retrieval.

The MRI flatbed slid out, and she sat up. Elijah nodded to her from the control desk. He folded and pocketed his phone as he stood up, and followed her out into the hall.

"What are you doing here?" June asked. She'd turned the hall lights on when she arrived, but they didn't keep the dark at bay. Smoke hung in the air at the end of the hall, and she felt an echo of the panicky feeling she got during Black Summer, of not being able to escape the smoke anywhere.

"Hannah texted me. Said you'd disappeared. I thought I'd better try to find you, and I guessed you might be here. I just texted her and let her know you're okay. *Are* you okay? Really?"

He said the last in a quiet voice, the expression on his face urging her to confide in him.

June considered his question, ignoring the tightness in her chest that came from the thought of him caring about her. She realised she was playing with the ends of her hair and made herself stop.

"Yeah, I'm all right. I closed the loop," she said tightly. "Today I was the one from the future meeting my past self in 1987."

They stopped in front of the external MediSlice door.

"Cup of tea?" Elijah said.

"Please."

She followed him to the break room and sat at the table while he made tea. He moved with an economy of movement, hands always dexterous, no matter if he was making tea, chopping vegetables, or petting an animal. She had always admired his hands; but he wasn't hers, so she had to stop watching him so closely.

"You came here after midnight to close the loop?" Elijah asked.

"No," June said. She rubbed her face with her hands, kneading it as if she could pull the skin off. "I came to change the past. To prove that I could. I mean, how can it not be changeable, right? It seems so easy. Take a bottle of nerve gas or something and break it in Times Square."

"You wouldn't do that," Elijah said, setting her teacup and saucer on a cork placemat on the table in front of her. No trace of doubt in his voice, just quiet warmth. Love, she would have called it.

She had been melodramatic all these past months; she knew it, she hated it, but she couldn't seem to stop.

"It makes sense that we can't change the past," Elijah observed. "The original model always felt crazy to me."

"Can I ask you a question?" June said.

Elijah put his cup of tea on the table and faced her. She tried so hard to ignore how attractive he was, every day, but she couldn't help noticing now. June stood up and closed the distance between them.

She paused at the last second to give him a chance to draw away, and when he didn't, she kissed him full on the mouth, surprising even herself. They fit together seamlessly, rightly, like the gentle click of the magnetic charging port and charger of a MacBook.

Elijah kissed her back, and in the aeons or perhaps seconds the kiss lasted, June felt urgent need rising, the red-hot desire to clutch him to her, but she kept her feelings buried and only allowed herself a kiss.

Elijah pulled away. He leaned back on the bench behind him and looked at her, serious. June sank back into her chair, maintaining eye contact. After a long moment, Elijah looked away.

"June," he said, in an exasperated tone of voice.

"I know, I know. We're finished. I'm sorry," she said with genuine remorse, because she knew she'd just stepped over the line. *But he had kissed her back.*

If June wasn't mistaken, Elijah was blushing. She watched as he took a sip of tea and settled himself at the table. Sitting opposite him felt as familiar as an old favourite song.

"What was your question?" Elijah asked. He held the cup to his face, letting steam rise onto his lips, nose, and closed eyelids.

"What?" June said.

"You said you wanted to ask me a question."

"Oh, yes. The question was, would you still have kids?" June asked. Then, hastily, remembering the last time she'd talked about children with him. "Not with me! I mean, knowing the Thwaites Glacier is collapsing."

Elijah's mouth set in a thin line. "Even though scientists got the timeframe wrong, and the West Antarctic ice sheet will break up over the next few decades, we know enough. We have enough time," he said. "We can move everyone away from the coastal cities."

"The cost of that would be in the trillions. I just can't—"

She broke off and searched for it on her phone. Mumbai, Guangzhou, Shanghai, Miami, Ho Chi Minh City, Kolkata, Greater New York, Osaka-Kobe, Alexandria, New Orleans. Amsterdam. Sydney. Melbourne. And so on.

"Where are all those people going to *go*?" June said.

"Inland. Money isn't real. With the technology we have, we can provide places for everyone to go. The real problem is political."

"It always has been. But that doesn't make it less of a problem," June said.

Elijah put his teacup down with a clatter. "Look at it this way. We were always going to have to abandon the cities, because in a geological time frame the coast isn't fixed. Twenty thousand years ago, so much ice was locked up that the sea level was one hundred and twenty metres lower than it is now. If the ice caps melt entirely, the sea level will rise by eighty metres, and Australia gets an inland sea. We're like hermit crabs who are washed out by the tide and wonder what happened."

"We're barely coping with the increased frequency and severity of natural disasters, and now we have to evacuate coastal cities as well?" June stood up and crossed to the sink, holding the edge, her back to him.

"Barely coping? That's not what the data says, June. Come on. There are more and worse disasters than ever, but fewer deaths, because we're better at predicting disasters, at protecting ourselves, and at recovering. You know that, right?" Elijah said.

June turned around to face him. "Tell that to the thirty thousand people who died in the Bangalore ultra-heatwave. Tell it to the people whose homes were burnt yesterday in New South Wales. Tell it to the billion animals that died during Black Summer, and to the animals that are dying as we speak," June said coldly. *Tell it to Zikshita,* she thought, but it would be wrong to bring up her death in an argument. She hadn't told him, or any of them, about Zikshita. It was too raw.

Elijah closed his eyes.

"I know. *I know.* I'm not saying we've done enough, or that we can afford to be complacent, but there are millions of people and organisations trying to do better. They've made amazing progress —despite the total lack of leadership on climate change—and they will continue to. The price of batteries has fallen ninety-seven percent over the last thirty years. Have you seen the response to Thwaites Glacier? People are paying attention. It's pulled humanity together in an unprecedented fashion. And I don't say that lightly —humans pull together when they face a threat. Throughout history, the rich crack down when there's a disaster, fearing looting, chaos. But largely a disaster is when people help each other—only a small minority will act badly. And that's why I'm hopeful."

June shook her head in disbelief, with a sense of exhaustion. This was just the same old argument.

"I don't think you realise how many changes have already been made," Elijah said. "How close we are to slipping through this crisis, even now—not unscathed, no—but not anywhere near societal collapse."

Elijah pulled his phone out of his pocket. "Look at this. It's basically magic. We are some mighty clever chimpanzees, when sufficiently motivated. There's going to be sulphate aerosols, and carbon capture and storage, and all kinds of geo-engineering. There has to be. There will be great loss of human life and biodiversity. But we'll survive."

June shook her head again. *Comforting lies.* The bubble Elijah lived in must make it so easy to sleep at night.

Elijah drained his tea and stood up. The clock above the sink read 2:48am.

"Do you want a lift home?" Elijah asked.

"Yes, please," June said. She could catch the bus in tomorrow. The idea of going to bed was suddenly attractive.

She rinsed both their cups in the sink, water hot on her hands. Elijah watched her silently. The cosy togetherness had evaporated, leaving something thin and grey in its place.

"I don't think I ever made it clear," Elijah said, and June started, looking at him. Elijah looked past her, out the window into the darkness made opaque by thick smoke. "I would have kids even if I thought the world was ending."

"I don't understand how you can say that," June said. The cup she was holding dripped as she put it in the drainer.

"Because you never know what will happen next. There's still beauty in the world, however this plays out. And . . . the inner light," Elijah said, and it took June a moment to realise he was referencing the *Star Trek: The Next Generation* "The Inner Light" episode in which the citizens of a doomed planet had children even though they knew their civilisation wouldn't survive. A shorthand he knew June would understand.

June dried her hands on a tea towel, but by the time she turned to respond, Elijah had left the room.

CHAPTER 16

Even inside Hannah's house, the smoke was thick enough to see in the larger rooms. A fire was advancing through the Lower Molonglo Nature Reserve, south of Canberra, although according to the news, the smoke in Canberra was mainly from the east coast fires.

"You don't have to go to work today. You could call in sick," Hannah said.

"I'm all right."

Hannah shook her head with a trace of amusement. "Most people wouldn't take off in the middle of the night because they remembered a bug that needed fixing," she said. Luckily, she'd accepted June's explanation, and even if it was strange, she'd put it down to June being strange.

"Next time, I'll message you before I leave," June promised.

Hannah handed June a mask as June left the house. The kids seemed fine; they watched television and didn't even notice that June was leaving.

June walked through the smoke to the bus stop. The PM 2.5 concentration was ten times the level needed to rate the air as hazardous. The squat cream cylinder of the bus stop loomed out of nowhere, much sooner than June expected. Rationally, she knew somewhere in the world it was winter, and the air there would be cool and fresh, but waking up to a city shrouded in smoke made it seem like the apocalypse had arrived.

The bus rumbled through a faintly yellow-tinted cloud. It was crowded with silent passengers, all masked, strangely blank to June because she couldn't read their facial expressions.

It reminded her of her first two years of university. As soon as Australia's Black Summer ended, Covid-19 hit. Masks, lockdowns, remote teaching, with no close friends and no boyfriend. She'd been in a deep depression, and hadn't minded Covid so much, because it isolated her from people, and people were more stressful than any pandemic.

The bus dropped June near Old Parliament House at 8:53am, and she walked to MediSlice to attend the morning meeting that Phoenix had called. Blythe was absent, having called in sick.

The only person who didn't have eye-bags and a glazed expression was Harry. He was immaculately groomed and had the same good-natured energy that he always had. Elijah had that argumentative look he got when his sleep had been disturbed.

"I'm sure you've all been thinking about this," Phoenix said, "but our mission has failed. As June revealed yesterday, we can't change the past."

"What *are* we going to do?" Elijah said. "Are we fired?"

The question sent a spike of fear through June. Not that she would find it difficult to get a new job, but she liked her co-workers and always had. She still missed her team at Deep Scan. She considered Blythe a friend now, and regarded Phoenix with affection. Family was family, but the work week was a significant portion of her life, and she came to like most people she worked with. She knew that she wasn't allowed to show it. Nonetheless, she didn't want things to change.

She especially didn't want to lose Elijah again. She couldn't follow him to another workplace—shouldn't have followed him to this one—so if he wanted to continue the relationship in any form, it was up to him. She understood that.

It was his move, but she didn't know if he would make it, or if he would disappear forever.

"Wait, surely we can do something," Harry said. "There's so much that's been lost in the past—answers to all kinds of questions. We have access to that."

"Which is interesting from a historical perspective, but answers that will save the world?" Phoenix said.

Phoenix's phone rang. An anonymous grey wraith holo twirled above the screen, indicating a private caller. Phoenix gave an apologetic grimace, answering it as he headed out to the hall. June caught the tinny "I care about the climate crisis" rote phrase from the phone before Phoenix left the room.

"The efficacy of carbon sinks around the world dropped before we had time to study them. I'm sure there are scientists who would sell their first-born to get access to a virgin environment," Elijah said.

"Yeah, send them to the End-Devonian," Harry said, chuckling.

Elijah and June exchanged glances—Elijah didn't appear to know what Harry was talking about either.

Harry seemed surprised they didn't understand him. "At the end of the Devonian period—Paleozoic era—there were waves of extinction which corresponded with glaciation events caused by the development of plants. As plants developed seeds, they spread across the globe, sucking too much carbon out of the atmosphere and causing the temperature to fall."

"I know planting forests helps draw down carbon, but surely plants don't draw down that much?" June said.

"No, they do," Harry said. "I mean, plants drew in enough carbon to cause an ice age. The Hangenberg Event, it's called."

"That's—are you saying *a mass extinction event* was caused by a screwed-up carbon cycle?" June said.

"They all were."

"What all were?" June asked.

"Every mass extinction event. Snowball Earths caused by a plummet, hothouse Earths caused by the amount of carbon dioxide soaring. Usually, volcanic emissions in the latter case, but also burning petrochemicals ignited by lava flow."

Elijah looked as shocked as June felt.

"I thought asteroids—" June said weakly, but Harry was shaking his head.

"Even in the End-Cretaceous extinction—the final days of dinosaurs—the asteroid impact probably exacerbated existing volcanic activity, with fatal consequences," Harry said. "Probably. We're not exactly sure. What's interesting is that there was an asteroid impact nearly as big as the one that wiped out the dinosaurs fourteen million years before the end Triassic, but it didn't even cause a minor mass extinction."

June glanced at Elijah.

"What scares me," Harry went on, "is that when climate change or ocean chemistry changes have been rapid in the past, the results are devastating. You can see the sudden flood of extinctions in the fossil record. And we are making fast changes now, with the very process that caused all the mass extinctions. We're a supervolcano, basically."

June played with the ends of her hair, waiting for the distress within her to subside. The room was so quiet and still that the clock ticks were the loudest sound.

Phoenix returned to the meeting room. "Sorry about that. That was Bennett and Sons, a law firm, delivering a message from June. A message from 15 October 1987."

They laughed, June most of all, which broke the tension in the room. At least June's attempt to get a message through would have worked eventually.

"Anyway," Harry said after a moment of silence. "So, we *are* fired?"

"Yes, essentially," Phoenix said. He sighed heavily, rubbing his hands over his face. "One month from now, I'm shutting MediSlice down. We'll work together and dismantle the time machine, and I'll sell the parts off."

Silence around the table as they all just sat, watching him.

"Time travel is a ridiculously big discovery, and you want to lose it forever? I say we give the time machine schematics to someone," Harry said.

"But we clearly didn't give it to someone," June pointed out. "This answers the question of where all the time-travellers are. They don't exist because we dismantle the machine."

So few trips, from such a tiny sliver of time.

"Let's pretend we have free will, though. Who would you want to give it to, Harry?" Phoenix asked.

"A university?"

"My best guess is that if we give it to a university, it'll be taken off them by the government. If we give it to a company, they'll use it for evil. By which I mean to generate profit for shareholders. Am I the only one here who thinks those sound like bad options?" Phoenix asked.

Around the table, eye-rolling and shaking of heads as they agreed with him. Harry seemed like he wanted to argue more, but he stayed quiet.

"All right then. I'm sorry," Phoenix said. "This isn't how I wanted this to end."

"I really wanted to visit ancient Egypt," Harry said wistfully. This brought forth an enthusiastic discussion about all the places in the ancient world that everyone wanted to go to, which surprised June. She had considered what it would be like visiting the Mayan empire in its heyday, but had decided that it would be too dangerous; she was a natural armchair explorer. But the others obviously felt differently.

"Do you know how much money we could make if we sold off artefacts from the past?" Elijah said. "What if we put a classicist into the library of Alexandria to digitise every scroll? We could sell footage of major historical events, watch Caesar be assassinated, the first performance of Hamlet, and so on. Or steal artefacts that have gone missing. If they're missing, we might as well take them, right?"

Harry was suppressing laughter.

"It's not what I wanted this company to stand for," Phoenix said finally. "We're here to fix climate change, not to make money, not to run a tourism business, and not to fence artefacts from the past. The billionaires who care about the planet still haven't managed to save it. The only way to fix the climate crisis is to change the past."

"I agree," June said.

"We *can* change the past," Elijah said. "We know that, because we *have* changed the past. Today's carbon dioxide level will still be four hundred and thirty-five parts per million, or whatever it is, but imagine if we went back and started a mining company. It secretly stockpiles olivine, a volcanic mineral that reacts with carbon dioxide, in huge quantities. Then next year it provides Project Vesta with all the olivine it has mined. Project Vesta is aiming to use olivine to capture carbon on a huge scale by dumping olivine on beaches and have the carbon locked up in the ocean. I mean, it doesn't prevent any of the damage we've caused already, but it gives us an edge."

June raised an eyebrow. Phoenix was nodding, eyes bright. "There are ways we could do that. Creating a lot of money in the past shouldn't be too hard—"

"But you're up against powerful fossil-fuel lobby groups who will outspend you by orders of magnitude," June pointed out.

"That's not the point," Elijah said. "What if we fund a group of researchers, researching in any area that can benefit us, who are forbidden to reveal their research until 2032? Maybe it will work, maybe it won't, and if it doesn't, we can try something else."

Phoenix's face was bright with excitement. June stared at the tabletop.

"June?" Phoenix said.

She shrugged. The facts around how screwed up the planet was were well established. Hidden research or projects would not significantly improve humanity's chances. But to continue working at MediSlice would be a good thing.

"So . . . we're *not* fired?" Harry asked, and Phoenix laughed.

"No," Phoenix said. "We'll continue."

––––––

June's new bed was a mattress on the floor of Rahul's room. She had to push the Lego out of the way to make room for it, and the bricks tumbling over one another made a noise like static. On her knees while she made up the bed, she saw the toys under Rahul's bed; a few books, a wheel, and clothing of some kind. It was cramped with two beds in Rahul's room, but not as cramped as the guest room was going to be with a double bed and a single squeezed in.

It was dark, but that was because the smoke had blotted out the sun.

She heard the front door open and steeled herself for an awkward encounter. What did you say to someone who had lost their three-year-old daughter in an ultra-heatwave? June couldn't even imagine.

But when June emerged, Pranav's sister, Rupina, had her head buried on Pranav's shoulder, sobbing. Her son, a six-year-old, held his father's hand. He wore a vacant expression, not looking at anything in particular, even as his father whispered to him. They were terribly worried about him, Hannah had told June a few weeks ago, because he didn't eat much anymore. He just wanted to sleep all the time.

June stood awkwardly in the doorway, watching the tableau. The air purifier hummed. Sitting in the corner next to the TV, the red light on the top of it was on, indicating poor air quality.

Probably because the door had been opened, bringing in smoky air; after ten minutes of filtering, it would return to green.

Ushadevi, Pranav's mum, let go of the handle on her suitcase-on-wheels and came over to June. June had met her before at Christmas, almost a decade ago. She gave June a tremendously kind smile and said something that June didn't immediately understand. After a few tries, June understood that Ushadevi was thanking her for letting them stay.

"It's not my house," June said, but that wasn't quite the right sentiment. "I'm glad you're here. I'm sorry for—for your loss."

"Thank you," Ushadevi replied, although June wasn't sure she had understood. Ushadevi clasped her hand, and June felt the woman trembling. What a long journey they had made, into a foreign land. June squeezed her hand tightly, hoping the woman would feel welcome.

———

The legend among Australian National University students was that if you hadn't started studying by the time the fluff tree seeds hit the ground, you were going to fail. During the November exam period, the light cottony fluff covered the ground like snow. As June emerged from the house, she thought immediately of fluff tree seeds, because a gust of wind blew something into her eyelashes. When she brushed her right eye, there was nothing but a smear of white ash left on her hand. She saw drifts on the ground, gossamer patches of grey, and black thread-like remnants of burnt forest.

"Wait! Take my car," Hannah said, coming out the front door after June and closing it behind her. Hannah held a cloth mask over her face.

The street trees on the opposite side of the road loomed out of the smoke, as if they were engulfed in thick mist, except that the smoke didn't have the purity of mist; it had a brownish tinge and burnt June's nose through the mask when she breathed. The trees thrashed as the wind changed direction.

June looked up at Hannah from the footpath leading to the porch.

"It's okay," June said, talking louder to be heard over the wind, and because her voice was muffled by the fabric. "I can catch the bus."

Inside the house, June heard a rapid-fire exchange in Kannada between Pranav and Rupina.

"No, it's fine," Hannah said. Her eyes were watery. June would have assumed it was from the smoke, except that she had sometimes heard Hannah screaming and crying during the night. Nightmares, her sister had admitted to June when she had asked. She would have left Canberra a week ago, travelled up north to escape the smoke, but Pranav didn't have any leave left, and accommodation and airfares were prohibitively expensive for a family of four, and it just wasn't clear what was going to happen next.

"They're not going to evacuate Canberra," June said. "Canberra is where they evacuate the regions *to*."

"June, for crying out loud, just take the damn keys," Hannah snapped. She held them out, her other hand still clamping the cloth over her face, which happened to be a dramatic gesture.

"*Okay*," June said, exasperated, and snagged the keys out of Hannah's outstretched hand. She was relieved not to have to walk to the bus stop; even with the smoke blocking out the sun, it was still pushing forty degrees Celsius today, and she was sweating already.

"Love you," Hannah said as June changed course to the light-blue Hyundai IONIQ Hybrid in the driveway. June held up her hand in a wave without looking back.

Pranav rode to work, just five minutes away, and their second car was in the driveway, so she wasn't leaving Hannah without a car. Hannah had even loaded the boots of their cars with wool blankets, June knew, which was recommended by emergency services for rural Australians. But this was Canberra.

She got into the driver's side seat of the car and closed the door, watching uneasily as a blackened half-burnt gum leaf landed on the windshield. Heat, westerly wind, and low humidity. An El Niño, following a drought, and a warm winter in which vegetation kept growing, sucking any remaining water out of the soil and producing fuel for fires. The conditions couldn't have been worse.

CHAPTER 17

At her computer, June scrolled through the logs and tried to blot the fires out of her mind. The light filtering in from outside still had that nightmarish dim quality that made her heart quicken.

She had to stop living at Hannah's house, and soon, especially now that Pranav's family had moved in. Find a share house, June supposed. She could date, if Elijah wasn't going to rekindle their relationship. Perhaps she could set up a dating profile online. Job: time traveller. Possibly time thief or project manager of a hidden network of researchers. She rolled her eyes.

Must not want children. There had been a window in which she wanted children, when she thought MediSlice could go back and change something so that the climate crisis wouldn't be upon them in the present. But that hope had evaporated with the realisation that the present was fixed; the carbon dioxide level was 435 ppm, and they couldn't change that.

The sky was orange, like Canberra had been transported to Mars. Blythe hadn't shown up for work, and neither had Phoenix, although Phoenix had said in the group chat that his mother was sick, and he couldn't come in.

Thunder rumbled, loud enough to make June jump. She reached for her water bottle.

Opening the wormhole length log file, June froze. She put her water bottle back on the table without looking at it. One of the wormhole lengths was wrong. At approximately 840 millimetres, it was huge compared to the other search lengths. She had opened the log file to check a discrepancy in timestamps across logs, but this was too strange to ignore. The search length of a trip to 1987 was two nanometres—about 0.000002 millimetres. The search length determined the time the operator would be sent to, with one second accuracy, because, as Phoenix had discovered, the wormhole length corresponded to the time. They used the search length to pluck the wormhole they needed from the seething quantum foam.

There was no way that wormhole length had been used. But she cross-checked the log files of the MRI machine to be sure and gaped in surprise. There was a trip that corresponded to that date and a trace file. She flicked through the slices the MRI had taken, all the way through the head, down the neck, and through the body. The person had breasts and wide hips.

A woman, presumably, who left on Friday 29 November, at 4:21pm. Almost four days ago.

But no one had made a trip at that time. Maybe the whole thing *was* a glitch.

Yet it looked less and less like a glitch. The only log that had been altered was the one that people were most likely to notice, as if someone were trying to hide the trip. All other indications were that the trip existed.

And it was definitely a one-way trip, because the wormhole length that stood out to June had only appeared once in the log.

It wasn't anyone who worked at MediSlice—because she'd seen all of them after the trip date, and whoever made the trip was still in the past: their trace was still on file. Who else would know about the time machine, let alone be able to use it? Mitch, the software engineer that had worked there, and Ted, the angel investor. Except that Mitch was in New Zealand, and Ted had died of cancer.

Thunder rumbled again. June expected to hear rain pattering on the window, but all she could hear was a faint howl of wind, presumably through a crack somewhere, and tree branches thrashing against the window, whipped into motion by the wind.

June calculated what the wormhole search length corresponded to in terms of time, an easy calculation, since it was linear: 289 million years ago. A quick search revealed it was the Early Triassic, but dangerously close to the End-Permian extinction. She immediately thought of Harry, the expert on deep time.

Hair rose on the back of her arms as she read about the End-Permian extinction, which was so bad it was colloquially called The Great Dying.

Friday 29 was when June had been rescued from the past, when they had sat around in the break room and listened to her talk about how the past couldn't be changed. Then they got the news about Thwaites Glacier, and they all left at around half-past three. Had they all left? Or was someone still in the office? Harry had definitely gone, because he and Elijah left at the same time. Blythe had changed out of her clothes and was in the break room when June left, June remembered suddenly. But even if Blythe had sent someone back, *why*? She knew how to send someone back, had the command line skills to delete the log from showing on the interface, but perhaps not enough knowledge to delete the myriad other logs that were created.

Not Blythe's ex-husband, because it was a woman.

June searched the Australian National Missing Persons Coordination Centre website, restricting by date so that it was after the trip was made.

A man with eye-bags and silver-white hair showed up, which June recognised, after a moment of confusion, as Blythe's husband. In the silence of the office, June breathed shallowly.

Obviously, this wasn't who was away on a one-way trip into the past, but it wasn't a good sign.

But who was missing? It wasn't necessarily an Australian. And it had only been three days. Perhaps the person hadn't been missed yet.

Phoenix wasn't answering his phone. With Blythe away, just June and Elijah were in the office. Harry had gone to the library; Elijah had told her when she ran into him in the break room earlier.

Then June remembered that Blythe had missed the last meeting, because she was sick. June had messaged her afterwards to find out how she was, and Blythe had messaged back. But June hadn't actually *seen* Blythe. She thought of Blythe's husband—missing—and tapped her fingernails on the desk.

June drew in her breath and called Blythe. Her hands trembled slightly as she held the phone up to her ear.

"Your call could not be connected, please check the number and try again," a robotic voice said, and the line went dead. June checked the number.

It was the right number.

June reached for her keyboard and searched for the Early Triassic, right after the End-Permian mass extinction. The mass extinction was the worst in Earth's history, June read. Why would anyone want to go there?

During the End-Permian, the ocean was as hot as a spa and devoid of oxygen, a condition that continued for millions of years. On land, the temperature was high enough to kill even insects. Mostly what showed up on the fossil record were fungi, feeding on all the dead bio-matter on land, the forests ravaged by acid rain and irradiated by UVB, until the rivers lost the boundaries defined by plants and just oozed across the landscape. The oceans emitted hydrogen sulfide—rotten egg gas—and carbon dioxide. Mega-hurricanes, big enough to wipe out entire continents, tore across the world with winds of 800 kilometres per hour.

The power went out, leaving June staring at her still-lit laptop screen, dark in the computer lab except for the light coming through the window. Red bulbs embedded in the ceiling switched on: emergency lighting.

An alarm blared. Four tones, then "Emergency announcement. This is not a drill. Everyone in the parliamentary triangle must evacuate. A fire is on the way. Visit esa–dot–act–dot–gov–dot–au for more info."

Someone shouted in the corridor outside MediSlice. The emergency announcement repeated. June listened with a creeping sense of horror and disbelief.

Elijah opened the door to the travel room. "Fires are breaking out all over the city because of the dry lightning storm. Black Mountain, the Arboretum."

"That's insane," June said, looking at a patch of green-patterned carpet near his feet, which looked black in the red light. "This is the heart of Canberra. We're right next to the lake. Hell, if we burn, new Parliament House burns."

"Come on," Elijah said.

What was she going to do? Evacuate, obviously. Blythe—if that's who was in the past—would still be there afterwards, provided the machine held her trace. The battery would preserve her trace for twelve hours; the power would be on long before then. June grabbed her bag and followed Elijah down Old Parliament House steps, part of the crowd of evacuees. The air glowed orange, and a wall of smoke blanketed the sky to the left. A great heaving cloud, lit with orange flames.

June heard someone sobbing behind her.

"I've got a car," June shouted at Elijah, as he turned towards the bike stand. He nodded and followed her to the carpark around the side, coughing deeply.

June climbed into Hannah's car, with Elijah in the passenger seat. The half-burnt leaf she had noticed that morning was still on the bonnet, she realised, trapped beneath the windscreen wiper.

She switched the lights on and drove out. The smoke was thicker than when she drove in that morning, and storm clouds darkened the sky, flashing occasionally. Plumes of smoke rose from Black Mountain.

"Where are we going?" June said. It was quiet inside the car. She slammed on the brakes as the cars in front of her stopped, and the car behind her honked.

"Um," Elijah said, frantically scrolling through his phone. "I'm not sure. The evacuation order was only meant to cover the suburbs on the Urban-Bushland interface, but now there's fires breaking out everywhere—and most of our firefighters are off fighting the fires in New South Wales—"

Canberra's bushfire plan was based on firebreaks, June was vaguely aware. If fires were starting due to lightning, all bets were off.

"I'm going to need some navigation," June said tersely. The cars in front of her started again. Farther down the road, a four-wheel drive veered off, mounting the curb and crossing the nature strip in an illegal U-turn before zooming away in the opposite direction.

Elijah was shaking his head. "I'd tell you if I knew. They say to stay with friends and family if possible. But that was before they expanded the evacuation zones. Um. Canberra Grammar looks like the closest—no, wait, a fire's broken out on Red Hill, they're closing that evacuation centre."

"*Red Hill?*" June said, keeping her eyes on the road as they rounded a bend. She sounded calm enough, but she was light-headed from breathing too fast. Red Hill wasn't far from Old Parliament House. She thought they had been evacuated just in case; it didn't occur to her that the fires would actually threaten Old Parliament House. If Old Parliament House caught fire, the time machine would burn. Blythe would be lost in time. She would die in the past.

But that wasn't June's problem. It was too risky to go back.

June knew who she was. Her world had careful limits. Sure,

there were many experiences that she'd never had and never wanted, like skydiving or going to a nightclub. But sometimes she hated herself. She was going to die of old age with no risks taken, no mistakes made, just a steady stream of managed experiences. Of caution and tea. Of cardigans and workplaces. And a few generations later, the world would end, and she could do nothing to prevent it. She wanted—*God, she wanted*—to not be powerless anymore.

There was no proof that Blythe died, therefore June might be able to bring her back. But probably not if the time machine burnt.

June braked, bringing the car to a dead stop in the middle of the road.

"What are you doing?" Elijah said.

June's heart pounded in her chest. She looked at him helplessly, no more able to formulate a sentence than compose an opera on the spot.

"June," Elijah said in a soothing voice, "we have to keep going. It's okay."

The timbre of his voice loosened the tightness in her chest. "We have to go back. There's someone out on a trip. I think it's Blythe."

"Are—are you *sure*?"

June nodded and Elijah groaned, rubbing his hands over his face.

"I could drop you somewhere—" June said.

"No. I'm coming with you."

A thick smoke plume was rising from Red Hill as they parked at Old Parliament House.

The front door was open. They ran through the deserted corridors into MediSlice. June set up the trip in less than a minute at the control desk, then went to the MRI. "It'll be okay," she muttered to herself. Elijah watched her through the glass from where he sat at the control desk.

She would mark where she landed, survey the surrounding area and find Blythe, then bring her back to the right spot to be picked up by the machine. If she couldn't find Blythe, she would leave. Either way, she should re-materialise in about twenty minutes, and then there would still be time to evacuate.

But her chest was tight; even though she knew she could breathe, she was struggling, because with every breath she was drawing smoke deep into her lungs.

The machine clanked as she dematerialised.

EARLY TRIASSIC, APPROXIMATELY 251.902 MILLION YEARS AGO, 2000 PPM CO_2

She was on her back, with the air whistling around her, falling—

She hit the ground, back and head smarting from the blow. The fall knocked the air from her lungs. She hadn't been winded since she was a child and had forgotten how painful it was. As she struggled to breathe, she focused on the tiny mossy plant next to her.

She probably hadn't been that high up, but it was enough to have flooded her with adrenaline. The dryness in her mouth wouldn't go away. She pushed herself up to standing gingerly. Her back was wet, as were her jeans.

The water she'd been lying in was barely a stream. More like a slow puddle, which spread out and seeped over the plain. Here and there clams lay in the shallows. The plain was carpeted entirely with fungus, great orange wings of it.

The putrid air carried the stench of something rotting, faintly bad egg flavoured. Perhaps it was from whatever was bubbling up from underneath the stream. The tiny air bubbles rose to the surface and popped. She heard each one because it was so damn quiet here. It was like she had dived to the bottom of a swimming pool.

The bright disc of the sun shone through a thick layer of clouds, the same sun that had beaten down for four point six billion years, and the same sun that would be shining in 2030 and for eight billion years after. She was sweating already, grateful for the thick layer of cloud; it must be at least thirty degrees Celsius.

She shaded her eyes and looked around. The landscape stretched away for hundreds of kilometres around her, crowded with low, smooth mountains. No trees or distinguishing features of any kind, just fungus. She was looking at what would eventually be the Australian Capital Territory, but she couldn't match up this landscape with the Canberra she knew at all, although the terrain was generally similar.

Behind her, about two kilometres away, was a rocky mountainside. Small green weedy-looking plants grew in some of the cracks in the rock. All one species, as far as June could tell, although lichen also clung to the rocks. So: lichen, fungi, clams, and a single species of weed.

She marked the spot where she landed by shredding some fungi. She was still in the turnaround time, but within twenty minutes the machine would switch to scanning and try to pull her back to her time. Unless it was scanning an area of sky above her, in which case she would die here, because there was no way to get up there.

The sensible thing to do would be to stay right where she was, but she couldn't see any trace of Blythe. From the top of the hill, she would be able to see much farther.

She'd looked up where Canberra was in the Early Triassic, assuming the time machine placed her down on the continent and not a fixed point in the world. She was on the supercontinent of Pangaea, somewhat inland. Between her and the sea was what would eventually cleave off and become New Zealand. If she crossed Australia, she could walk right onto Antarctica. But she wasn't going to do that; she was just going to go up the hill and see if she could spot Blythe.

She walked up. Stepping on rocks was okay, and the strange-looking weeds bounced back if she trod on them, but the fungi squished in a way that made her think of stepping on human flesh, so she tried to avoid it. As she walked, she felt herself unwinding. She felt safe here, in a world so obviously empty. No fire, no smoke, no alarms. She cleared her throat and breathed properly; by the time she reached the top of the hill, she was even humming.

But then she saw the ruins of a crudely built hut. Made of rocks and mud, the roof—if there had been one—had long disappeared, and the walls were crumbling. June pictured Blythe living here in this empty world, building shelter with rocks and dirt, drinking from braided streams no deeper than a hand's depth, and eating clams and weeds.

Something stirred behind a ruined wall at chest height for June, and June fought the urge to scream and run away. The visceral sense that this place was so terribly far from home struck her with the force of a physical blow.

Rustling, scratching, from behind the wall.

"Hello?" June said in a thin, reedy voice. Her words were swallowed into the nearly empty continent, across the nearly empty world. "Is anyone there?"

She felt ridiculous, talking as if she were looking for a friend at the supermarket on this planet where she was the only human, or one of two.

A dog-size creature emerged from what used to be a door at the side of the ruined hut. Primitive fear shot through June's limbs, leaving her trembling and frozen in place. She felt an urgent need to pee. This wasn't her Earth, where predators had been driven to extinction or trapped in small, safe pockets. She was nothing but a meal to most animals for much of Earth's vast history.

But the dog-like thing—which didn't look like a dog at all, really—just waddled up to her and bared its toothless gums, in the parody of a grin. Tusks grew either side of its face, although the one on the left seemed flat and shorter than the right. June stayed very still. The yellow fur on its back ran down its sides before turning beige. Small, black eyes glinted at her, wide apart above its square snout.

It honked before turning and trotting away down the opposite side of the hill. Maybe it was relieved to see someone else alive. There sure weren't many creatures left.

June took a deep breath, and then another. She relieved herself in the ruins of the hut. Obviously, Blythe wasn't here, and hadn't been here for some years, maybe even decades. If she was dead, June couldn't rescue her, because it had already happened, but June hadn't seen any remains.

Blythe had had time to build a hut. That meant that June was already too late to whisk Blythe back a few minutes after she arrived. But maybe June went back farther in time and rescued her, leaving her hut to decay, and that's what June had just discovered.

June reached the stack of fungi she had created and suddenly she was staring at the ceiling of the MRI.

The smoky room was a nightmare in the red light that did nothing to dispel the darkness. She banged the inner cylinder of the MRI scanner, as if she could wrench it open and escape. Then the bed started sliding out and her hands slid along it.

June sat up on the flatbed. "The fire," she said, coughing, as Elijah approached her.

"It's okay," he said. "The wind changed, so it's not advancing. But it could change again at any moment. Did you get her?"

"I was too late. The machine sent me too late."

She pushed off the bed and rushed to the control desk. Why had the machine sent her to a different time when she used the exact length that had been set on the previous trip?

She checked the logs and spotted the problem. The wormhole that had been plucked out was infinitesimally longer than the search parameter she had specified, because—she found, drilling frantically down through functions until she found the code controlling wormhole search—there was a tolerance set, because you'd never find a wormhole *exactly* the right length, that was close to impossible. And the threshold was working fine, for the trips they'd gone on, because there were trillions of wormholes to choose from.

The wormhole search had taken six milliseconds longer than usual. Which didn't sound like much, but it was huge. It was like a person with a cube and a sphere in front of them taking minutes to decide which was the cube.

"June!" Elijah said. She glanced at him, having forgotten he was there and that the fires were getting closer.

"There must be far fewer wormholes to the deep past than there are to the more recent past," June said, realising.

"Great theory. Well, no rush, why don't we work out the exact distribution of wormhole length?"

"Oh," June said in surprise. "I'd love to, but I don't think we have time for that."

"*Sarcasm*, June," Elijah said wearily.

She shook her head, dismissing him. It was then that she half-remembered a conversation with Blythe, when Blythe rescued her from 1987. Hadn't Blythe said something about the wormhole tolerance length? They had to adjust it because there were fewer wormholes in the near-present. Well, there were even fewer in the ancient past, so the tolerance was still too high. She reduced the tolerance to a millionth of what it had been—in lieu of working out what it should actually be, because she didn't have time for that—recompiled, and deployed.

While the binaries copied over, she calculated what the new wormhole length should be in her head. She couldn't use the original length, because she'd already seen the hut, so the woman had to be there long enough to build the hut.

"Okay," June said, punching in a new trip.

As she climbed onto the flatbed, she glanced at the battery and froze in shock. It was at about twenty-five percent. Elijah must have seen the look on her face, because he came over to see the battery.

"But it's supposed to last twelve hours," June said.

"Powering the machine, waiting to bring someone back. Not

powering multiple round trips," Elijah said grimly. "But there's plenty of juice for you to make it back again."

June nodded. She climbed onto the flatbed.

"Good luck," Elijah said over the speaker, as the flatbed slid into the scanner. The MRI bed was covered in dried mud that had flaked off her clothes. Great waves of sound swept over her, and she squeezed her eyes tight shut.

CHAPTER 18

END-PERMIAN, APPROXIMATELY 251.8 MILLION YEARS AGO, 8000 PPM CO_2

She was floating—drowning!—in water. Panicking, she struggled to her feet, vomiting, emptying her stomach in the fetid, neon-green, algae-choked water. As soon as her head was above the water, she was blasted by a wall of sound; a crackling, thundering roar.

She stood calf-deep in a body of water. The world was an oven, boiling her alive. In the distance, the sky was black with thick smoke clouds above a raging fire.

The time machine wasn't going to bring her back for twenty minutes, but she wouldn't last twenty minutes here, she was being baked—

A rotten-egg stench filled her lungs. She tried to breathe through her mouth. Her heart rate jumped until she thought her heart would give out. Was this a panic attack?

Something hit her neck, and she floundered around to see a black lump the size of a baseball sinking into the water. Behind her was land, but the surface of it was just a mess of unidentifiable muck. And behind that, a hurricane, impossibly huge, ripped across the land like an angry God flinging debris and *boulders.*

"Elijah," she whispered. "I'm going to die."

White spots floated in front of her eyes. Her tongue became stuck in the dry cavity which was her mouth. The roar in her ears faded out, replaced by the whine in her head, and she swayed and stumbled, putrid water splashing her.

TUESDAY 3 DECEMBER 2030 AT 11:16AM, 435 PPM CO_2

She was suddenly lying on the brown hexagons on the floor by the flatbed, with no sense of any time having passed and no memory of what had happened. Elijah kneeled next to her, his eyes full of concern. She coughed until she retched. Elijah gave her a bottle of water, and she sipped it. Her jeans and T-shirt were as wet as if she had bathed in a river, but only partly from the anoxic ocean she had landed in; the rest was sweat.

Her face and arms were painfully red, an extreme sunburn. She couldn't see properly.

"I might have miscalculated," June said, her voice croaky.

"You did," Elijah said. "I recalculated after you were gone. You were off by about ten million years. I set the machine to scan for as soon as you arrived—which in practice was two minutes."

"You saved my life," June said gratefully.

She reached up to embrace him, but Elijah drew back and looked away.

"End-Permian, was it?" Elijah said, as if she hadn't tried to hug him.

"Yeah," June said, trying also to pretend nothing had happened. Her voice shook.

"What happened?"

She didn't answer, because she didn't exactly know how to interpret what she had seen. She knew that in Siberia, during the End-Permian, volcanoes spewed out enough lava to cover whole continents kilometres deep. There were also exploding bombs of petrochemicals ignited by lava flows. Probably ten thousand gigatons of fossil fuels were ignited in the End-Permian, or maybe five times that. Lava also reacted with salt deposits, creating gases that destroyed the ozone layer, so that the surface was irradiated with UVB.

The carbon dioxide concentration had probably been somewhere in the order of 8000 ppm, June realised, and wondered if the concentration was high enough to be hazardous. Probably not for the limited time she was there, even though 8000 ppm sounded ludicrously high to her. Carbon dioxide in the atmosphere in 2030 was 435 ppm, having been 200–280 ppm for the last few million years before the industrial revolution.

In the End-Permian, it was sixty degrees Celsius on land. Forty degrees in the ocean. June shook, partly chilled from her wet clothes, and partly from shock.

She knew they should leave. Travelling in deep time was dangerous. Just being in Old Parliament House was dangerous. Even if the building didn't catch fire, the smoke could kill them. But she changed clothes, using the costumes from the Ikea cube storage. Elijah turned his back, but she could see his eyes reflected in the glass partition of the control desk, and he was watching her. Not with desire, but with concern.

It struck her, then, that he didn't want her back, and wouldn't want her back even if she single-handedly saved the world. Her cheeks warmed with mortification. She was stupid for worrying about love when the world was on fire.

She put on the 1980s outfit, the floral skirt and blouse that she had worn to the café when she closed the time loop, surely the most impractical costume to wear back to the Early Triassic.

"You look beautiful," Elijah said.

"Smooth. All this dating is giving you lots of experience in flattery, is it?"

Why would he say such a thing to her? Why now?

He stared at her in consternation; it wasn't like her to snap at him.

June took a deep breath. She was still trembling, despite the dry clothes.

"Okay, sorry, whatever, send me back," she said.

"Are you serious? You nearly died! The fire is practically upon us. We're almost out of time to evacuate. You want to go back again?"

"You evacuate. I have to try to save Blythe."

She went to the flatbed, but Elijah grabbed her wrist. His grip bound her more tightly than she could ever hope to break; as she knew, he'd spent many hours with his body hanging from that hand, fingers wedged in a tiny crevice, while rock climbing. The steady sound of the battery beeping was the only noise.

"She's gone, June," Elijah said.

"Only because you've given up on her."

"The battery is down to fourteen percent. You'll never make it back. We're not even sure what time she was sent to."

June laughed unsteadily, her eyes watering. He hadn't worked out the worst of it, she noticed. That she might not come back, not for years or perhaps not ever, because someone built that hut, and it could have been her.

It could *be* her.

She desperately wanted to go with him. Once upon a time, being alone in the world might even have appealed to her, but now she was terrified of it. But—

"I'm setting the trip," June said. Elijah loosened his grip.

"Please don't do this," Elijah said. "It's not like you to play the hero, and I can't help thinking that you're doing it to try to get me back, but I'm *not* coming back, June." He was nearly crying. "I'm so sorry," he said hoarsely. "I know what breaking up has done to you, and it's absolutely the last thing I wanted. I still care about you, but I just can't—"

He made an indecipherable gesture. She realised, with a wave of nausea, that all the tension between them the last three months hadn't been sexual tension at all. On Elijah's part, it had been guilt. Stomach-clenching, soul-rending guilt, because he had cast her adrift and left her lost. He wasn't cruel, June knew that. Maybe some part of him was flattered that she still paid attention to him, but she could see so clearly now that he had been trying to reject her, in the kindest possible way.

"It's all right," June said, as calmly as she could. "This is something I need to do. You should go. Evacuate."

"No, I'm staying," he said. "All right. I'll be at the control desk, waiting for you, I promise."

June nodded and climbed onto the MRI bed. *Please God*, she thought. *Please don't strand me in the Early Triassic.* She wasn't religious, but everyone has to appeal to someone when they're in need, and June was never more in need.

EARLY TRIASSIC, APPROXIMATELY 251.902 MILLION YEARS AGO, 2000 PPM CO_2

She had been in a state of terror in the MRI machine, lying still with her heart racing. Part of her thought it would send her back to the End-Permian, and the animal part of her brain was urging her to escape.

She was falling—

And *splat*, here she was in the Early Triassic, staring at a clear sky. In wet clothes yet again because she was lying in a stream. The sun burnt down. She hoped the ultra-violet radiation wasn't high enough to damage her skin.

With a sigh, she got up, marked the spot, and started walking. Dread made her limbs heavy. A missing hut meant she might be stuck there, destined to build it herself.

Somehow, she expected her skin to have healed, but of course it still stung. Her wet skirt stuck to her legs as she climbed the hill, but it dried as she walked. The wind buffeted her; it was the only sound in the world. Not even the walk soothed her this time, because her future was about to be decided.

The hut was there and in good condition.

June cried out when she saw it, and her knees suddenly gave way, plonking her to the ground. She laughed unsteadily.

Next to the hut was a knee-height cube made of mud bricks, perhaps a kiln. Smoke rose from a chimney at one end of the hut. Interlocked clam shells formed the roof. June stood up and approached the hut. No door in the doorframe, just a screening wall in front of the opening, to keep the wind out.

Inside the hut, the translucent clamshells glowed with an uneven pink-purplish colour. Flames flickered in an alcove near the back. Next to the fire lay a stack of dried fungi. In the corner, a blanket of fur rested next to several pots. Maybe the fur was from a creature of the type June had seen last time. One of the pots had a stew, which seemed to be made of weed and clams.

The fire crackled. June whirled around as the hut darkened, Blythe blocking the light from the door. But it wasn't Blythe.

"Huh—who—" The woman's voice was rough.

Her hair was matted, her clothes torn and dirty. She was skinny, but she didn't look starving. The woman stared at June. June's social anxiety turned up to ten, because she had absolutely no rulebook for how to talk to someone who had been stranded in deep time. This was going to be awkward.

"Hi, I'm June. Have you been here long?" June asked.

The woman shook her head.

"Oh, good," June said.

The woman looked enraged. "Yes, I *have* been here a long time," she said. "I mean, *obviously*!"

June realised the woman had been shaking her head in disbelief at June's question rather than trying to answer in the negative.

"Oh, okay," June said weakly. "Sorry. How long?"

The woman burst into tears, stumbling forward and hugging June. She smelled surprisingly clean, considering her surroundings. A strong human scent, better than the ambient rot-and-hydrogen-sulphide combination.

The woman sobbed uncontrollably for a few minutes, while

June awkwardly patted her back and hoped she would stop crying soon. June wondered where Blythe was.

Eventually, the woman wiped the tears off her face with the back of her hand and sniffed.

"I'm Maddie Park. I've been here about a year. I think. I lost the stone I was first marking during an earthquake," the woman said. "Then there was a flood, and my hut was swept away, but I got the new stone back. I can't believe this is happening. I keep thinking I'm going to wake up. Where am I? What the hell happened?"

"You're in the Early Triassic," June said.

"The early what? *How*?"

"I'm not sure. You were sent on a trip through a time machine, which I guess you don't remember. For us, that was only three days and ten hours ago."

Maddie grabbed June's arm. "A time machine! I thought this was an alien planet. But *can you get us back*?" she said urgently.

"Yes . . . yes, that's what I've been trying to tell you," June said.

Maddie grabbed a rock from beside the fur blanket. The rock had been carved into a lifelike face.

They left the hut. June picked her way across the uneven ground, but Maddie moved like she was born there. June wondered if she could go back in time, arrive earlier so that Maddie wouldn't have to be there so long, but she couldn't, could she? Even if the battery allowed another trip, she'd already spoken to Maddie now, so it had happened.

As they walked down the hill, June spotted a figure far away; too far away to be sure it was a person at all, except that there were no trees around, nothing upright, so it was hard to see what else it could be. She stumbled, righted herself, and stopped; when she looked again, the figure was gone. Maddie stopped beside her.

"What is it?"

"I thought I saw a person, over there, but . . . I must have imagined it," June said. She scanned the landscape one more time, but no one was there.

"I see people all the time. People from back home, mostly, but sometimes strangers." Maddie said. "They talk to me, but I can't hear what they're saying. And they disappear if you look away."

"Okay," June said. That was probably normal for someone who had been alone for so long, she guessed.

"Who sent me here?" Maddie said.

"I . . . I don't know, exactly. Perhaps a colleague of mine. Blythe."

A friend, June thought, but wondered if that was still true; whether it had ever been true.

"I wondered if it might be her. I've had people yell at me before, threaten me. Didn't figure Blythe would be a problem, though. She didn't seem the type."

"I'm sorry?" June said, not following.

"I was investigating her," Maddie said. "I was a private investigator. Mostly, I worked for the government. You know, seeing if someone was playing football when they were meant to be too ill to work. But also, private work. Cheating spouses, that kind of thing. Sometimes they spot me, get angry."

"Were you hired by Blythe's ex-husband?"

"What? No. My client, Daniel Taylor, was trying to bring a lawsuit against her," Maddie said absently. "He invented KestrelWare VR, and she stole it and took all the credit. And the profit."

June nodded slowly. Maddie stopped, and June waited for her, but she just stood there.

"Three days I've been missing, you said, right?" Maddie said.

"Actually—" June said, about to correct Maddie to *three days and ten hours*, but she remembered just in time that people liked approximations, so she finished weakly—"about that, yes. You weren't listed as a missing person yet."

"No, I wouldn't be," Maddie said bitterly. "The only person who'd miss me if I was gone for months would be my landlord."

Then something in her face changed. A light had gone on behind her eyes.

June wasn't sure what to say. She shifted from one foot to the other, anxious to keep going. She had to hurry, because Elijah was waiting for her in a building threatened by fire. But she could stay here for years and still be pulled back to that moment, so she forced herself to stillness, to wait for Maddie to be ready.

"Can you send me back in time to the year 2008?" Maddie asked. "There's a mistake I need to correct."

"It doesn't work like that—"

"How does it work?"

June sighed. She pointed to a rock nearby, and they went and sat down, and June explained how time travel worked. You couldn't go back and take a different path in your life, she explained. You couldn't change the past. Maddie looked thoughtful, excited even.

"How do we get back to the present?" she asked eventually, eyes narrowed.

June pointed to the pile of shredded fungi nearby. "We stand near that."

"What happened to your skin?" Maddie asked. "Is that part of the time travel?"

June explained about how she travelled to the End-Permian temporarily, and Maddie nodded. They arrived at the pile of shredded fungi that June had made, and June woke up in the MRI.

CHAPTER 19

June jumped off the flatbed as soon as it wheeled out, returning her to the red-lit, smoke-filled room with the beeping battery. Elijah was gone. Perhaps he'd decided to evacuate without her; there did seem to be more smoke now. She held on to the edge of the glass wall separating the MRI from the control desk as she was overcome by a rush of vertigo.

The flatbed slid back in, and the morse-code tones of the machine started again, recovering Maddie. June clapped her hands over her ears, leaning against the glass wall.

The door to the travel room opened. June's lips parted in relief as Elijah entered. He hugged June tight, but before she could hug him back, he released her abruptly, as if realising it was inappropriate.

He shouted over the noise of the MRI. "Phoenix messaged the group chat, said he was coming in to quench the machine. But I'm here, so I can do it. Phoenix hit the roof when he found out we hadn't evacuated. But anyway, apparently there's no power to the cold head, so if we don't quench it—release the cryogens—it will quench itself. Which could kill any firefighters trying to defend the building, if there are any."

The smoke was acrid in her nostrils. She was so sick of the smell of smoke; it made her rage with claustrophobia, turned her stomach. *Danger*, the smell said, and her body responded to it. There was a faint white haze at the end of the room, or perhaps she imagined it.

The MRI quietened, Maddie appearing on the flatbed, and then the flatbed slid out with a whine. Elijah took an incredulous look at Maddie, then at June, but he didn't ask.

"Is the building on fire?" June said.

"I don't know, but if it's not, it soon will be," Elijah said, but his attention was on the instructions on the box mounted on the wall near the door. *Maybe they should use the time machine to escape the fire*, June thought, but when she glanced at the battery, she saw there was probably only enough power for one trip, which meant only one of them could use it.

"Wait!" Maddie said, as Elijah drew his arm back to smash the glass pane on the box. "Send me back," Maddie said, sitting on the edge of the flatbed, eyes focused on the button.

"*What?*" Elijah said, hand still hovering over the red button marked "PUSH" below a sign reading "EMERGENCY."

June inhaled sharply. "Maddie, you know you can't change the past. Your younger self will still be—"

"I know." Her face was stony. "But there's a mistake I made that I think I can correct."

"It'd be a one-way trip," June said, glancing at Elijah. His face was grim and set.

"That's fine!"

June hesitated. "You don't have to decide now, we can come back after the fire passes—"

Maddie rolled her eyes. "Assuming the time machine still exists then. It's not looking too good. No. You owe me. I survived a year in that godforsaken place, and now I have the chance to find someone I love. Send me back now."

Elijah raised his eyebrows at June, tilting his head slightly, which she knew meant *okay-with-it-if-you-are.*

June sighed. "Okay. What's the exact date?"

When Maddie gave her a date, June sat behind the control desk and authorised the trip. "I can't believe I'm doing this," June mumbled to herself.

"Good luck," she said over the intercom.

"Thanks," Maddie said, as the flatbed slid into the MRI. Elijah stood by the door with his hands on his hips as he waited. June held her hands over her ears and shut her eyes for the few minutes it took for Maddie to dematerialise.

As soon as she was gone, Elijah smashed the glass over the button labelled "PUSH."

It hissed like a pressure cooker releasing steam. The cryogen vent pipe above the MRI began leaking gas, like smoke but whiter, and flowing down rather than rising as smoke would. After a few seconds, liquid began dripping from the rim of the pipe, presumably condensation.

"Let's go," Elijah said urgently. He opened the door, and they rushed out into the hall outside the travel room. June's phone had been sitting on the windowsill. The holo above it was red with missed call notifications and unread messages, but she only had time to grab the phone, and then she raced after Elijah, catching up to him in the corridor. They headed away from the main entrance to the fire escape at the side of the building.

The smoke was thicker there. Elijah dropped to his knees and crawled along the floor, and June followed. She wanted to ask if they should shelter inside, but was coughing too much to talk. They reached the end of the carpet and crawled onto the marble floor, which hurt her knees. She tried to put more weight into her palms, but they smarted too. Finally, Elijah stood up in front of her and pushed out of the fire escape. Five concrete steps, and they were outside.

June was expecting fresh air, but there was just smoky wind that blew grit into her eyes. Smoke rose from the roof of Old Parliament House. Uphill, in the direction of new Parliament House, a wall of brown smoke rose, until it merged into the orange sky. The sun was a dim flat disc, more like the moon than the sun.

The building exploded above them. June looked up to see glass showering down, and black smoke and flames billowing out the blown-out windows, before Elijah pulled her away. They held hands awkwardly as they sprinted towards Hannah's car.

An ember landed on the brown grass beside the car as they entered it, and the fire spread, a black growing circle outlined in crimson. They accelerated away from the fire.

———

The nearest evacuation centre was at the Australian National University. June headed towards Commonwealth Avenue, going no more than fifty kilometers per hour. Elijah stared out the window with wide eyes. June drummed the steering wheel, frustrated with how slowly they were going. But the smoke was like thick fog; it would be easy to crash.

"Can you check my phone?" June asked, and she dug it out of her pocket and handed it to him.

"Missed calls from Pranav. Messages from Pranav . . ."

"What is it?"

He didn't respond.

"*What?*" June asked more forcefully. A helicopter thrummed overhead, then rose, vanishing into the smoke. The wind gusted, rocking their car. They slowed to a crawl while driving over a broken branch.

"He wanted to know if Hannah was with you," Elijah said.

June looked at him, startled.

"Several messages. The last one was thirty minutes ago. He can't find her, or Rahul."

"Oh God," June said. "Ask him—"

"You have zero connectivity."

A giant lump lodged in her throat, making it near impossible to swallow. They had to be okay . . .

The trees either side of the road thrashed. With the next gust, one of them uprooted, crashing into a power line. June braked sharply. The power line split, dropping a cable across the road. The cable appeared no more dangerous than a rope, except that every few seconds it crackled and spat a firework of sparks onto the road.

"It's fine," June said, doing a U-turn. "We can cross at King's Avenue."

But King's Avenue was blocked by a fallen tree, and she ended up heading down Parkes Way, a long route around the lake. Soon the smoke had cleared somewhat, so June drove as fast as she dared.

"I want to go to Hannah's place," June said.

"You know we can't do that," Elijah replied. Lightning flashed, followed closely by a drawn-out splitting thunder that June felt deep in her stomach.

"Yeah," June said after a moment. Her instinct to find Hannah was compelling, but she recognised it as unreasonable. "Okay. The uni evacuation center, then."

A white car loomed out of the smoke suddenly, driving the wrong way into oncoming traffic.

June swerved left. The white car swerved right, tires screeching, and they missed each other by centimetres. June's heart thudded. The white car didn't even stop. June realised belatedly that Elijah had been swearing the whole time. He opened the door, and shouted after the car, while June sat there staring at the steering wheel, trembling.

Elijah was shaking his head when he came back in.

"It's chaos," June said.

"What did you say?" Elijah yelled.

The wind gusted, shoving the car sideways. Even inside the

car, the roar of the wind and nearby fires drowned out their speech. June repeated herself, and Elijah nodded in agreement.

June caught a glimpse of the lake—of boats, of heads above water, swimming perhaps—before the bush obscured her view again. *That would be safer than the road*, June thought, and wondered where Hannah was, trying to imagine where she would be. They would have evacuated at the first sign of trouble. They had Pranav's car. And Pranav was at the hospital. They'd be all right.

Elijah cried out something incoherent, and June jumped.

"Did you see that?" he shouted. Lightning flashed across the sky. Elijah ducked his head low to look out her window. June took her eyes off the road for a second and glanced right. A hurricane of dark smoke rising from Black Mountain, ten kilometres high, writhed like a decapitated serpent. June gasped, clutching the steering wheel so tightly that her hands ached. They sped away from the hurricane.

Elijah twisted around in his seat to look behind them. "You missed the turn-off," he yelled. He looked at the offline map on his phone; they were now surrounded by bush. June wasn't sure where she was, although she knew the lake was on their left somewhere. The winds outside roared and spat a tree onto the road. They both yelled as June swerved, narrowly avoiding it.

Elijah scrolled on his phone. June slowed down; the car was buffeted by wind, which was making the scrub on either side of the road bend and thrash as if possessed by demons. Lightning flashed. Tree branches fell across the asphalt road.

"I don't know where we are," Elijah shouted.

"Okay," June shouted back. It didn't look familiar to her either. The road cut through thick bush, but that was true of many roads in Canberra. Sweat dripped down her back.

Maddie made a good call, June thought grimly.

The smoke became denser until the darkness triggered the overhead streetlights. June slowed down as her view of the road dwindled. She dodged the larger branches and imagined she could feel the smaller ones crack as she drove over them, but she heard nothing but the roar of wind and fire outside, which was as loud as a jet engine. They rounded a bend and June braked. Ahead, flames advanced down the hillside on their right towards the road. Even from a hundred metres away, June could feel the heat on her face and hands, like standing in front of an open oven. She jumped as a burning branch hit the bonnet of the car, followed in quick succession by several more cracks; it was raining burning debris.

The streetlights cut out.

June glanced at Elijah, feeling the car rock against the wind as it pushed the car this way and that. Elijah held the grab handle above his door with white knuckled strength and braced himself against the dashboard. Wordlessly, June did a three-point turn, reversing direction carefully and accelerating away from the fire. But the fire front still advanced, a sweltering fury of black smoke and dancing flame advancing down the slope towards them, now on their left. Tiny fireflies of embers danced in the dark smoke.

The road was increasingly blocked by burning branches and trees. *They weren't going to make it.*

There was a clear area to the right of them. June drove onto the gravel, wheeling the car around so that it faced the oncoming fire. The windshield was tougher than side windows, so it would be less likely to break. If the fuel tank vented, the wind from the fire would blow the vapours away from them. Also, this would hope-fully minimise the amount of radiant heat entering the car. She had practiced these steps many times in the early hours of the morning. Her mind would tell her: you're caught in a bushfire, in a car, what do you do? And she would have to think through the steps, lying in the dark with a dry mouth and heart pounding, and then maybe she could sleep. Telling herself she was safe never had any effect.

"What are you doing?" Elijah screamed.

"It'll be on us in minutes! We have to prepare!" June yelled.

She put on the parking brake but left the engine running. Unbuckling her seat belt, she activated the hazard lights. The headlights were on already, shining a metre at most into the impenetrable smoke.

The aircon was off, but now she also closed all the aircon vents on the dashboard to prevent any more smoke getting in. It was dark as night outside, except for the orange smoky glow ahead of them and the ever-moving tiny embers.

Elijah's eyes were wide. "We have to abandon the car, run to the lake!"

"We'll die if we're caught outside."

If they left, they would definitely die—fried in the radiant heat of the fire—but if they stayed, there was a chance of surviving this. June gave a silent prayer of thanks to Hannah, who never drove her car without a woollen blanket in the boot; Hannah's paranoia might just save their lives.

She drew her seat forward as far as she could, to create a space behind it, and crawled gracelessly into the back seat. But she couldn't get the seat down to access the boot. Elijah slid into the back too, knocking June's shoulder with his knee. He yanked at the strap that held the seat up, but it didn't budge.

"We're dead," Elijah shouted.

"No! You can't know that. It's not over until it's over," she shouted back. This wasn't the first time she was in peril in the back seat of a car; she remembered the heaviness that came over her limbs last time, when she was trapped in the flooded car, and the sense of doom that left her paralysed.

This time was different: she was ready to fight until her last breath.

"I'll be right back," June yelled, although she wasn't convinced Elijah was going to be able to hear her over the crackle. She opened the backseat left side door into smoky hell and slammed it behind her.

The radiant heat baked her. She was pelted with sticks,

burning or already burnt, as thick as fingers. They rained down on the car and bush, starting fires in the bush where they nested in the flammable leaf litter. Embers whirled in the wind, mapping the eddies and gusts; like a campfire at a million times the scale.

The trees nearby writhed as if in pain from the flames sweeping through them, every leaf becoming a candle. Her eyeballs were dry and gummy.

The wind tugged and threw her as she made her way to the boot. The super-hot air burnt her throat. She extracted the wool blanket and a plastic bottle of water mostly by feel, then slammed the boot.

By that time, her eyes had watered so much she couldn't see anything. She was light-headed, close to passing out, but she slid along the side of the car—the metal almost burning hot—until she found the handle.

Falling inside, she pulled the door closed behind her.

Elijah took the green blanket from her while she coughed and spread it over them; it was king-size and soft, easily large enough to cover them both. She lay on him. They were both below the level of the windows, but uncomfortably cramped, legs drawn up and wedged against one side door, head pushing against the other. June couldn't remember if she was meant to lock the doors.

"How will we know when the fire is here?" Elijah said. He didn't have to shout; his mouth was right next to her ear. June tilted her head up.

"It's mostly here already," she said. Then her skin prickled with heat. Even under the blanket, it was like baking in the summer sun.

The car rocked violently. She thought it would tip over, but it didn't. The crackling roar got louder, the smoke more intense, and the crack of sticks hitting the roof and windows increased in frequency. *Ten minutes*, June thought, *maybe twenty*. Survive that, and they would be okay. They were lucky to be inside a car, rather than in the open where the oxygen would be sucked towards the fire front, leaving them gasping.

The smell of burning plastic stung her nostrils. Elijah's body was solid beneath her, his arms cradling her. Almost delirious, she laughed.

They made it through that moment, and the next, and then the next. The heat lessened. Eventually, June sat up, pushing the blanket off. The air in the car was still superheated and was foul: plasticky and smoky. But outside, the visibility had improved.

Elijah tried to open the door and cried out, drawing his hand away; the handles were burning hot. The passenger seat window had cracked, and some of the front dashboard had melted.

June's mouth was glued shut, but she forced it open to drink from the water bottle she'd found in the boot. She drank half the bottle, and Elijah drank the rest. The water was hot. She opened the door gingerly.

Black tree trunks faded to grey and then vanished in the distance, hidden in thick smoke. Small fires glowed throughout the bush. Flames flickered in hollows, at the base of trees, and on fallen branches. The roar of fire sounded far away. For now, they were through the fire.

———

June didn't know what to do. They sat in the front seats with the engine running—no aircon, it made the car even more smoky—and stared at the bush. Elijah had a stunned, almost dumb, expression on his face. June guessed she looked similar.

Neither of them had any connectivity. It seemed safer to stay in a burnt-out area than to venture farther and maybe cross paths with the fire again, and besides, the road was impassable because of the fallen trees. It was around one in the afternoon, and they sat there quietly until after two. The sky gradually lightened, but there was still a tremendous amount of smoke. The lightning storm seemed to have dissipated.

The car was silent except for the sound of them breathing. Elijah fidgeted. June stared at him unhappily.

"June—" Elijah said, but June held her hand up as if she could stop him talking, and apparently it worked, because he did stop talking. June bunched her hand into a fist and held it clenched as she dropped it to her side. She was sick of him, but she needed him; she could see that he didn't need her. She was sticky and her skin hurt.

She got out and leaned against the car, trembling. Hannah and Rahul were missing. Who knew where Blythe was.

Elijah opened the door. "I got the radio to work!"

Hannah's radio had never worked, that June could remember, so she hadn't even tried it. She slid back into her seat and listened. The announcer sounded calm, but with a frazzled undertone.

The fires were mostly under control. The announcer listed the suburbs that people were allowed to return to. Dickson, where Hannah lived, was one of them. But they still couldn't go anywhere, because the road was blocked. And their phones didn't have any connectivity.

It was nearly 8:00pm before an SES truck came through, splitting the fallen trees with a chainsaw and hauling them off the road. The SES volunteer they spoke to, an exhausted-looking woman who seemed barely out of her teens, refilled their water bottle and gave them muesli bars before taking off.

Elijah drove carefully, dodging the small branches and leaves that were strewn across the road. The road was sprinkled with sawdust where the SES had cleared away fallen trees. June sat with her shaking hands wedged between her knees.

It was dark when they entered Lyneham, a suburb adjacent to Dickson; the sun had set. June cried out. Some houses were smouldering ruins. Others were untouched.

Elijah said nothing, just drove with a glassy-eyed expression. They pulled up in front of Hannah's house. None of the houses in her street had been burnt. June sat watching the lights inside the house for a minute, her brow painfully knotted, before she unbuckled and went in. She couldn't bear to lose Hannah. Elijah followed June, as close as her shadow.

But Hannah was there. She screamed when she opened the door and engulfed June in a hug, crying. June tried to ask whether Rahul was all right, but she couldn't; wordless tears streamed down her face. It was only then that she realised how blackened and smoky she and Elijah were. June's face stung from the UV burn she'd received in the End-Permian, but she guessed her burns would be attributed to the fires.

Rahul appeared. "It's Elijah!" he said excitedly to the others in the room, making June smile, because Rahul showed no reaction to her presence. Pranav appeared, looking relieved to see June, and talked to Elijah. Rupina and her son were there, and Ushadevi was cradling Amy. Elijah accepted the dinner he was offered and joined them at the table, talking to them. June winced as she over-heard him ask Rupina how many children she had; glimpsed the grief-stricken look on Rupina's face as she answered that she used to have two, but now she had one.

"Pranav said you and Rahul were missing," June said to Hannah.

Hannah's smile twisted, then disappeared. "Rahul had an asthma attack. I left Amy with Sarah from next door and rushed him to hospital. There weren't any ambulances. It all happened very quickly."

June nodded. "But he's okay?"

"We all are. Until the next time, I suppose. Dinner?" Hannah said.

June's stomach turned; she hadn't eaten since breakfast, except for the muesli bar the SES volunteer had given her, but she couldn't imagine eating, nor going into the crowded, noisy dining area. Hannah understood; of course she did.

June stumbled down the hall towards the shower, face crum-pling from the deep hurt inside her. Even her eyeballs felt grimy. In the mirror, she saw pale channels running down her cheeks where her tears had run.

She undressed mechanically and stood under the cold water, her skin stinging, sobbing, until she was spent. Her snot was black, the water puddled near the drain a dirty brown from her filth. It felt like the end of the world.

The fires were under control, but the smoke would linger for some days, or longer. The smell made her want to vomit. When she emerged from the shower, she went into her—and Rahul's—room, and closed the door. She was asleep within minutes.

CHAPTER 20

The whole country was in chaos after the fires; day cares and schools closed, so Hannah took leave. Construction tape and traffic cones marked off burnt-out buildings all over Canberra.

Phoenix messaged them the next morning to let them know the time machine was out of commission. If they hadn't quenched it, it would have exploded, he said. Even so, the roof over the collider had collapsed, and some components had melted. He thought he could repair it eventually, but didn't sound overly confident. MediSlice was closed, he said. Don't come in—except Blythe, if anyone has seen her.

But no one had seen Blythe, and her phone was disconnected. June worried, but perhaps she had escaped again with her family, changed her name and moved back to New Zealand. Or somewhere else. She hadn't messaged June, and June found this surprisingly painful, because she thought they were friends. It was like Elijah all over again; June drank tea and sat at the table in Hannah's dining room, watching the smoky orange sky outside, miserably wondering if she'd failed Blythe as a friend in some way. Which of her many flaws was so terrible that Blythe would leave without saying goodbye?

For the next five days, June stayed home. Her dreams were dark and claustrophobic. Waves of panic passed over her as she wandered strange empty lands. But gradually she became calm. She had survived yet another climate disaster, and that was something. The skin on her face and arms peeled off, leaving her itchy and tender, and she could not stop picking at it.

The smoke that had pervaded the air in Canberra gradually cleared. Rupina and her family were able to move out of Hannah and Pranav's house, into housing provided to refugees, and Ushadevi went with them. The house was suddenly quiet, although they visited frequently. June moved back into the guest room.

Thwaites Glacier was still collapsing. Australia's fires were still burning, but they were under control. A cool change had come through, bringing rain. Canberra's fires had burnt right over the top of new Parliament House, leaving little damage. The building's bunker-like design had been criticised. Some people talked about how Canberra was getting what it deserved—the media used "Canberra" to mean Federal Parliament, to the annoyance of Canberrans—but although the present federal government had not done enough, more blame was attached to the previous climate-denying government.

Nonetheless, the politicians must have been shaken, because there was an uncharacteristic amount of attention paid to climate change, and to helping those affected by bushfires.

No one had thought Canberra would burn, and the accusations flew in the post-mortem. As with most disasters, it was a line-up of failures that looked preventable in retrospect. The irrigation mandated by the bushfire management plan had been neglected because of the drought. The tree canopy cover boosting program had seen large numbers of trees planted close to buildings, and while the trees successfully provided shade and cooled the city, they provided a disastrous amount of fuel for fires. The trees were mostly eucalypts, because non-natives were politically unpopular and higher maintenance, but eucalypts, also known as "gasoline trees," were incredibly flammable: their peeling bark turned into embers, they dumped kindling in the form of dry leaf litter around their base, and their oil-rich leaves burnt readily. Why did Canberra have huge dry nature reserves running through the city? Especially in a place where the steep rough terrain made it susceptible to pyroconvection, where storms were created by fire. And so on.

ACT Fire and Rescue formally apologised for having the bulk of its force out in NSW when Canberra needed them the most, but public reaction was sympathetic. You couldn't leave firefighters in reserve when there were fires that needed attention elsewhere, and no one had expected the fires in Canberra to multiply so fast, or to become out-of-control so quickly. The whole system was designed based on the idea that there wouldn't be too many emergencies at any one time; an assumption that was no longer correct.

———

On her last day of leave, June reached the top of the Arboretum, pedalling hard. She was meeting Elijah, at his request, but she was early. The east side of the Arboretum was closed, only the blackened stumps of trees visible beyond the barriers, but most of the Arboretum had escaped. From the west end, the top of Dairy Farmer's Hill, the city was laid out around her. The lake reflected heavy grey clouds. She could see blackened nature reserves and burnt-out buildings throughout the city. Gentle hills rose on the outskirts, covered with the grey green of old pasture, or black ashes where the fire had raged.

Wind blew across her face as her breathing slowed. At a bench nearby, a woman wearing a headscarf was glued to her phone. Farther down the hill, two cyclists had stopped and were looking at a single phone screen.

Cold, slippery fear began to build in June's belly. *Was it the AMOC?* Or some other disaster? If the AMOC shut down, it would severely disrupt rain in India, South America and West

Africa, leading to famines. Temperatures would plummet in Europe at the same time as storms increased. And it would probably be the end of the Amazon rainforest and Antarctic ice sheets.

But no one looked upset.

June pulled out her phone and unfolded it. The breaking news on the Australian Broadcasting Corporation website was about COP35, a speech by US Senator Alejandro Gomez. She played the video file.

It started in the middle of a fight. Alejandro stood behind a podium.

"—the US delegate will yield the floor!" a voice off-camera cried out.

The contemptuous look Alejandro gave the source of the voice would have set stone aflame.

"I will not," he thundered. "I will not yield the floor."

He took a sheaf of paper and tried to rip it, inexpertly, whole pages falling on the floor. Cries sounded around him. The camera zoomed to his face, which was dark with rage.

"This is what our agreement is worth, and it is past time we recognised it. We're all waiting for someone with the authority to step in and save us. If it's not us, if it's not *now*, then who? And when?"

Applause from somewhere, but also booing.

No one believes they have their hands on the levers, June thought. *Even Blythe, with her billions, didn't believe she could do anything.* Human societies produced emergent behaviour beyond the control of any single member.

"It is clear, now, that two degrees was a dangerous amount of warming to aim for. We have to cease all greenhouse gas emissions *immediately*. Economic development has been decoupled from carbon combustion, so now is the time."

Alejandro cleared his throat. "Modern civilisation *is* intense energy usage. While we have many technologies that will seamlessly replace their fossil-fuel equivalents, the speed at which they are being adopted isn't fast enough. The future—especially for those of us in rich countries—has to be less comfortable and convenient than it is currently. That is not up for debate!"

He had to shout the last part as someone yelled something over him.

"The solutions to our crisis are clear, even if they are unpalatable. Who will dare implement them? Only countries whose citizens *demand* their leaders act."

Two men came up—perhaps security guards—and tried to wrest the microphone off him. He deftly dodged the first and gave the other a shove that sent him sprawling.

A murmur of shock came from off-camera.

June was surprised no one had cut off his microphone yet, but it was entirely possible someone was fighting to protect him from that; the higher the stakes rose in the climate crisis, the more climate activists there were. Every disaster spawned more.

"We thought in 2025 that we'd won, because we'd committed to a path to zero and we'd reduced emissions for the first time. Nothing more needed to be done. But the hard work has not been done, because action has not followed commitments. The hard work must be done," Alejandro said.

He gripped the podium, ignoring the security guard who was helping his colleague off the floor. "Treating climate change as an emergency will have an impact on par with a natural disaster. It will be chaos, but business-as-usual will be chaos too, because that's the future we chose when we failed to address this issue from the start."

"It wouldn't have been possible ten years ago," June heard someone say behind her.

"But we're so close now," a woman replied. June's heart pounded.

"Mass electrification—" Alejandro said, then shot a worried glance at four new security guards who had just entered the frame and changed tack. "I once met a woman who had been caught in one of Australia's savage bushfires as a child. Terrible, I thought, the scar she bore from it, running all the way down her arm."

June drew in her breath; she felt as if the people around her should be pointing and staring at her, but they weren't. Her scar seemed to tingle in the strangely numb sections where the hair never grew back, even though she was sure it was just the sensation of the breeze on her bare skin, brought to her attention by Alejandro.

"But the real scars were inside, the look of desolation in her eyes, the same look I see in so many young people today. Knowing that how we live destroys our future. The real impact of the climate crisis is that we're *destroying our humanity*."

The new security guards grabbed him roughly and began to pull him away, but Alejandro took the microphone with him and kept talking.

"I don't have the power to make the changes that need to be made. Obviously," he said, with a wry glance at the guards forcing him out. "But if enough of you want change, you can make it happen. We can reverse the terraforming that began with the start of the industrial revolution in 1760 and make this planet habitable for humans again. Help me!"

The room exploded in clapping and cheering. Alejandro, still being hustled away, seemed at first disconcerted, then delighted.

The video ended.

June sighed. The speech would change nothing, surely, because there had been many speeches before, just as good or better. And yet, something about the way Senator Gomez spoke made it all seem possible.

Thunder rumbled. It would rain soon. June mounted her bike and pedalled towards the Village Centre where she was meeting Elijah.

———

The massive windows of the Village Centre captured the view of the city. The building was shaped like the top of a hill, the gentle curve supported inside with timber struts and tree-like pillars.

Elijah sat at a table near one of the windows, watching the grey, brooding sky. June ordered at the café and crossed the vast stone floor, clutching the buzzer they'd given her.

She weaved through the crowded tables to join Elijah. A manila folder sat on the table in front of him; Elijah liked physical items, even when digital would have been more appropriate.

"How are you? And your family?" Elijah asked. He wore a button-up shirt, the brown plaid one she'd always liked. His hair was freshly combed. She caught a hint of his laundry powder over the smell of hot chips and coffee coming from the café.

She waggled her hand from side to side, her smile wry. "Yourself?"

"All right," he said. They had to talk loudly; the acoustics in the vast space led to a general babble of noise. Conversation and a child crying, a coffee machine humming, a door slamming.

"Your dad?"

"Coping." His hands cradled his white porcelain cup of tea.

"Have you heard from Blythe at all?" June asked.

"No. But I dropped around to her house, and it's empty. A real estate agent was showing prospective tenants around. She said the previous tenants had broken the lease."

June nodded. Phoenix had Blythe's mother listed as next of kin, but when he called her, Blythe's mother had just said that Blythe was fine and hung up when Phoenix asked where she was. Her phone was still disconnected. Based on that, June guessed she had run again, into a new life. Her ex-husband was still listed as a missing person; June checked periodically.

A woman asked Elijah if they needed the extra chair at their table, and he told her to take it. June shuffled her chair forward to give the woman more space to carry it.

"So why am I here?" June asked. A few weeks ago, she would have been wildly excited about being on a date with him, but she knew she wasn't there for a date.

"I tracked down Maddie," Elijah said. "I met her."

June sat up straight, excited. "Yes?"

He slid the manila folder over to her, and she opened it. There was Maddie, looking down at a newborn in her arms with a doting expression. She was perhaps forty, not significantly older than June remembered. The next page was a photocopy of an adoption record. June skimmed through it, frowning. "Josephine Park adopted a girl from . . . Madeline Park—wait."

Elijah smiled. June flipped back to check the date on the adoption record. Madeline Park was eighteen when she gave up her child, June read, and that was in 2009.

"Maddie adopted her own baby?"

"Yes. She's working as a nurse these days. And she got married. Anyway, she seems happy."

"She knew," June said, realising. "When I told her about time travel. She had some inkling that the person who adopted her baby was her future self . . . maybe she left herself a hint."

She put the adoption record aside and saw another photo, this one a selfie with Elijah and a Maddie who looked like she was in her sixties. A shy young woman stood behind them.

"Her baby, Sun-Hi, is now twenty-two, home for a break. She's studying architecture in Dublin," Elijah said. "Maddie's very proud."

"That's great news!" June said.

Elijah smiled, but he looked uncomfortable. He studied the massing clouds through the window. She'd seen that expression before when he tried to break bad news. *This relationship isn't working out for me*, for example. June waited.

"The le—"

June's buzzer went off. "Hold that thought," she said, and she went to the café to collect her drink. At the next table, a young girl was smearing foam from her babyccino all over her face; the father watched—amused? Or resigned—a pack of baby wipes on the table beside him.

"What is it?" June said to Elijah when she returned. Her cup was warm in her hands.

He was still gazing out the window, where a few drops of rain had started to fall.

"After some deliberation, I've decided to return to Melbourne," he said, turning his attention to her. "Back to Deep Scan. Starting after Christmas."

June's response to this was a rush of confusing emotions, which, experienced all at once, were hard to identify. Trying to project calm acceptance, she smiled slightly, and although the tension in her forehead probably gave her away, it didn't feel like a false smile.

"Don't worry, I will not be following," she said wryly. "Give my best to everyone, won't you? And I hope it all goes well for you."

He laughed. "Thanks. And if you want to keep in touch—as friends—"

"Sure," June said, knowing that she wouldn't.

They finished their tea. The father at the next table over wiped his daughter's face and left, holding her hand.

The skies opened and rain poured down outside. Something loosened inside June. The rain would finally clear the last of the smoke that was hanging around, she hoped. The humid air was scented with earthy petrichor when she emerged into the stone-lined alley outside the Village Centre.

She rode away in the rain, sheets of it splashing down on the roads and drumming on her back. The rain leaked through her jacket and wet her neck and her sleeves. But her eyes were dry and clear.

At home, in Hannah's guest room, she opened the box on her bedside table and plucked her engagement ring out. She snapped a picture with her phone and had an ad online in minutes. *Engagement ring for sale. It didn't work out. Hope you have better luck.*

CHAPTER 21

Two days later, June woke to the news that an eighty-seven-year-old woman in Ireland had declared that she was going to wear a green armband until the climate crisis was addressed. A picture of her sitting at a bus stop with her arms folded and her mouth set stubbornly made the news. It was all over social media.

A man on the bus wore a green armband. June heard a teenager say "Good on you, mate," as he passed him.

June got off the bus and walked up the stairs to Old Parliament House. Phoenix was in the travel room, at the control desk, typing. His face was in shadow, out of the light cast by the desk lamp, but even so, the dark circles under his eyes were obvious. He'd had Covid, he'd said in the MediSlice chat.

"Phoenix?" June said.

He turned away and coughed into his elbow, before acknowledging her presence. The waveform on the oscilloscope jumped and plunged.

"Are you going somewhere?" June asked, suddenly uncertain. Why else would he be at work, if he was still sick? For a crazy second, she wondered if Black Death or the Spanish Flu was in fact Covid-19, spread by Phoenix travelling to the past, but no—the Black Death had been in medieval times, she was sure, and the Spanish flu later than 1830. Besides, researchers would have noticed. And there wouldn't have been a pandemic in 2019, because the emergence of a novel coronavirus would have been into a population primed with antibodies.

"No, just running diagnostics," he said. "I haven't fixed the time machine, anyway. It's going to take a while."

She laughed in relief. "For a moment, I thought . . ."

"That I was going to inflict mass death on the past?" Phoenix said, smiling. He pulled a tissue out of his pocket and blew his nose, then binned it in a receptacle under the desk. He used the hand sanitiser that sat next to the monitor.

"Of course you can't." If he tried, something would stop him. Maybe a meteorite would hit MediSlice in the next two minutes, destroying everything. Something.

"I'm not infectious anymore. It's an interesting thought experiment, though, isn't it? What would happen if I went back to, say, 1830?"

"Was Old Parliament House even built then?" June said, fascinated.

"No, Canberra was just sheep farms in the parish of Queanbeyan. But say I risked it. It's 1830, and the world's population is one billion. The industrial revolution has started—it started in 1760—but if I go back earlier than 1830, there's a Ngunnawal settlement in the place where Canberra was built, which raises a different set of problems. So, a deadly virus is unleashed on Australia, then spreads by ship overseas. Who knows how many people it kills? Healthcare is primitive in 1830, so the mortality rate would likely be higher than when Covid emerged in 2019. It would be a significant proportion."

"Then what?" June said. She loved the way he thought, the interesting and comfortable conversations she had with him. Maybe, now that she had let go of Elijah—maybe—

"I don't know, and I wouldn't believe anyone who claimed

they did know. But after the Spanish flu, people were disillusioned by science. And that was in 1918. During the Black Death, there were bands of people who flogged themselves to atone for their sins, to repent so thoroughly that God would forgive them. A pandemic would be considered a message of some kind, and what kind of message would they think it is, in 1830? Germ theory is in its infancy."

"You don't know that they'd blame science," June said.

"No, I don't. The industrial revolution had been in swing for seventy years, and I don't really know—no one knows—how people back then would react."

"It wouldn't bother you that you would be safe while the bodies piled up around you? Their deaths caused by you?" June asked. She was curious, not criticising him, and wondered how she would feel. Empathy was something she learnt, painfully. How to make the right face, pick the correct sophistries when someone related their suffering. It was some time before she felt genuine emotion behind it; she had to understand suffering first, to suffer herself, then to consider how others wished to avoid suffering.

"It would bother me, of course. But essentially, it's re-rolling the dice; changing some parameters early and running forward. Maybe there wouldn't be a Great War," Phoenix continued. "Or, as it's later called, World War I. Perhaps no World War II. Yes, Covid would cause great suffering, but I think those poor people were in for a lifetime of suffering anyway. And if it altered history, so that today we're not facing the death of the planet, wouldn't it be worth it?"

June didn't reply. She knew it wasn't possible to change the past. But if it were possible—if they knew that this timeline had no future, would she roll the dice again?

No. She wasn't a doomer, not anymore. She had thought the world needed to change for her to be rid of that suffocating feeling, but it hadn't changed, and yet she was free.

"Most likely humanity would just continue with the industrial revolution once the pandemic passed, anyway," Phoenix said. "They'd return to science, pumping out carbon dioxide until they're drowning in it just like we are."

June nodded. She looked down at her lap where her hands were gripping each other, despite her being barely aware of them. "It's inevitable that science will continue to advance once the seed is planted," she said. "But here's the thing: I believe we can change the future, starting now. Without the time machine."

"Do you? Because I had the impression that it was Elijah who believed that, and that you disagreed with him. Vehemently."

"You should have seen the Early Triassic," June said softly.

The desk lamp caught Phoenix's eyes. His gaze reminded her of when she was dating Elijah, early on, when he didn't understand her fully and hung on her every word, hungry to know her. Some part of her ached.

"It was devastating," she said, and she paused. "It was *devastated*. The media says the sixth mass extinction is here, but it's not. Count how many species there are, just within walking distance of Old Parliament House. Hundreds? In the Early Triassic, I saw perhaps five. We're terraforming a new world, but it's not here yet. If it were here, we'd be fighting to save cockroaches and rats from extinction. We can keep fighting."

"But there's an invisible line, a tipping point, and once we cross it, there's no saving us," Phoenix said. "We might have crossed it already. Perhaps it was the Thwaites Glacier?"

June was silent. The tipping points were dominos. The AMOC, the West Antarctic ice sheet, the Greenland ice sheet, the Amazon rainforest, permafrost and methane hydrates, coral reefs, and so on. Some scientists thought some had already been tipped, others thought they were highly likely to tip, but either way, once they started tipping, the others were likely to follow. A non-linear response; a breaking down of ecosystems, completely out of control, leading to an irreversible catastrophe.

A cascade of tipping points could lead to a hothouse Earth, something like the End-Permian. Although 2030's CO_2 concentration of 435 ppm looked measly compared to the End-Permian's 8000 ppm, humanity was adding CO_2 ten times faster than was added during the End-Permian era. Speed was everything. Add CO_2 slowly enough, and the effect would be counteracted by the carbonate-silicate cycle. Warmer, rainier weather with more acidic rain led to more weathering of rocks, which removed carbon from the atmosphere, stabilising climate.

Too bad it would take 100 thousand years for weathering processes to remove the carbon dioxide humans had added to the atmosphere.

"I don't know what happens five minutes from now—no one does—and maybe I can't change the future. But I'm damn well going to try, no matter how many tipping points we cross," June said.

"Very inspiring," Phoenix said.

"Thank you," June said in surprise.

"I was being sarcastic," Phoenix said, sounding a bit embarrassed.

"Ah."

Phoenix stared into space. "Can I show you something?" he said abruptly. June nodded, but he didn't move immediately.

He stood up.

Inside the travel room they had been completely cut off from the sounds of the outside world, but as soon as he opened the door, June heard rain beating down, caught the scent of it.

She went with Phoenix to his office, where he searched through his stacks of books and handed her a book with a cloth cover. Old, the red cloth faded to maroon. *Mycoremediation and Other World-Saving Uses of Mycelium*, it said in almost-illegible gold text on the front.

June looked sharply at Phoenix, dismayed. It was the book Harry had been holding the night she saw him in Phoenix's office. The book which had a chapter by Richard Simpson, who looked so much like Phoenix.

June had forgotten to ask Phoenix about it. She opened the

book at the bookmark—a torn-off piece of paper, heavy with Greek-alphabet equations—and found herself at Chapter Six, at the picture of Richard Simpson.

"Richard Simpson's not your relative?" June said. Her voice broke slightly, and she cleared her throat. The books stacked on his desk had titles like *Ectomycorrhizal Fungi in the Field, Mother Tree, On Photoassimilates.*

"No, he's me," Phoenix said.

"Are you sure?"

"It's my style, and that picture is me. I've always been interested in fungi, actually. If I hadn't gone into physics, mycology would have been my second choice. I borrowed these books because I thought perhaps we could send some research back in time, but when you came back with the news that we couldn't change the past, I thought I'd better find a new research interest. After what Harry said about forests drawing down carbon . . ."

He shrugged. June nodded slowly.

"Have you heard of the Wood Wide Web?" he said.

"No."

"Fungi connect plants together in a network, sometimes kilometres wide. Carbon produced by trees is transported around the mycelial network, to feed smaller plants, shaded plants, or deciduous plants which have shed their leaves. It goes to where it's needed, as do other nutrients. Ecosystems with sufficiently large mycorrhizal fungi networks store eight times more carbon than those without. I was wondering if we could increase that even more. And we can. With this research, the carbon stored is closer to *twenty times more* than a forest with no fungi. My contribution was to show we can extract carbon from the Wood Wide Web—to act as a parasite, a myco-heterotroph—thus encouraging trees to remove more from the atmosphere to boost the mycelial network's overall supply."

June kept still.

"This is world-changing. We're going to have to suck large

amounts of carbon dioxide out of the air, and increasing the efficiency of cheap self-replicating machines that already do it could make a huge difference. Because I went back and researched this area, the technology is there to do it today."

"But the research is published here . . . so you've already done it. Can't you take it back, publish it, and retire?"

Phoenix laughed. "Researchers don't make much money. Australian researchers, anyway. Yes, technically I suppose I could. It seems like cheating, though. I've avoided reading it, other than the abstract, but I've been reading a lot of background. And getting my affairs in order."

He stared out into the hall. June swallowed.

"Did you look up Richard Simpson?" she asked.

"No. If I can't change the past, I don't want to know."

"At least you live to a fairly advanced age. Looking healthy, too," June said, with only a faint edge of hysteria in her voice.

"Maybe I don't go back to the past until I'm sixty," Phoenix said, and to June it sounded like he was offering a hope they could both cling to.

The nameless thing that existed between them—lust, recognition, above all *potential*—hung in the air like mist. The palest of hopes, now, which hurt June. She guessed maybe it hurt Phoenix more; his decade-long date with a pile of books, following the sacrifices he had already made to build the time machine.

Phoenix's phone rang, and he looked at June apologetically.

"My sister," he said, and answered it. He sat in his office chair, swivelling around so his back was to June.

She returned to the computer lab and sat in front of her computer, but she had trouble concentrating. Rain beat down outside, quiet and steady.

How did it feel to know that your fate was written? She hit compile on the core modules. While she waited, she searched for Richard Simpson.

He had his own Wikipedia page. Early life, some vague stuff

she was sure was made up. Personal life. She saw with surprise the entry said he was bisexual, but he married a woman, a rather attractive French microbiologist with her own Wikipedia page. Three children. He won awards for his research, and for his work promoting Indigenous participation in STEM. In the picture of him sitting around a campfire, being presented with a trophy decorated with Aboriginal art, he looked delighted.

Phoenix entered the open door of the computer lab, and June hastily switched back to the second desktop to hide the browser. He noticed her sudden movement and stopped.

The expression on his face was hard to read.

"June, I was wondering if you wanted—wait, were you searching for me?" he said.

"Yeah," June admitted, trying hard to keep her tone neutral, to not let any information leak.

"Oh," Phoenix said. He frowned and paced back and forth. "*June,*" he complained.

June smiled. "It's okay," she said.

"It is?"

She raised her eyebrows significantly and gave the smallest of nods.

"Pretty good life?"

"Oh, yeah. From what I can tell, anyway."

Phoenix nodded slowly. "You're not—are you? I mean, you're not part of it, by any chance . . .?"

It took June a moment to parse the question. *He wanted to know if she went back with him.* Her look of surprise must have told him the answer, because his expression became inscrutable. She hadn't thought of going back in time herself, but when she did, she wished she'd read about herself in the Wikipedia entry.

June tried to compose a hint for Phoenix that didn't reveal too much. "You . . . won't be lonely in the past," June said.

Phoenix looked up with amazement. "Yeah?"

June nodded, biting back a smile.

Phoenix grinned, and June recognised it as the mischievous

grin that Richard Simpson wore in the author photo; a knowing grin, because Richard Simpson knew his past self and June would see the photo.

June had the feeling Phoenix would smile a lot more in the past.

CHAPTER 22

There were already global strikes, mostly organised by the School Strike 4 Climate movement, but the number of participants was unprecedented. About forty percent of the people June passed in the street wore green armbands. June joined one of the marches, walking beside Hannah and Pranav in the sun, but she only lasted half an hour before she became overwhelmed and left; it was electrifying, but too much.

Phoenix, Elijah, June, and Harry planned for more missions, even though after Christmas Elijah would be going back to Melbourne. The missions were of a different type, now; knowing they couldn't change the past, but looking for ways to use the past to nudge the future or create pleasant surprises. They couldn't enact any of their plans, because Phoenix was still trying to fix the time machine, but they wanted to be ready.

They all wore green armbands except Elijah.

"We're overreacting," Elijah said to June. He sat at the break room table, in the morning sun. "What you people are asking for is ridiculous! We can stay under two degrees *without* shutting down all fossil-fuel burning immediately. I mean, yes, we need stronger regulations, but a complete stop is a disaster."

June slid her lunchbox into the fridge. "Stronger regulations have not been forthcoming over the last fifty years politicians have had to act, and I'm sick of waiting. It's 2030, and the government is still approving permits for new gas and coal projects! I don't trust the government to regulate industry properly, and if it's not properly regulated, it's better to shut it down. Anyway, risk is the chance of something happening multiplied by the consequences. If we reach a threshold where tipping points fall, that's a huge consequence. Recovering from that would be difficult, right?"

"Yes," Elijah admitted. He broke off a chunk of chocolate chip biscuit and dunked it in his tea.

Harry came in carrying a coffee cup and rinsed it under the sink.

"So, the risk is high, even though the chance of reaching a tipping point is small. Although, as far as I know, scientists don't know what the chance of reaching that threshold is," June said.

Elijah nodded, reluctantly acknowledging her point. The sunlight caught his eyes, bringing them a clarity that made June think of high-resolution prints in glossy magazines.

"I suppose so. On the other hand," Elijah said, as she knew he would, "you have to weigh the chance of reaching the threshold against the cost of acting. The actions people are demanding are not warranted according to science. It's a trade-off, and one I feel we're about to make poorly. We're asking for unnecessary pain. To force people to live impoverished lives, and to damage our economy. The very economy we need to be strong, in order to invent and upgrade ourselves out of this mess."

Harry just shook his head.

Governments around the world—including the Australian government—watched with dismay as the GDP fell to levels not seen since the 2019 pandemic, because of the number of people withholding their labour. Alejandro's speech to COP35 was blamed by some. There were counterstrikes too. A surprising number of people seemed to believe in conspiracy theories and marched wearing yellow suits, giant menacing bobble-headed dolls holding signs "STOP THE ICE AGE"—which the conspir-acists believed would follow the switch to renewables.

Far more concerning, some forty-seven percent of people didn't want change, according to polling, and the more enthusi-astic of them emerged in force, facing off against green-armband protesters. They were a conglomerate, representing different and slightly confused beliefs. The world was doomed anyway, climate change was a hoax, others were just upset at the idea that they would be forced to change their behaviour.

"Fools!" June said in agony to Phoenix, after watching the footage of their march on the White House in America, and on houses of government around the world, including Parliament House. She was sitting at her desk in the computer lab.

Phoenix watched grimly over her shoulder.

Worse was the feeling that, had she never interviewed for the job at MediSlice, she might have been among them. Not marching, but quietly supporting them; certainly not wearing a green armband. She had believed the world was doomed, and if it was, what was the point of desperate flailing about?

"If only they could see what I saw," June said, thinking of the End-Permian, and the Early Triassic. She stood up, grasping Phoenix's arm. Elijah glanced at her from his desk.

"They can," she said.

"You mean film it?"

June laughed, because that was a great idea, and it hadn't occurred to her. "Well, yes, that would be fantastic. But what I was thinking was that we should open-source the time machine."

Elijah gave her a sideways glance.

"We release the schematics, code, and documentation to as many people as possible. Then it won't be owned by just one group," June said.

"We can't let just anyone use it," Elijah said.

"How many people have a few million dollars lying around that they could spend on parts—not to mention tritium—and the expertise to build it? It wouldn't be just anyone, it would be companies and universities and governments. But it could still be used for ill," Phoenix said. "Used voyeuristically, or for theft. The past will be treated like a playground by those with money. I hate to think."

"It probably would be used for those things," June said. "But maybe it could provide some much-needed perspective for humanity. And I'm not worried it would be used for nefarious purposes, since the past can't actually be changed."

Elijah and Phoenix glanced at each other. Harry entered the lab, carrying a stack of books. June waited, the atmosphere electric.

"What did I miss?" Harry asked curiously, putting the books on his desk.

"We're open-sourcing the time machine," Phoenix said.

Nudging the future, June thought. It would change the path they were on, maybe for the better, maybe for the worse, or perhaps neither. But it was worth doing.

They couldn't release it as open-source immediately; they didn't even have a functioning time machine, and without that, they'd be dismissed as crackpots. Anyway, they needed detailed specifications, and clean, well-documented code. But then what would happen, assuming that they could prove it worked? Phoenix thought the government would probably come and take over the machine. June had a feeling, not for the first time, that they were terribly naive. But then they were engineers, except for Harry. They were way outside of their field of expertise.

In the meantime, a ceasefire was declared in the India–Pakistan war. Green-armband strikers continued, as did the counter-protests. The Australian government folded, declaring an emergency. Government advertising was everywhere, on the web, and signs on bus stops, highways, shops, and businesses. You couldn't miss it. "Climate Emergency," the signs read, then detailed the changes that were coming. It was like when Covid-19 swept the world; everything upended.

Every time period feels like it will last forever, June thought, *but the world does nothing* but *change, always*. Quickly, or slowly; and right now, it was quickly. Over the next two months, June's life changed completely.

June had the option of claiming meat and dairy rations. The meat ration was redeemable for five hundred grams of beef or lamb every month, or a chicken or five hundred grams of kangaroo every fortnight, or five hundred grams of fish a week. The dairy ration was for two litres of milk per week or an equivalent amount of dairy products, such as cheese. Choices had to be made. Two litres of milk, or two hundred grams of cheddar. Many people complained about this, saying that the government was starving them or that they couldn't get enough protein. Counter-protesters rioted, smashing shops and burning buildings, and a black market thrived. Regardless, sales of beans, chickpeas, and lentils soared, as did plant-based meats and cheeses. As a vegetarian, June rented out her meat rations, but kept her dairy ration and supplemented with soy milk when she ran out. Her diet didn't change much, but she appreciated the extra sixty dollars a fortnight she earned from her ration. Hannah, a vegan, held onto hers, because she said it meant she was saving an animal each week.

Presents and decorations for Christmas were homemade, because supply chains were broken or unreliable, but that was okay. Elijah left for Melbourne after Christmas. The rest of the MediSlice team felt how tenuous the changes were and were keen to get the time machine fixed and released to the world.

The police offered a reward for information relating to Blythe's missing ex-husband, which was picked up as a nationwide news story. June expected that the police would interview her, and the MediSlice team, but they never did. Perhaps they hadn't connected Alisha, Blythe's real name, with Blythe. Despite Blythe claiming to have given away all her money, she had evidently kept enough to buy herself and her family convincing new identities. Madeline Park appeared beside Blythe's missing ex-husband in the database, although June never saw the case mentioned in the news. Perhaps, as Maddie had said, her landlord had reported her missing.

June kept thinking she saw Blythe—in the supermarket, or on the street—and would be ready to call out her name, but when she got closer, it wasn't Blythe after all.

In February, the gas network shut down in Canberra. Hannah's gas stovetop and hot water stopped working. They used the microwave and oven and had sponge baths with water heated in the kettle. It was summer, and most days were over thirty degrees Celsius, so sometimes they just had cold showers. Some counter-protesters broke into the Lodge, but the prime minister's security staff fended them off, and he and his family were unharmed.

Pranav tried to buy a heat pump to replace the gas instant hot water system but was put on a waitlist and told it would be months. Likewise with an induction cooktop. The upgrades would cost thousands; Pranav and Hannah's combined income was too high to qualify for subsidies. June increased the amount of rent she paid them.

Money and resources had been thrown at the government's ambitious power grid mega-project for months to get it to completion and, finally, the Oceania grid came online. In the short term, there were shortages, because Australia's grid now supplied billions more people, and coal-fired power plants were taken offline. Electricity rationing started.

On sunny days there was plenty of power generated from solar, but the amount of power available to Australians fluctuated from day to day. Vulnerable people were given greater rations— the old, the sick, and the young. Hannah, June, and Pranav sat down to work out an electricity budget.

After several days of trial and error, they worked it out. The hospitals, exempt from power restrictions, had to kick out people trying to charge their laptops and other gadgets. A volunteer community group, Insulate Canberra, came around and insulated the whole house for free—roof, walls, floor—and made a number of other changes such as adding shade cloths over windows, pelmets to curtains, sealing doors, and installing fans. It was uncomfortably warm in the afternoons if power rationing was in place, because the air-conditioning had to be off, but with ceiling fans and a cold cloth on the back of the neck it was all right.

The number of counter-protesters grew, and the government talked seriously about restoring coal-fired power stations, to the alarm of green-armband supporters.

June and Pranav both joined Insulate Canberra and spent their weekends insulating and refitting other people's houses, when the organisation had enough materials; supply chains were unreliable, and many raw materials were impossible to get. It was fun work; June made some friends, and because it was a work environment rather than a social activity, she didn't find it intimidating.

One evening when June was fitting door sweeps to an ex-government house in Ainslie, a man approached her with an armload of insulation.

"You!" the man said, spotting her sitting on the step of the laundry.

She stared at him in surprise. *Was he a university classmate?* But he was too familiar to be just a classmate.

He stood silhouetted against the sun, his heavy workboots crusted with mud. She shaded her eyes to look up at him, confused. The heat of the sun had lessened, leaving the land relaxed. Clouds glowed with the colours of the setting sun, colours that leached into the air itself.

"June," the man said, with a sense of triumph, and she finally recognised him. Vivid memories of the flood in Merton surfaced. The smell of sewage, the freezing-cold currents sweeping her away, and the relentless ache in her arms from where she had clung to the tree. It was *him*, the man who had pulled her out of the sinking car. That day, almost five months ago, felt like a fever dream. But here was proof that it was real.

He grinned, one corner of his mouth quirking. "You don't remember me, do you? I'm—"

"Yarran," June said, finally remembering his name. Yarran's grin widened.

A group of pink-chested galahs roamed the lawn, making *chet-chet* noises. The yard was mulched with sugar-cane straw, with young natives planted at intervals. A paved path led to a Hills hoist clothesline.

Yarran put the bale of insulation down. "What are you doing here?"

"I'm installing a door sweep," June explained. She held up the door sweep so that he could inspect it. The concrete she sat on was hot, like an electric blanket; it had been in the sun all day.

He raised his eyebrows, and kneeled on one knee on the path outside the door, resting on his heels. His eyes had the same brown colour and clarity as Phoenix's. "I mean in Canberra," he said.

"Oh! I live here. I was in Merton visiting my Aunt Katie."

"That explains why I never saw you again," Yarran said. "I didn't know you were related to Katie. After you got swept away, I called the SES, and they sent a dinghy after you. They told me they rescued you. I'm glad you were okay."

"Thanks," June said awkwardly. "Likewise. But what are *you* doing in Canberra?"

"Studying medicine. And insulating houses, obviously."

June nodded. She was having trouble getting a grip on this conversation. She barely knew him, but they had survived a flood together, so she felt she knew him well. She peeled the backing tape off the door sweep and lined it up carefully.

"Anyway," Yarran said. "I better get this insulation installed."

"Okay," June said, but she was sorry he was going.

Yarran stood up and grabbed his bale of insulation, scraping his boots at the door before entering the house. The galahs took off noisily, wheeling across the sky with grey wings outstretched.

———

June didn't like change, so it was an unsettling time for her, but in this case, the changes gave her a sense of hope. Following a flurry of construction, there was suddenly enough power, and rationing ended; supply had increased, but also people had become accustomed to using less.

In her work for Insulate, June often ended up teamed up with Yarran, and got to talking while installing insulation in ceiling cavities. Yarran was also a keen reader of fantasy and was easy to talk to. They were an effective team; she felt unaccountably comfortable around him.

At MediSlice, Phoenix was struggling to fix the time machine. That was why June wasn't surprised when she found him in the break room one day, sitting at the table with an untouched cup of tea and staring into space.

"Not going well?" June asked, as she printed herself a blueberry protein bar. Harry was at the library, so MediSlice was empty except for the two of them. The room was dim, blinds drawn against the heat. Lights off, because that made it feel cooler.

"I was able to recover the logs," Phoenix said, which didn't sound like bad news and didn't match the crease between his eyebrows. His face was bisected with a white line of light from one side of the blinds. The protein bar printer dashed around like an elite athlete, depositing layers of bar.

"Okay," June said. She stood in the gap between the kitchenette benchtop and the small table, facing Phoenix.

Phoenix pressed his palms together and touched his fingers to his lips. "Blythe is out on a trip."

June stared at him in consternation. There was no way they could recover her, even if Phoenix managed to fix the machine; the machine had lost power and with it her trace.

"But—" June started. The protein bar printer beeped, telling her it was finished.

"She's been dead fifty-three years," Phoenix admitted with a sigh. The blinds swayed as the wind blew, clanking back against the window; Phoenix squinted as the line of light danced across his face, into his eyes. He pushed his chair out, moving himself into the relative darkness. "The trips didn't show up in the interface. It looks like Blythe was tampering with the logs. Early on December third—the day of your Triassic trip—three people went to 1947. A child, and two adults, using Blythe's authorisation code. So, assuming she was in the past, I googled her."

Phoenix ran his hands over his face. "June, Blythe lives out the rest of her life and dies there. We couldn't bring her back even if we wanted to. She's on Wikipedia. She didn't even change her name."

June sank into the chair opposite Phoenix, blocking the line of light. Using her phone, she searched for Blythe. What would a software engineer do in 1947? Not work, because she was a woman, but she appeared on her husband's Wikipedia page. Ollie Evans was listed as a famous author, known for his futuristic science fiction, which predicted many inventions and discoveries.

She snorted.

"I know, right?" Phoenix said quietly. He reached across the table for his tea. June's back and neck were overly warm from the tiny sliver of light the blinds let through; she tossed her hair back to try to block it.

Blythe and Ollie had another two children, both boys. Blythe was known for her work with charities. Died 1978, age seventy-two, missed by all. But her daughter, Lucy, had a blue link.

June followed the link. Lucy had died at age eleven after being stung by a box jellyfish.

"How old is Lucy now—how old was Lucy, when she went back?" June asked Phoenix.

"Seven, I think."

She would live out four years in the past before dying. The scent of blueberries hung in the hot room.

"But a box jellyfish sting shouldn't be fatal—" June broke off and searched for box jellyfish antivenom. *The box jellyfish antivenom became available in 1970.* Blythe made her choices, and now she'd have to live with them; June couldn't imagine a worse punishment.

"She might have died even with the antivenom," Phoenix said. "Box jellyfish venom can cause cardiac arrest within minutes."

"Maybe. But maybe not. Dammit. Lucy shouldn't have had to pay for her mother's stupid decision."

Phoenix nodded. His face gleamed with light sweat. June shut her eyes. The protein bar printer beeped again, reminding her she'd left a bar in there, but she was no longer hungry.

———

In Australia, with only one month's notice, driving was practically banned in cities. The age of the private vehicle was over. It had already happened in major cities all over the world. For some of them, it happened decades ago, as part of the New Urbanism movement. Counter-protesters clogged the roads for days. Many people ignored the car ban, continuing to drive after the deadline had passed. The number of hit-and-run incidents soared; it seemed the only way some people could express their frustration was through attempted murder. But after a few weeks, those still driving petrol cars ran out of petrol, and it was impossible to get more. That got rid of sixty percent of offenders, and the police managed the rest.

Country towns were now crammed with Teslas, purchased cheaply. And the population of those towns increased dramatically, as those who didn't want to live without cars abandoned the cities.

Cyclists rode freely on roads that were never built for them. It was like playing in a giant's playground. Since there weren't cars, roads were far too wide, and were rezoned into tramways, cycle paths, and walking paths. The space alongside roads was sold for housing and businesses, in narrow lots, three to eight stories.

The scale of Canberra began to change; no more huge swathes of pavement, more narrow laneways and dense, pretty streets. Suddenly there seemed to be children everywhere, out running in the streets until dark. The smaller the streets got, the more cared-for they appeared; the weed-infested roadsides and unmown grass that used to be ubiquitous vanished.

It was utterly silent in the MediSlice computer lab. Silent everywhere. June had never realised how loud cars were. She saved a file and closed it; she had finished documenting the code long ago, and her changes were just fiddling. Having finally admitted to herself that she had no more work to do, June set up a dating profile online, something she'd been meaning to do for a while. Just out of curiosity, she searched for Yarran on the site, but he wasn't there.

The dating profile asked her if she wanted children, and she hesitated. *Undecided*, she put eventually, but later she thought she should change it to *Wants Children*. Even though they couldn't change the past to prevent the carbon dioxide level from being 435 ppm in 2031, she could sense the potential for change in the present, and from that stemmed hope.

She heard the chirp-THUMP of the MRI calibrating and headed over to the travel room. Phoenix stood behind the control desk, grinning. It smelled chemical in there, over the ever-present charred smell Old Parliament House had taken on. Some lubricant, perhaps.

"Fixed it!" Phoenix said, pumping his arms in the air in celebration. "*Finally*. I knew I had to be able to fix it, because otherwise, how would I be able to go back and research fungi in the past? But frankly, I was beginning to doubt."

June walked forward into a pool of light created by a downlight. "Do you need a guinea pig?"

He regarded her. "You want to make a trip?"

"I want to see Blythe."

"There's nothing we can do, June," Phoenix said, dropping into the chair behind the control desk and logging in to the computer there. "There's an obituary for her daughter in the paper. It definitely happened."

"I know," June said. She leaned her shoulder against the edge of the partition, peering around at Phoenix. "I'm not going to try to change the past. I just want to talk to her."

Phoenix hesitated. The swaying waveforms appeared on the machine to his left. "Are you going to tell her about her daughter?"

"Of course not," June said. "I just want to see her, that's all."

Phoenix thought for a moment. "All right."

June pushed herself off the partition and lay on the flatbed. The ceiling moved as the bed gave an infinitesimal jerk and slid her headfirst into the scanner.

CHAPTER 23

June lay on the green-patterned carpet, three figures looking at her. The travel room had become a phone booth once again, and they were crowded in. Blythe, Lucy, and her husband, Ollie. Lucy looked at June, her face apprehensive. Ollie had one hand on the doorknob and in the other, a large trunk.

"June," Blythe said, setting down the suitcase she carried. She wore a V-neck dress, hemline to the knee, blooming roses pattern on cotton fabric. No piercings. She'd cut her hair shorter, too, and made it curlier.

Housewife, June thought, standing up.

"Guys, why don't you wait in the next room?" Blythe said to her husband and daughter. She would sound incongruous to people in the 1940s until she learnt not to speak like a millennial engineer. Lucy looked at Ollie uncertainly, but Ollie just nodded and went—limping slightly—and so she followed. June tried not to look at Lucy.

"When are you from?" Blythe said, passing the chair to June and sitting on the built-in desk. June felt a million years older. So much had changed in the world, and yet it hadn't been that long. Blythe probably wouldn't even believe her if June told her all that had changed. Driving banned? Fossil-fuel power plants shut down? They'd finally declared war on climate change, yet June would have said it was impossible, right up to the point where it happened.

"Two months, one week." June caught the amused smile Blythe gave, because Blythe was always a bit fascinated with June's odder tendencies, such as her habit of giving precise times and dates. June sat sideways on the chair Blythe offered her and rested her elbow on the back of the chair.

"You can't stop me," Blythe said. "I will spend the rest of my life here. It's already happened. Look me up."

"I'm not here to stop you. I just want to understand."

"Then you know what I did," Blythe said, looking down. "In my defence, I didn't think Ethan would die. Must have been a heart attack. Tasers can cause that, right?" Her legs dangled in the air, and when June glanced at them, she crossed her ankles.

June didn't say anything.

"I sent him—his *body*—back to 1978, because that's what the machine was set to, from my mission to dump a bunch of academic papers. Stupid! I thought it would be fine, because they didn't have DNA tracing back then. But they do now, and they're testing the cold cases. They'll figure out who he is. Who I am. I should have sent him to the deep past."

"Like where you sent Maddie Park?" June asked.

"Is she the private investigator?" Blythe asked.

When June nodded, Blythe's mouth twisted. "She turned up a week after Ethan died, tried to force me to come with her. We struggled, we lost balance and we both fell, her beneath me. She hit her head on the edge of the desk and was knocked unconscious. I didn't know what else to do."

Call an ambulance? June thought. Stick the woman in the time machine and send her back to dinosaur-land wouldn't have been June's first thought. Hell, if Maddie had a pacemaker, she would have died.

"The private investigator will be fine. I sent her to the Early Triassic, to buy me and my family time to escape. You can recover her minutes after she arrives. The time machine can be used to suspend people in time, in a sense. I left a note on Phoenix's desk before I left."

"He'd been out sick, but we retrieved Maddie. Not before she'd been there for more than a year, though. If I hadn't managed to get her when I did, she would have lived out the rest of her life in the Early Triassic, because we almost lost the time machine."

"I'm sorry," Blythe said. "But I wasn't about to be tried for murder."

"You know she had nothing to do with your ex-husband," June said.

Blythe looked sceptical. "She must have been there about Ethan. Why else would she—"

"She was hired by your ex-classmate," June said. "The one who wanted to sue you."

Blythe, obviously shocked, had tears in her eyes, which made her look strangely like an actress from an old film; women dressed like her always seemed to be crying on camera back then. She hadn't known.

It wouldn't be enough, June thought, not for what she'd taken from Maddie. For the manslaughter of her husband and attempted murder of Maddie, or forced imprisonment, or whatever you charged someone with when they stranded a person in the past.

But June knew of the punishment that waited for Blythe; one that she had invited.

"Why the Early Triassic?" June asked.

"Safe, because there weren't many species and very few carnivores. Harry told me about it."

June nodded slowly. The Early Triassic was safer than most time periods, she guessed. It wasn't Blythe's fault June had visited the End-Permian mass extinction by mistake.

"The private investigator showing up made me realise that I wasn't safe in the present anymore. So, I started researching what time period to move to. But then I thought, what if I already did it? I looked for evidence I'd gone back in time, and I found it. I'll die at seventy-two of pneumonia. My husband gets cancer, but he survives, lives to eighty-five."

June said nothing.

"It's confronting reading," Blythe said. "I mean, anyone's life would be, if you stack up all the tragedies and read them all at once. But there are a lot of years where Wikipedia has nothing to say. Which means that in our lives, there were years where nothing happened but Christmases and birthdays and picnics in the sun, and that doesn't sound so bad. Ollie has always wanted to write. I think I'd make a good housewife. Some quiet gardening and housekeeping might be just what I need. Seventy-two is younger than I wanted to die, but at least I know I have that long."

"What about your daughter?" June asked carefully. She laid her cheek in her hand, leaning onto the back of the chair with her elbow.

"I didn't have the heart to look up what happens to her," Blythe said. "I know she's there with me. That's enough."

June nodded, knowing that someday Blythe would look back at this conversation and wonder whether June knew. She was struck by how happy Blythe looked; her perpetually haunted expression had vanished, leaving a warmth that June had never seen in her before. All it had taken was a murder or two.

She hoped Blythe would understand that there was nothing June could do about Lucy. But June thought Blythe would cope; that the rest of her days—her remaining thirty years—would be mostly happy ones, even with the weight of the grief that she would bear to her grave.

Maybe June looked upset, because Blythe smiled at her.

"We'll be all right," Blythe said. "It's safe here. Maybe it didn't feel so at the time, but you have to agree, in hindsight, it's looking pretty good. I've researched the era, and it wasn't so bad. A lot of the events they were scared of back then never eventuated. No nuclear war. No reds taking over the world," Blythe said.

June's grandmother had written letters to the paper about the dangers of communism. Quaint, with the benefit of hindsight. Maybe someone would find worrying about climate change quaint someday; June didn't think so, though.

"Good luck," June said.

"I'll miss you," Blythe said.

They hugged, then Blythe left the phone booth. June sat in the chair waiting for the machine to pick her up. Every part of her itched to run after Blythe, to shout at Lucy that she was never to swim in the ocean. But it wouldn't work, would it? Even if Blythe understood what June was saying, even if Blythe forbade Lucy from swimming in the ocean, it would still happen. Maybe June trying to change the past would just become a part of why it happened; Lucy's swim a rebellion against her mother.

The silence rang in her ears. The booth felt private; the wood-panelled walls were comforting in some way that she didn't understand.

Phoenix was at the control desk when June returned. He came out from behind the glass.

"Did Blythe leave you a note when she left?" June asked.

He looked baffled. "Not that I'm aware."

June checked Phoenix's office, searching the stacks of books and the desktop. Finally, she found it: a note in blue biro, a terse summary of what had happened between Blythe and Maddie, which had fallen between the desk and the wall.

June crumpled up the note and put it in the bin, throat hurting, eyes stinging as unwelcome tears welled up. She sighed deeply.

After a long moment, she returned to the travel room, sitting at the control desk and watching Phoenix work. She guessed that even if they DNA-tested Blythe's husband's corpse, a cold case from 1978, and even if it matched the DNA from a missing person case in 2030, it would be dismissed as a mistake. Until they released the time machine, perhaps, and after that they might have to answer some questions . . .

The time machine specs were ready to release onto an unsuspecting world. And now they had a functioning model, they could start missions again, except that "they" would be her and Harry, when Phoenix left. Since Harry was non-technical, she would be in charge, Phoenix said. She would be tasked with hiring people; she really had no idea whether that would be difficult for her.

Phoenix placed a panel back on the side of the MRI, clicking it into place.

"When are you going back?" June asked Phoenix.

"Keen to get rid of me?" Phoenix joked. "Soon, soon."

He didn't seem to be in any hurry. A few days later, he was still making adjustments and testing. June wondered if Richard Simpson's Wikipedia article would say how old Phoenix was when he left, but it was too vague to tell. While she was on the page, she scrolled down farther to read the end. Richard Simpson died—when? June realised with a shock that he was not dead, although the Wikipedia page didn't have any information on what he was currently doing. He was eighty years old.

———

The retirement home was surrounded by conifers. By the entrance, a bronze statue of Mary Poppins floated over a pond, holding an umbrella. As June approached the pond, she saw a flash of brilliant orange-gold underneath the statue as a fish sped away. Ripples spread across the pond, lapping at the rocks that lined the edge.

June passed reception into a room filled with comfortable padded chairs around well-spaced tables. Skylights admitted a cool glow from the overcast sky. June had phoned ahead and arranged to meet him, but somehow, she didn't believe he would be there.

But he was. Richard Simpson sat at one of the tables near the long picture windows overlooking the gardens. His back to her, hand over his mouth. Same long neck, same dark, intelligent eyes.

He stood unsteadily as she weaved between the empty tables.

"I'm Richard, and I care about the climate crisis," he quipped.

She gave a faint smile.

A crutch rested against the arm of his chair. June was suddenly aware of the weight of four decades between their ages. She was a teenager again, hopelessly inadequate and set adrift in a world she didn't understand.

Phoenix—*Richard*—had aged gracefully, but even so. The haggard folds of his skin, the mass of ashen hair, and the way his bones pushed against the thin layer of his skin was uncomfortable to behold. She looked away in confusion, out the back window at the ever-moving, wide green leaves of an ash tree.

"Ageing is terrible, but it's better than the alternative," Phoenix informed her dryly. June laughed at that and was able to look at him again. His grin hadn't changed at all.

"I didn't think I would ever see you again," Phoenix said. "Can't let the wife hear me say this, but—I've never forgotten that kiss."

June tried to figure out whether he was joking. She cocked her head, eyes widening.

"Looks like *you've* forgotten it. Wait—I'm too early, aren't I? Hasn't he left yet? Damn," Phoenix said, chuckling.

"Humph," June said. "All right. I'll look forward to it."

She smiled at him, and it was his turn to laugh, which made him wheeze. Bucolic landscape prints hung on the exposed-brick walls; the nearest to June was a boy fishing in a river, dog sitting by his feet.

"I know you travelled to the past, but here you are, a wise old man with my immediate future in your memory," June said.

"I know what the future holds," Phoenix said. "A cuppa and a Tim Tam. The kitchen's over there." He pointed. June made them both tea and came back with a selection of biscuits.

"You're not worried anymore?" June asked, meaning about the future.

"No," Phoenix said.

"Because you'll be long dead when the future comes around?"

"God, I'd forgotten how blunt you were," Phoenix said.

"Like you can talk," June replied, laughing. He was wearing a strange costume of age, but it was him.

Phoenix leaned forward conspiratorially. "Has Harry left yet?"

"Left to go where?"

"Back home," Phoenix said. "Back to the future."

"*What?*"

Phoenix laughed at the look on her face, but it turned into a coughing fit so bad, that a nurse came over from reception to check on him. The nurse gave June a severe look before leaving.

"Harry's from the *future*?" June whispered.

They were alone in the sea of tables, the nurses at reception in the next room over, but she felt it was worth keeping her voice down.

"You'll have to speak up," Phoenix said.

She put her elbows on the table and leaned towards him. "Harry. From the future?"

"Yeah. Yes! Cheeky blighter. He's a historian. He never lied about that. Came here to see the tipping point."

June had a moment of confusion, because Harry couldn't use a time machine—he had a pacemaker. *He'd lied*, she thought, amused. Although perhaps he hadn't. He might have a non-ferrous pacemaker, or perhaps his time machine didn't use an MRI.

"The Thwaites Glacier?"

"No," Phoenix said. He looked at her with watery eyes. "Our time travel. Your trip to the past, to the café. The speech Alejandro made. That was humanity's tipping point, after which non-linear action was taken regarding climate change."

June nodded slowly, then faster as she understood. She remembered Harry's strange behaviour and understood, because she had closed a time loop herself; the weight of doing things right, trying not to second-guess herself, and panicking when things didn't go the way she expected. Harry should know that time couldn't be changed, but so had she, and still she worried. Or perhaps—it occurred to her then—he was starstruck. Maybe June was famous, but whether it was for her role in MediSlice, or for something she hadn't yet done, she didn't know.

"What's the future like?" June asked.

"Harry wouldn't say. He just said we had to keep fighting for a better future."

She thought of Harry blurting out that the AMOC had shut down as if it were an event that had already happened and was quietly terrified. Was that what they were in for?

"You're disappointed," Phoenix observed after a moment.

"A guaranteed utopian future would have been nice," June said. But if the future was malleable, she could try to change it, and she would. She was already trying. But either way, she no longer carried the weight of the doomed planet on her shoulders; anything could happen. "I joined some local groups. Software Developers for a Carbon Negative Future, Half Earth Canberra chapter, and Insulate."

"What does Software Developers for a Carbon Negative Future do?" Phoenix asked.

"Oh . . . we ran a hackathon. My entry was an app where you could press a scream button—to show your feelings about climate change—and it would display a map of who else pressed the button. It only got seven downloads though. I've done a lot more good insulating people's houses."

Phoenix grunted. "My son is in the Insulate Canberra chapter," he said. "Actually, speak of the devil."

June turned in her seat to find a man approaching the table. Phoenix's son, Yarran.

She should have guessed. He had Phoenix's smile, Phoenix's eyes, but with a strong nose that could only be from his mother.

"June. Sorry to startle you," Yarran said. He looked from Phoenix to June and back again, clearly struggling to work out why she was there.

Phoenix grinned widely.

"Well, I should leave you to it," June said, feeling herself blush and hoping it wasn't obvious.

"You'll visit again, though?" Phoenix asked her.

"Of course I will."

June said goodbye to them both; Yarran looked as if he wanted to say something, but she left before he could find the words. As she walked out past reception, she glanced back to see Yarran in her chair. Phoenix was talking, waving his arms around as he did, but Yarran was watching her. She would see him at the meeting on Wednesday, she knew.

As June passed the Mary Poppins statue taking flight over the pond, she smiled to herself. Some workers were ripping up the carpark; it looked as if they were putting in a bike cage and a seating area, and more trees. This wasn't the end of anything; it was the beginning. She was going to change the world, nudge by nudge, like she already had.

June mounted her bike and rode away. The wind tugged at her hair and made her feel like she was flying.

AUTHOR'S NOTE

For an independent author, reviews are like gold-pressed latinum, so please consider leaving a review at the bookstore you purchased this book from.

Subscribe to my newsletter at www.rebeccadengate.com to be the first to know when I release a book, or feel free to email me at rdengateauthor@gmail.com. I love to hear from readers!

ALSO BY REBECCA DENGATE

On a hostile planet, an AI-equipped Environment Suit struggles with its wearer and with its own conscience. It can't even move. How can it make things right?

A science fiction adventure novel for fans of Murderbot and Becky Chambers.

https://books2read.com/envydengate

ACKNOWLEDGMENTS

Thank you to my family and the Human Disasters Creativity Club for beta reading and general support: Sue, Howard, and Arran Dengate; Miles Gantney, CeCe Philpott-Cummins, and Tammy Pinto. You are the best! I look forward to seeing *Heart Leech* and *Hamartia* in print (no pressure).

My editor, Kim Smith, improved my novel immeasurably and was a joy to work with. Thanks, Kim!

Finally, thanks also to my husband, Tom, my best friend and the kindest man I know.

The following non-fiction books were instrumental in writing *Traces of June* and I highly recommend them:

- *Losing Earth* by Nathaniel Rich
- *The Ends of the World* by Peter Brannen
- *How to Build a Time Machine* by Paul Davies
- *Firestorm* by Greg Mullins
- *Great Australian Flood Stories* by Ian Mannix

ABOUT THE AUTHOR

Rebecca would have applied to Starfleet Academy if it existed. Since it doesn't, there was an ill-fated attempt to become a ballerina. This was followed by an Engineering degree at the Australian National University, majoring in Mechatronics, then a highly enjoyable career developing software.

She lives in Canberra, Australia, with her husband and two children.